SARAH
HAGGER-HOLT

THE
FIGHTS
THAT
MAKE US

USBORNE

"So much of our history is forgotten or just not told, but what even is history anyway? It's this moment. Right now. Every second we live becomes history, and life continues."

Closing words from Adam Zmith on The Log Books podcast

"There is joy, there is light, there is positivity in our community. Yes, there's a fight we're trying to win, but it doesn't mean that everything has to be doom and gloom all the time [...] it can be fun. It's not *all* rainbows and glitter – but it's a *lot* of rainbows and glitter."

Shivani Dave, non-binary producer and presenter (from the Pride and Progress podcast, April 2023)

LISA'S MIXTAPE

01 Heart and soul – T'Pau

02 Heaven is a place on earth – Belinda Carlisle

03 Lean on me – Club Nouveau

04 I still haven't found what I'm looking for – U2

05 Who's that girl? – Madonna

06 Respectable – Mel and Kim

07 Out with her – The Blow Monkeys

08 Causing a commotion – Madonna

09 Too good to be forgotten – Amazulu

10 Walking down your street – The Bangles

11 Turn back the clock – Johnny Hates Jazz

12 Crush on you – The Jets

13 Sing our own song – UB40

14 Never can say goodbye – The Communards

15 It doesn't have to be – Erasure

16 What have I done to deserve this? –
    Dusty Springfield and Pet Shop Boys

17 Manic Monday – The Bangles

18 With or without you – U2

THIS DIARY BELONGS TO LISA SCOTT

STARTED ON MY 15TH BIRTHDAY
Monday 24 August 1987

KEEP OUT
PRIVATE

This includes you, Matthew Scott. If you dare even THINK about reading this, I'll find out and you'll be DEAD. I mean it. And I'll tell Mum about the you-know-what hidden under your bed and then she'll kill you and you'll be dead twice. And I will find out if you read it, you know I will.

01 HEART AND SOUL

"Oh," says Mum, sitting down suddenly. "Oh, that *is* sad."

There's something about her voice which makes me stop what I'm doing – making my favourite breakfast of Cheerios, Rice Krispies and corn flakes mixed together, mashed up with a spoon and drowned in milk – and turn to see if she's all right.

Mum is always exclaiming about something. Tutting over the news on her phone or laughing at some supposedly funny video that one of her friends has forwarded her. People who complain that teenagers are obsessed with social media haven't met my mum. But this is different from the usual running commentary of sighs and groans and "here, Jesse, you'll love this baby panda falling over".

"What is it?" I ask, putting my bowl down on the table

next to my glass of orange juice.

"Oh," she says again. "Well, I just opened this letter and, here, look… It was just a bit of a shock, that's all."

She hands me a sheet of paper.

I read it quickly. A few phrases jump out: "sorry to let you know", "memorial service", "donations to Cancer Research". But I don't recognize the name or the address.

"Who's Lisa Scott?" I ask Mum.

"Lisa? Lisa's my cousin." She pauses. "*Was* my cousin now, I suppose." She rubs her hands over her eyes. She looks tired.

"I didn't know you had a cousin called Lisa," I say, surprised. "You never talked about her. Have I ever met her?"

Mum leans back in her chair. "No, you haven't. It's years since I've seen her, she was quite a bit older than me, you see. I didn't even—" She stops, takes a deep breath. "I didn't even know she was sick. I should have known, I should have kept in contact… Oh, I don't know."

I look at the envelope. It isn't addressed to Mum. Instead, it's been forwarded to us from Gran's old address.

Mum nods. "Yes, it was sent to Gran. She was always one for keeping in touch with everyone, wasn't she?"

She smiles, but she looks sad underneath. Maybe this is why Mum's so upset about someone it sounds like she hardly knew. Because it reminds her of last year, when Gran died.

Gran said that she wanted us to think about her after she'd gone, but she didn't want us to be sad when we did. She wanted us to remember the happy times and how she made us laugh. Although she wouldn't have said it like that – she didn't say "gone" or "passed away" or that sort of thing, she just said "when I'm dead". Everything dies in time, she used to say, flowers and leaves and birds, people too. No point pretending they don't. That's part of what makes them so precious. Death is just a natural part of life, she told us, that's why you have to cherish being alive, and live the best you can, every single day.

But when you feel sad, you can't just decide not to feel sad any more. At least, that doesn't work for me. But I can try not to think about it, or to hide it so that no one notices.

I don't know what to say, so I lean over and rest my head on Mum's shoulder, just for a moment. She squeezes my hand in reply.

"Well," says Mum firmly. Her voice is calmer now. "We must go to the funeral, of course. I'll have to book tickets to London, find somewhere to stay, ask for the time off work… 20th February, that's in half-term, isn't it?"

"Would Dad and I have to go too?" I ask.

"It depends if he can get the time off," says Mum. "You wouldn't *have* to go, but…I'd like it if you came, Jesse. Gran would have wanted to go. As she can't, I think we should be there to represent the family, don't you? For all I know, we might be the only family there."

Mum's right. Gran would have wanted us to be there.

But that doesn't mean that *I* want to go. There are so many reasons not to. I hate dressing up and formal stuff and having to be polite to people I don't know. I know Lisa is part of our family, but I've never even met her. And Simran and I have got our joint history project to do together over half-term. And…

"Would I have to wear a dress for the funeral?" I ask, feeling breathless at the thought.

Mum snorts. "Where did you get that idea? When was the last time anyone got you to wear a dress? Don't be daft. You just need to look smart, that's all. Well, smartish."

I breathe normally again. I knew she'd say that. I knew it would be okay. But that didn't stop me from worrying.

Even thinking about wearing a dress, or a skirt, makes me feel uncomfortable. Maybe I'll want to one day, but right now, I tense up and it makes my chest feel tight. Like when someone uses my full first name or like when I used to have long hair and could feel it on the back of my neck. It just feels wrong. I know the opposite feeling too. When someone listens to me and takes me as I am, without any fuss, then my whole body relaxes.

"Actually, this could be a good thing," continues Mum. "We've been talking about making a trip to London for a while, haven't we? We could stay a bit longer, see the sights, maybe go to some museums and get ideas for this history project you keep talking about. What do you think?"

"Yeah, maybe," I say. I'm still not that keen.

"It would be some time together, just you and me, g—" She pauses, swallowing back her words. I can tell she was just about to say "girl time" before she stopped herself. "Together time," she says firmly.

Since I told Mum and Dad I'm non-binary, they've both been trying so hard to say and do the right things. To be fair, they usually do okay. Once, when I borrowed Mum's laptop for something, I saw she had a website open, with blogs from parents of non-binary kids. It was nice to know she was trying to understand it better, but kind of embarrassing too.

I'm not sure they totally get it though – that it's not just about clothes or using the right words or any of the outside stuff – it's about how I feel on the inside. Not like a boy or a girl, not totally anyway, just like me. Jesse. Those labels are fine for some people, I guess, but they don't make sense for me. And when I realized that I didn't have to accept the labels – that some other people choose not to either – then I could show people the person I was but had kept hidden away. Right now, changing my hair or what I wear is one part of feeling more comfortable in who I am, and in showing that to the world, but it's not the only way.

"So, what do you think – a trip to London, you and me?" asks Mum.

Maybe she's right. About the museums anyway. I'm in dire need of inspiration for our history project. Ms Grant says that each pair can do whatever we like, as long as we investigate something that matters to us and use our history skills to examine evidence and sources. It's exciting, but hard too. Especially when Simran and I have zero ideas so far. But I want Ms Grant to think our project is the best in the class, the best ever. She's only taught us for a term and a bit but she's totally different to any teacher I've had before.

She came striding into that first lesson back in September, her red skirt swishing and huge hoop earrings swinging. Everyone was chatting and messing around as usual; it was the first week of Year Eight and no one was used to being back in school yet. The noise in the classroom made my ears ache. Even so, we all paid attention when she slammed a large pile of textbooks on her desk with a bang.

"Right, Year Eight, are we ready?" Everyone shuffled slowly back to their seats. My best friend Simran and I were sitting together as always.

She waited for silence. Dylan and Conor were the last to stop whispering. "Good. I'm Ms Grant, I'm looking forward to getting to know all of you this year. Let's begin."

She picked up one of the books from the pile and waved it at us.

"This is our textbook for the year. Who's this on the cover?"

I watched a surprising number of hands go up.

"To help me get to know you, when you answer a question, please tell me your name too." She looked round the class and pointed at Ella.

"Ella – it's Henry VIII," Ella said, looking pleased with herself.

"Exactly, Ella, Henry VIII. We've all heard of Henry VIII, haven't we?" Lots of nods. "So, this is a bit harder, how many people were living in England and Wales when Henry was on the throne?"

Everyone stopped nodding and looked at her blankly.

I don't usually put my hand up, but there was something about Ms Grant, the way she *expected* us to know things and to *want* to know things, that already made me want her to notice me.

I did a rough calculation in my head, then I put up my hand, but not too high, so it looked like I could just be stretching.

When she nodded in my direction, I checked behind me in case she meant someone else before saying, "The population's about seventy million now, and there were a lot less people then, what with plagues and no proper healthcare and everything, so maybe half that?"

Simran stared at me. She was surprised to hear me say so much in class.

"Good deduction, er...?" said Ms Grant, nodding.

"Jesse," I said.

"Well done, Jesse. Not quite that many though, but thanks for starting us off and for giving us your reasons. That kind of analytical thinking is really important for a historian." She smiled at me and I couldn't help smiling back. "It was actually more like 2.5 to 3.5 million." My smile disappeared. I was way off, she must think I'm really stupid. "So, why, when there were millions of people living in Britain, do we only ever hear about one man?"

It was a real question, but no one knew how we were supposed to answer it. Of course, Dylan had a go. Whether he knows the answer or not, Dylan always has something to say. It's like the contents of his head just pours straight out of his mouth.

"It's not just Henry VIII though, is it? There's his wives. You learn about them too, Miss. Oh, I'm Dylan, Miss."

"Exactly, Dylan, we do. We hear about women who die, get cast aside or killed. But that's not *all* that women did in Tudor Britain. Or what women do today. At that time, out of those two to three million people, only a few of them had the power to make decisions which affected the whole country – only the men who owned land, no one else…"

"What?" said Jasmine. "That's so unfair."

"Exactly," Ms Grant acknowledged, before continuing, "which means that those men *wrote* the history, and that, even today, we forget that other people, other histories ever existed. But they did.

"So, we *will* be learning about Henry VIII," she sighed, "and his wives. But we'll also be learning about influential women like Margaret Beaufort, who had a huge impact on education at the time. We'll look at the range of roles, from sailors to seamstresses, that Black people took in Tudor society. And uncover queer history too, like the relationship between royal musician Arabella Hunt and her 'husband' Amy Poulter."

Jasmine made a face when Ms Grant said "queer", then she nudged Ella, stared at me and Simran and whispered something. Just like always.

"We'll be looking at who writes history and why, how it affects us now, and whose voices are missing. We'll discover how we're all part of making and recording history." Ms Grant paused and looked around again, making sure everyone was watching her. We all were. "Who keeps a diary?"

I kept my hand down this time, but a few hands did go up. One of them was Simran's. I glanced over at her. I didn't know she wrote a diary. I wondered what she wrote about me.

"Or writes a blog? Or emails or messages on social media? That's all history, it's you recording history, what matters to you, what changes you see, the details of what your lives are really like."

A list of sentences appeared on the whiteboard. I scanned them quickly.

History is boring.

History is all about the past.

History is about kings and queens.

History is about power.

History is about facts.

History depends on who tells the story.

History affects my life now.

History is written by the winners.

"In pairs," said Ms Grant, "I want you to discuss these

statements and pick one you agree with and one you disagree with and why. You have five minutes, go."

Simran turned to me. "Wow," she said after a moment. "She's awesome, isn't she? And a bit scary too. Did she really say we'd be studying queer history?"

"Yeah," I said, not really listening to Simran.

I wasn't worried about whether Ms Grant thought I was stupid any more. I was thinking about what she had said and how it made me feel – that the people and events that everyone said were so important weren't the only ones that mattered. So maybe there was a place in history for people like me, not on the edges of the story, but right in the centre.

Thanks to Ms Grant, history lessons soon became the best part of the whole week. But that's all going to change soon.

A few weeks ago, when we were all excited about the projects, she told us that she'll be going on maternity leave after Easter. I can't imagine having an ordinary teacher for history again, not after how brilliant the last few months have been with her.

Ms Grant says we'll put on an exhibition to display all our projects before she goes. We'll make the school hall into a gallery, like a real museum, so that our families can come in and see what we've researched. Maybe looking round museums in London will give me some ideas to share with Simran for our project.

The doorbell rings. Mum looks surprised.

"It's just Simran," I say, shovelling the last few spoonfuls of cereal into my mouth as I get up from the table. "We're going into town, remember? Her dad's dropping us off."

"Oh," says Mum. "Yes, of course, I'd totally forgotten…"

She sits there, staring at the letter. Not saying anything about me talking and eating at the same time or nagging me about putting my dirty bowl in the dishwasher.

"Mum, are you okay?" I ask. This letter has really shaken her. She's gone all vague and dreamy, like she was in the weeks after Gran died. "I don't have to go…"

"No, no, I'm fine." She waves her hand at me.

The doorbell rings again. Long and shrill.

"Go on, off you go," she says. I pick up my bowl. "Leave it, I'll sort that."

"Thanks, Mum!" I put the bowl back on the table, shove my feet into my trainers, down the last of the orange juice and give her a hug on my way out.

02 HEAVEN IS A PLACE ON EARTH

"At last," says Simran when I open the door. My laces are still undone. I have to shuffle carefully down the path after her so as not to fall over. "Dad's got the twins in the car. God, they never shut up. He's taking them swimming after dropping us off."

"I'll sit in the back with them," I say. "I don't mind."

"If you're sure," she says, opening the passenger door.

I like Simran's brothers. They badly wind her up, but they make me laugh. I'm jealous of her being a big sister, instead of the baby of the family like me. When I was younger, I used to plead with Mum and Dad for a little brother or sister. But there was only me and Tom – and he's gone away to uni now.

"Hello, Mr Gill," I say, fastening my seat belt. "Thanks for the lift."

"My pleasure, Jesse." Simran and I have been friends since we were younger than the twins and I've barely heard her dad say more than a couple of sentences at a time. Simran and her brothers more than make up for it though.

I've been collecting some really good jokes for Ranveer and Parminder, but first I let them try out their jokes on me. I always laugh, even at the rubbish ones or the ones that make no sense, despite Simran's sighs from the front seat.

"Which Roman emperor always has a cold?" asks Ranveer, wriggling with excitement.

I make a show of scratching my head and pretending to have no idea, even though I first heard this joke when I was in Year Four like they are. "I don't know, which Roman emperor always has…"

"Julius Sneezer!" shouts Parminder before I've even finished, and then does a huge pretend sneeze.

"Hey," protests Ranveer. "That was my joke! Dad, he did my joke!"

"Boys!" says Mr Gill, quietly but firmly. "Stop showing off."

"It's okay," I say to Ranveer. "I didn't hear properly, you tell me the answer." Ranveer repeats the punchline,

I smile and tell him it's a good one. Then, when he's looking out of the window, I wink at Parminder.

I'm so obsessed with this history project that even Ranveer's joke makes me think about it. Hurston used to be an important town in Roman times. There are Roman ruins in the park on the way to school and signs telling you what used to be where hundreds of years ago. Simran and I *could* do something about the Romans, I suppose, if we get really desperate. Maybe…but it doesn't feel personal enough somehow.

"Dad, let us out here," says Simran as we reach the high street. "Please, I can't bear any more of those jokes."

"But I've got a really good one," pleads Parminder.

"Next time," I tell him with a grin. "I promise. Thanks, Mr Gill." Simran slams the car door behind her before I've even undone my seat belt.

Out on the street, Simran takes my arm and steers me through the door of the hospice shop. She loves charity shops, mixing and matching, cutting and stitching, and turning second-hand clothes into something entirely unique.

I don't.

"I thought we were going to Over the Rainbow, not going shopping," I say.

"In a minute, just a quick look round. I need your help."

I sigh. "No really, Jesse." She already has a top in each hand. She holds up one in front of her, and then the other, and then the first one again. "What do you think? Which one's best?"

I shrug. Simran looks great whatever she wears. Not like me. I'm better at knowing what I *don't* like, rather than what I do. And, anyway, it's only recently that I've started looking in the mirror and recognizing the person looking back. Simran calls it "finding my style". But I think it's more like finding a part of myself.

She snaps her fingers in front of my face. "Come on, Jesse." I look properly this time.

"The first one," I say at random.

"Hmm…" says Simran. "I'm not sure…" She puts both tops back on the rail. I drift over to look at the books. I'm flicking through some old Lemony Snickets when Simran taps me on the shoulder.

"What about this?"

She puts a hanger into my hand and steps back, nearly knocking an extremely ugly royal jubilee teapot off the shelf behind her. I lean forward to catch it, but it just wobbles then rights itself again.

I look at what Simran's handed me. "For you?" I ask, surprised. It's not her usual style.

"No, course not, for *you*." I run my fingers over it. The

fabric on the front is so soft, but the back is silky smooth. It's grey, but not dull. The colour is dark and deep, but warm too. It's...beautiful. It's like Simran's reached into my head, found a style that I didn't even know I had and then conjured it into reality. She's grinning like she knows it too. Only Simran would think of picking up a waistcoat.

"Put it on," she says. And I do.

I normally prefer clothes that are too big for me, where I can hide inside them, but this fits perfectly. Simran claps her hands. "I'm buying it for you! Early birthday present."

"But my birthday's not till July!"

"Whatever, it's yours!" I don't even try to say no. I want it.

Once we get to Over the Rainbow, I tuck the bag under the table. We're sitting by the window, but I am more interested in what's happening inside the cafe than looking at the street outside. This is the place I love most in the whole world. We never bump into anyone else from our year in here. They're all in the shopping centre, in McDonald's or Starbucks, not this little bookshop cafe on a tiny side street. I don't have a problem with any of them – well, except maybe Jasmine – I'm just glad that this is mine and Simran's special, secret place.

The bunting that decorates the walls is in the colours of the non-binary, trans and Pride flags. It was this bunting

27

that first made me stop and peer through the window a few months ago. I couldn't go in because Mum was in a rush. We were cutting through a new shortcut she'd found back to the car park.

The next weekend I made Simran walk past with me five times, just so I could peek inside, until she got fed up and dragged me through the door.

As soon as we walked in and saw the people and the books on the shelves and the brightly coloured posters on the walls, Simran turned to me and said, "Jesse, this place is for *us*."

The chairs and tables, glasses and plates, none of them match, but it doesn't matter. I like it that way. The shelves are stuffed with books and magazines and it's okay to flick through them even if you're not buying one. Maz, who owns the place, is always pressing her favourite books into people's hands, even if they've just come in for a takeaway coffee.

Also, people talk to each other here, even if they don't know each other. At first that kind of freaked me out, but now I'm used to it. It's the first place I saw two men holding hands, or someone wearing a badge saying "she/they". Hurston's too small to have its own Pride, but instead we've got Over the Rainbow. And I think that's even better, because it's here all year round, not just for one day.

I slurp my banana milkshake. You can get milkshakes here in every colour of the rainbow, even green, it's so cool. Simran leans forward and looks at me expectantly. "Go on then, put it on."

"Are you sure? What if I spill something on it?"

"You won't, go on."

I slip off my hoodie and put on the waistcoat instead. I feel a bit self-conscious at first. I mean, what twelve-year-old wears a waistcoat? But then I look around at what everyone else in here is wearing and start to relax. No one's going to notice or care what I look like. And it feels good. It makes me want to throw my shoulders back and sit up taller.

"Now," says Simran. "Half-term's only a week away. I was thinking – we've got to do something good. You and me. There's no way I'm spending the whole week stuck at home, trying to stop Ranveer and Parminder destroying the place while Mum and Dad are working. I don't even get babysitting money. They say being a sister isn't a job, it's a blessing." She snorts. "So, what do you think? Would your mum and dad mind me hanging round at yours?"

"Course they wouldn't," I say. "But who'd look after the twins?"

"Not. My. Problem," says Simran fiercely. Then she softens. "Actually, Dad is working at home a bit and I'm sure for a couple of days they'll be round at friends' houses anyway. I can help out when they're not. I mean, they're not so bad really."

"Come to mine whenever you like, we can do our history project."

"What?" exclaims Simran. "I swear you're obsessed with that project. Obsessed." She shakes her head in pretend despair.

"I'm not *obsessed*," I tell her. "I'm just *interested*. I mean, it's loads better than normal homework, isn't it?"

"*Interested* in the project or *interested* in Ms Grant?" asks Simran, grinning.

"In the *project*," I say firmly. I look over my shoulder, pretending to be distracted by who's coming through the door, in the hope that Simran won't notice that I'm going red.

When I look back at her, she's smiling an annoying smile, but she doesn't say anything.

"So, have you had any ideas about what we can do it on?" I ask her.

Simran stretches back like a cat and flicks her long black hair over her shoulders. "Dad thinks we should do the Sikh soldiers. From World War One."

"What Sikh soldiers?"

"Exactly. As Ms Grant always says, no one tells you

about them, do they?" Simran waves her finger at me. "Dad says one in six of all the soldiers fighting for Britain in World War One came from India and loads of them were Sikh, just like my family. They were really brave and everything. Some of them fought with actual swords."

"No way!"

"Uh huh. Dad's got these history books full of ancient photos. He got really excited when he thought I might be interested. I suppose it is kind of cool, but I'm not sure. I'd like it best if it was our idea, not someone else's, not even Dad's. What do you think?"

I try to imagine Simran's dad as one of those soldiers, going into battle brandishing a sword. But it's much easier to picture him sitting in the big battered armchair in Simran's living room, with a mug of tea in his hand, reading books about old battles as the twins climb all over him.

"It's the best idea we've got so far," I say. "My dad thinks we should do it on the history of flood defences in East Sussex."

"Yawn."

"He says they've got archives at his work we could go and look at."

"Stop talking about that this second, or I'll fall asleep right now," threatens Simran.

03 LEAN ON ME

"Hello, hello," cuts in a cheery voice behind me. "How are my favourite customers today?"

"Leo!" exclaims Simran and jumps up to air-kiss him.

I raise my hand in acknowledgement. "Hi, Leo."

"Hi, Jesse." He smiles.

"Are we *really* your favourite customers? Really truly?" Simran asks.

"Of course," he replies and Simran beams. Talk about *interested*. Simran is definitely *interested* in Leo. But she doesn't have a chance with him. He's a whole four school years above us. And he's gay.

I recognized him from school when we first started coming in here, but I was too shy to speak to him. It's not like Year Eights ever really talk to sixth-formers. But Simran wasn't shy. And now Leo greets us like his best friends whenever we come in.

"More banana milkshakes?" he asks, clearing away our empty glasses. "Or...how about today's special?" He lowers his voice, like he's about to offer us a secret deal, and looks round as if he's afraid of being overheard. "It's a kale and spinach milkshake. We're trying out some new options for the green one."

"No thanks," I say. "I'm okay."

"Sorry, Leo, that sounds rank," says Simran. "But maybe we'll have a brownie or something? To share?"

"Brownie. Good choice," says Leo, but he doesn't sound like he means it. "I mean, that is, if 'good' is enough for you. But if instead you're looking for spectacular—" He pauses dramatically and nods over at the counter. "There's a white chocolate and raspberry tray bake that I *happen* to have had a hand in."

He leans in. "Maz says I can do more in the kitchen, instead of out the front, if the cakes I make sell well enough. She'll start training me up properly and everything. I've got loads of ideas for developing the business too. I think we could bring in loads more customers." His voice is excited. Leo's dream is to run his own cafe one day. Probably a whole chain of them.

"Wow, it sounds amazing," says Simran. "We'll definitely have that. Right, Jesse?"

"Sure," I shrug. "Whatever."

"What's up, Jesse?" asks Leo, looking concerned. "You okay?"

"They're moping about homework, would you believe?" says Simran, and she explains all about the history project and how we still haven't found the perfect topic.

Leo looks thoughtful. "Ms Grant...the A-level group have her too. She's great, isn't she? I think she might be one of us, don't you? She's got that kind of...I don't know...that kind of vibe about her."

"Ms Grant? You think she's LGBTQ?" I stare at him. "But she can't be, she's pregnant."

"So?" he retorts quick as a flash. "It's not just straight people that have kids, is it?"

I don't say anything. My head is spinning with the idea that Ms Grant might be gay or bi. It's none of our business really, and I know what Mum says about talking about people behind their backs, but it would be so cool if she were.

"If it were my project, I'd do something on food," Leo continues. "Maybe some old recipes from World War Two or something and the stories behind them. People were so creative – making whole meals out of potato peelings and powdered eggs."

34

Simran makes a face. "Yuck. I hope there's no potato peelings in your tray bake!"

"You see," I say gloomily. "That's a brilliant idea! And you don't even *need* to come up with anything!"

"You'll both think of something awesome," says Leo, putting his hand on my shoulder. "And if you don't, you can have my idea, if you like. I'll bring you your *delicious* tray bake. No potato peelings in sight. Gotta dash, I don't want to get into trouble for chatting!" He nods over at Maz standing behind the counter. She looks really fierce, with her buzz cut and tattoo-covered arms, but under the surface she's really kind. Just not in a gushy way. She might talk tough, but Leo's not scared of her really.

"We've got loads of time over half-term to come up with something," says Simran, once Leo's gone to get our cake.

Then I remember the letter that came this morning. And the funeral. And Mum's plans for family bonding time over half-term.

"Oh no, hold on, I might be away. It's the funeral of Mum's long-lost cousin and we've got to go to London for it, even though I'd never even met her. Mum wants to make a thing of it. It's not just the funeral, we'll stay over, go to some museums and stuff... I mean, that's okay, just as long as she doesn't try and take me shopping."

"That's brilliant!" Simran exclaims, clapping her hands together.

"What? Why?"

"I could come to London with you. Why not? You and me. It would be magic." I stare at her for a long moment. The only words I've said that have registered with her are "London" and "shopping".

"Simran, you can't just randomly turn up at the funeral of someone you don't even know. That's weird."

She shakes her head. "It wouldn't be random. Or weird. I'd be with you, supporting you. Anyway, you said *you'd* never met her, that means that I know her just as well as you do."

"Yes, maybe," I say uncertainly. Simran has years of practice in out-arguing me. "But—"

"I came to your gran's funeral, didn't I?"

I remember Simran's hand slipping into mine as we took our seats at the crematorium. And I remember grabbing hold of it so tight when I caught sight of the coffin at the front. I wanted to be there, to say goodbye and to remember Gran, but I couldn't believe, I just couldn't believe, that it was Gran in there. All the life and colour and noise of her, shut away in that wooden box. That I would never hear her tease me or ask me about school or call me "Messy Jesse" again. It was just wrong.

And I remember that Simran never let go of my hand, not once, during all the blur of songs and speeches and readings, even though I must have nearly squeezed her fingers off.

It *would* be magic, Simran coming to London with us over half-term. With her there, I'd feel better about going to the funeral too.

For the first time since the letter arrived, I let myself think about the real reason why I don't want to go. A funeral. A coffin. Black clothes. People crying. What if being there made me think of Gran, dead, when I've been trying so hard not to forget what she was like when she was alive?

I shake my head to scatter those thoughts away.

"I don't know," I say. "I don't know what Mum will say. You know what she's like about quality family time. No offence, Simran."

Simran shrugs. "It'll be fine. Your mum loves me." She says it like it's a fact. Which, to be fair, it is. Mum *does* love Simran.

Simran and I started Brownies together when we were seven. We were the only two new kids that term. Simran's mum and my mum didn't know each other but they stood together, watching nervously from the edge of the hall, worrying whether we'd settle in well, whether we'd make friends.

We played some games which were okay, and then the leaders got out paper and coloured pens and asked us to draw our pets. I think it was for some project on caring for animals; I can't remember. I sat there for ages, not drawing anything, wondering if I should draw Cookie, my guinea pig, even though she'd died last year. And then I started feeling sad about Cookie and thought I was going to cry and that would be awful on my first week when I didn't know anyone and then Mum would worry about me and…then I saw what Simran was doing.

She had collected all the green pens that no one else was using for their boring kittens and gerbils and goldfish, and was drawing the biggest, fiercest, greenest crocodile ever, with huge snappy jaws.

I couldn't stop myself saying, "You can't draw that, you don't have a pet crocodile."

She stared right back at me, looking nearly as fierce as the crocodile she'd drawn and said, "Who says? I can have a pet crocodile if I want, can't I?"

Then a huge mischievous grin spread over her face.

"Have you got one too?" she asked me. "Because, maybe if you had a crocodile, they could be friends. Mine won't bite – I tamed it myself."

In that moment, I decided I wanted this fierce, grinning, crocodile-taming girl to be my best friend.

"No," I said, grabbing a grey pen and starting to draw. "I haven't got a crocodile, but I have got an ostrich. She runs super-fast and lays huge eggs. Could she be friends with your crocodile?"

Simran looked thoughtful and then nodded, like she'd made an important decision. "Okay then."

A couple of other kids gave us weird looks, but we didn't care.

Our mums were relieved that we'd made friends, although slightly bemused by the pages of drawings we brought home of unlikely zoo animals forming cross-species friendships. And that was it, since then Mum has been Simran's biggest fan.

Even though we went to different primary schools, Simran and I have always been close. Now it's brilliant not just to be in the same secondary school, but to be in the same form! Then, last year, we got even closer.

I was on a sleepover at Simran's house. We were snuggled under the duvet, eating strawberry laces, chatting, and watching this interview on YouTube with a fashion designer that she likes. It was getting late and I was drifting off to sleep. Then suddenly she said, "I think that's like me."

"What?"

"Are you still awake?"

"Er, not really." I tried to focus my tired eyes on the screen. "What's she saying?"

"She's talking about being pan."

"What?"

"Pansexual. It means you can like anyone, it doesn't matter what gender they are. It's not like being just gay or straight, it's different."

"Oh, okay." I yawn. That made total sense, even to my sleepy brain. I didn't know it was something that had a name though.

"You don't think it's weird?" she asked.

"No," I replied. "When you think about it, it's more weird that everyone *isn't* like that. I mean, people are people."

Simran sat up and gave me a hug. She looked relieved. "I guess so, but I think most people are in one box or the other." She nodded at the screen, where the designer was still talking. "She says you shouldn't put people in boxes at all."

That idea stuck with me. I thought about it the next morning and the day after and the day after that. I read more and watched more and found out more stuff, and things started to make sense.

I didn't want to be in a box either. Not because of who I might one day fall in love with but because of who I was inside. I found some words for it too, words that seemed to fit. And other people online who seemed to see themselves the same way as I did. All because of Simran. I don't think she was at all surprised when, halfway through Year Seven, she was the first person I told that I was non-binary. And telling someone else, especially telling her, felt brilliant.

"Hey, Earth to Jesse!" calls Simran and waves a hand in front of my face.

"Er…what? Oh yes, I'll ask Mum. About London."

"I'll ask my mum and dad too. I'm sure they'll say yes!"

Leo reappears with a plate of the most amazing looking cake and two spoons.

"Voila," he says with a flourish. Then he looks at me. "Nice waistcoat, Jesse. I meant to say before."

I feel myself blushing. I always feel self-conscious when people comment on how I look, even in a good way. I worry if they might be judging me for not looking feminine enough, or for not even trying to.

"I chose it for them, you know," adds Simran, leaning forward, keen to enjoy some of Leo's approval.

"It's really cool," says Leo. "I mean it."

But even so, half an hour later when we get up to leave, I slip the waistcoat off and put it back into my bag.

It's just that, after the last few months in school,

sometimes I simply want to fade into the background. But being the first, the only, person to come out as non-binary in my year – maybe in the whole school for all I know – has made it hard to keep a low profile. I never want to make a fuss or to be noticed; I just want to get on with my own stuff. It's other people that make it a big deal, not me. That's why Over the Rainbow is so important – it's somewhere I feel like no one's staring or questioning, somewhere I really belong.

04 I STILL HAVEN'T FOUND WHAT I'M LOOKING FOR

"I *love* this room!" says Simran for about the tenth time today. "I could *live* here."

She flops down on one of the hotel's twin beds and sighs happily, unwrapping a packet of three fancy-looking ginger biscuits, shoving one in her mouth and waving another at me. I take it and then turn back to the mirror. She's right. Anything that comes with free biscuits has got to be good.

We only got to London a couple of hours ago, and already the TV's on and our stuff is scattered everywhere. Mum's room is next door, with a door connecting to ours, but she's got a double bed and a fancier bathroom. "Might as well treat ourselves a little," she said, when she booked it last week. Simran and I have our own bathroom, just

43

for us, and our own door with our own key card.

I try not to get biscuit crumbs on myself because I've already got changed. It's only a few minutes till we have to leave for the funeral. Mum's been going on about how we have to be ready on time because you never know when the tubes in London might get delayed and she isn't sure where the crematorium is and does not, I repeat not, want to be late, not for a funeral.

But then, after today, we've got another day in London to do exactly what we like.

"Do I look okay?" asks Simran. I turn to look at her. She's wearing a black dress, black tights and she looks good. Like she always does.

There's a knock on the connecting door. After a moment, Mum sticks her head through. "Ready to go?"

She looks me up and down. I can see her taking in my smart black trousers, white shirt, and the waistcoat from Simran with my "they/them" badge pinned on it. I wait.

"You both look really smart," she says. She's smiling but still looks a bit anxious. "Now let's go, it's already after two."

It's actually really easy to find the place. We only have to change trains once to get there. Once Mum's sure that we're not going to be late, she's more relaxed.

"Are you two all right? Are you sure you're okay with this?"

Simran and I both nod and we all walk together through the gates and down the long path to the chapel.

We find a spot near the back. I flick through the order of service booklet that we were given on the way in.

The photo on the front is of a woman with short grey hair and glasses. I look closely, trying to pick out any family resemblance between Lisa and Mum or me, but nothing stands out.

I turn over the booklet.

There's another photo on the back. In this one, Lisa looks just a little older than me. She's got red hair like mine, but it's cut in a terrible style, even worse than Mum's hair in her old school photos. Her eyes are sparkling, and she's got the most enormous grin, like she's just heard the best joke in the world. I can't have done, but I'm sure I've seen her somewhere before.

Simran nudges me. I scramble to my feet. Everyone stands up as the coffin is carried in.

I don't want to look, but when I do, what I see takes me by surprise. This doesn't look like a coffin. It's rainbow-coloured, more like a basket than a box, carried by women who look like they could be Lisa's friends. It's actually beautiful, which feels a weird thing to say about a coffin, but it's true. I'll never meet Lisa, but this makes me wonder about the sort of person she was.

We all sit down and the woman at the front starts speaking. I can't concentrate. I keep looking at the order of service, wondering why I recognize the girl in the photo. Suddenly, it clicks into place.

"Mum," I whisper, as soon as some music starts playing.

"What?" she whispers back. Everyone else has their eyes shut or is looking seriously down at their laps.

I hold up the order of service and point to the picture on the back. "I recognize Lisa, even though I've never met her. There was a photo of her and you on Gran's bedroom shelf, wasn't there?"

Mum peers at the booklet. "Oh yes. Gran's photo must have been taken around the time Lisa came to live with us. She looks about the same age in this one."

"She came to *live* with you?" I ask. "Really? Why?"

Mum's never said anything about that before.

The music has got to a quiet bit. Mum lowers her voice further, so that I have to lean in to hear her. Simran shoots us a questioning look.

"I don't know," she whispers. "I was probably only four or five. I don't remember. She just appeared one day. She must have stayed for weeks, I suppose, maybe longer now I think about it. You know what your gran was like for taking in waifs and strays." She smiles, but in a sad kind of way. "I guess we'll never know for sure now."

"But, she—" I start, but the music is finishing. Mum shushes me as the woman at the front starts speaking again.

I was going to say, "but she looks so young". She can't be more than sixteen in that photo, so why was she living with Gran and Grandad and not at home with her parents?

A couple of Lisa's friends stand up and tell stories about her life. About how she drew little cartoons in her Christmas cards. About how she was a great host but a terrible cook – that bit made everyone laugh. About how she was always taking part in one campaign or another, and trying to help other people, even when she was really ill. But nothing about her family. Nothing at all. And certainly no clue about why she might have gone to live with Gran all those years ago.

At the end of the ceremony, Simran and I head for the loos. There's only one and it's unisex, which is a relief. No worries about getting funny looks in the queue. While we wait, I tell her what Mum said about Lisa having lived with her and Gran, and how weird it is that Mum has no idea why or how long for or anything.

Simran shrugs. "It probably wasn't that long. Maybe she just came for a holiday or something. You know what little kids are like. They haven't got a clue. I swear my brothers are so obsessed with Minecraft they don't even notice what goes on half the time."

"They didn't have Minecraft when Mum was little."

"Well, duh," says Simran. "You know what I mean."

My phone buzzes. "You go first," I say to Simran while I check my messages.

There's one from Tom. It's short, just hoping the funeral went all right. I send him a thumbs up back. We're not the kind of siblings who message very often, but it feels good to hear from him now. He understands, without me having to say, how worried I was that today might make me sad about Gran all over again.

But, now the funeral's over, I can't think why I'd got myself worked up about it. I'm always going to be sad about Gran not being here, that's just how it is, but today hasn't made it any worse. In fact, it feels good to have learned something new about Gran from Mum, something that reminds me how warm and kind she was, even if I don't know the whole story of her relationship with Lisa.

When I come out of the loo, I look around for Mum and Simran. They are standing by the big doors which lead out to the crematorium gardens. Mum's talking to two women.

"Yes, I'm Ali, it was me that got in touch, and this is Sam," says the taller of the two, as I reach them. "Lisa didn't really talk about her family, and we never pried, did we, Sam?"

The other woman nods, making her curly hair bounce up and down.

"Everyone has their reasons," Ali continues. "But, towards the end, Lisa gave us her address book and asked if we'd contact everyone, including her aunt." I realize that she means Gran.

"The letter was forwarded to me," says Mum. She falls silent for a moment and then says, "Lisa was lucky to have friends like you. I'm sorry that I never really knew her. It's been years, since I was a child really… Anyway, I'm glad we're here today."

Sam smiles. Ali reaches over and squeezes Mum's hand. "You must come back to the house. There'll be something to eat, a few drinks. You'd be really welcome. You're the only ones from Lisa's family who were able to come. Her brother couldn't make the journey from Australia and, to be honest, I don't think there was much love lost between them."

That's so sad. I grip the phone in my pocket. I can't imagine losing touch with Tom like that.

I'm ready to leave. My smart shoes are pinching my toes, and I've had enough of smiling at people I don't know. And yet…I kind of want to find out more about Lisa and why she lost touch with all of her family. Like Ms Grant says, there's always a story behind the story, if you look hard enough. So what's the story here?

Plus my stomach's growling. The idea of food sounds really good. If it gets awkward, we can just eat and leave.

"Oh, I'm sorry," says Mum suddenly, as if she's only just noticed we're standing behind her. "This is my youngest, Jesse, and their best friend, Simran."

"Good to meet you," says Ali. "Please do come back. All of you. A few of Lisa's friends are helping clear her house. I'm sure she'd have wanted the family to have a memento or something."

Ali gives us directions. It's only a short walk to the house. It's pretty – and old too. It feels more like a cottage than a house. I didn't think they had cottages in London, but maybe it was built before this was proper London, just some little village that eventually got swallowed up by the big city.

Inside, people are talking quietly, either perched on the small sofa, leaning against the one cosy-looking armchair or standing round with drinks in their hands. Some of the shelves are still stuffed with books. Others have already been packed into boxes. Same with the pictures – some paintings are still on the walls, others have already been taken down and covered in bubble wrap.

It makes me feel kind of sad, seeing someone's life being packed away like this, even though it's someone I never knew. All the things that were special to them aren't special any more, because no one else cares about them in the same way.

Simran grabs my hand and pulls me towards the kitchen. We have to squeeze past people to reach the table. We're loading up paper plates with sandwiches and crisps when Ali appears behind us.

"Ah," she says. "Just who I was looking for! Could you help me out for a minute? I need a couple of people who are strong and fit and, well, not too large."

"That's us," says Simran through a mouthful of crisps. "What do you want us to do?"

"Would you be able to pop up into the attic and have a look round for us? We'll need to clear it all eventually, but we don't even know how much is up there, let alone if there's anything valuable or important. I don't much fancy my chances of getting through that hatch to have a look, not someone my size. There should be a light switch, but you might need to crawl around a bit to find it."

"Will there be spiders?" asks Simran.

I give her a look. "Don't be such a scaredy-cat. It'll be fine."

I'd much rather be exploring the attic, even if there are a few spiders, than making boring small talk downstairs. You never know what interesting things might be up there.

The noise of chatter fades away as Ali leads us up the steep stairs. The doors to the upstairs rooms are all shut. No snooping here. There is a stepladder waiting under a hatch in the ceiling.

I push the hatch back and pull myself into the attic, sneezing as the dust I've dislodged swirls around me. I feel around in the gloom to find the switch. At last, the light buzzes into life. A harsh fluorescent glare reveals cardboard boxes, suitcases and bulging files. The nearest ones say things like "tax returns" and "bills". I don't know what I expected, but it all looks disappointingly ordinary.

"Is it okay?" calls Simran from below me. "Should I come up?"

"Yeah, come on." I grab her arms and heave her in. She brushes the cobwebs off her dress. I start wandering around, taking a few pictures on my phone to show Ali.

"I bet there's mice up here," says Simran uncertainly. "Maybe even rats…" For someone who's usually so confident, it surprises me how anything creepy-crawly or small and furry totally freaks Simran out. Hardly anyone sees this side of her.

Right on cue, there's a scuffling noise in the far corner of the attic. I must admit it does sound a little bit like tiny mouse feet.

"I'll check it out," I say, picking my way through the

boxes towards the far corner. Simran doesn't reply. I turn round to check she's okay. She's disappeared back down the ladder. I guess I'm doing this on my own then.

I move a box to one side with my foot. It says "1987/88" on the top in spiky blue writing. I try to be gentle, but it's so old and packed full of stuff that some papers slide off the top when I move it. I pick them up and glance at them quickly. Then I stop. There's a photograph of Lisa, with a small hole from a drawing pin at the top.

She looks just the same as she did in the photo in the order of service. But in this picture, she has her arm thrown around a girl with dark curly hair and glasses. They both have the same enormous grin on their faces. Even though the quality's rubbish and the picture's faded and it's probably been hidden up here for years, happiness shines out of it.

I peer more closely, trying to work out where they are, but all I can see behind them are crowds. It could be anywhere.

I sit down on an old suitcase and carefully open the box, taking care not to break or rip anything. I wonder if there are more photos in there, or anything from the time Lisa came to stay with Mum and Gran. On the top are some exercise books, then a textbook or two – including a history one with pictures of kings and queens on the cover that I bet Ms Grant wouldn't approve of. Why would you keep your school textbooks for nearly forty years?

I stick my hand deeper into the box and rummage around. There's something soft – clothes maybe? – more books and loose paper, and a few hard objects too. I can feel the edge of a biscuit tin, I think.

I pull out an exercise book at random. It has spiky writing on the front, just like the writing on the box. It's as difficult to read as mine! Maybe terrible handwriting is a family thing. I open it on the first page. This is not just another school book. It's a diary.

THIS DIARY BELONGS TO LISA SCOTT

STARTED ON MY 15ᵀᴴ BIRTHDAY
Monday 24 August 1987

KEEP OUT
PRIVATE

This includes you, Matthew Scott. If you dare even THINK about reading this, I'll find out and you'll be DEAD. I mean it. And I'll tell Mum about the you-know-what hidden under your bed and then she'll kill you and you'll be dead twice. And I will find out if you read it, you know I will.

It feels like spying, even though I know that the "keep out" isn't really meant for me. I guess Matthew must be her brother, the one who is now grown up and living in Australia. I wonder what terrible thing he had hidden under his bed.

I flick through the pages, trying not to feel guilty about reading someone else's diary. As far as I can tell it's mostly Lisa moaning about the things her parents won't let her do, about homework and about how annoying her brother is. It's a bit like listening to Simran, except she has two little brothers to complain about instead of just one!

The handwriting's hard to read, but there are drawings everywhere. Some just doodles, others really detailed. They are all brilliant. The people she draws look so real. I don't know who they are, but I bet I'd recognize them straight away if I met them in real life, just from Lisa's drawings.

On the back cover there are two names written in block capitals:

LISA MARIE SCOTT

LOVES

NICOLA ANNE BURRIDGE

Along the bottom, she's written "Lisa and Nicky" over and over again, surrounded by lots of hearts of different sizes. Most of the page is taken up by a single drawing. I recognize the curly hair and big grin. It's the other girl from the photo.

I stare at the page for a minute. What does this mean? That Lisa was gay, or just that she had a girlfriend in school? Maybe only that she had a crush on another girl? Did Mum know this about Lisa? Did Gran? And why did nobody tell me? I mean, if I'm not the only LGBTQ+ person in the family, I wish someone had mentioned it.

This part of Lisa's life mustn't be left to rot away in a dusty attic or cleared out and sent to the dump! That would be so sad, like her dying all over again. If these were my diaries, I might not have wanted anyone to read them when I was alive, but I certainly wouldn't want them to be forgotten after I'd died.

"Hey, Jesse, have you been eaten by rats?" calls Simran through the hatch. "What *are* you doing up there? You've been ages. Nearly all the food's gone. I think Ali's worried that you've moved in or something."

"Just coming!" I shout back. Now that I've started reading it, I don't want to leave the diary or *any* of the contents of the box, not until I've found out more about Lisa.

Then I remember that Ali said I could choose a memento.

56

I wonder if it would be okay to take this whole box. I guess I can ask. I wrap my arms around "1987/88" and heave it towards the hatch.

"Sim!" I call, loud enough for her to hear me from the bottom of the ladder. "Can you just help me get something down? You'll need to come up a couple of steps and grab hold of it. There are no rats, I promise."

"Have you found treasure?" Simran asks eagerly.

I don't reply, I just pass her the box. She wobbles a little under its weight, but nothing falls out. "What on earth is this, Jesse?"

05 WHO'S THAT GIRL?

"When she said 'memento', I imagined something like an ornament or a piece of jewellery, not an old cardboard box," says Mum.

We're sitting in mine and Simran's hotel room, drinking tea, eating the last of the free biscuits and chatting about the funeral.

"You don't mind, do you?" I ask. "It *was* okay to ask if I could have it?" I'm suddenly not sure – what if I've been rude without meaning to? All I know is that rescuing that box out of the attic felt like the right thing to do.

Ali had seemed fine about me taking it. She even said how pleased she was that someone in Lisa's family was interested in her life. I didn't specifically mention the diary to her, or to Mum or Simran. I just said it was some old books and papers and clothes. I don't know why. It felt more respectful to Lisa somehow.

"Of course it's okay," smiles Mum. "I hope you find something interesting in there. Now, if you'll excuse me, I'm washed out, I'm going to lie down for a bit and then call your dad. Then how about the three of us go and get something to eat? Those sandwiches were a long time ago."

She *does* look tired. Maybe it's just the journey down to London and meeting all those new people. But, I mean, Lisa was her cousin, even if Mum hadn't seen her for years and years. And she died so young – only ten years or so older than Mum. It must feel strange for Mum, knowing that she'll never have the chance to see Lisa again.

Once Mum's gone, I tip the contents of the box out onto my bed. Clouds of dust fly up and Simran starts sneezing. There's a denim jacket with badges on, some Dr Martens boots and other clothes (obviously they are what Simran's most interested in), ancient-looking magazines and leaflets, a biscuit tin stuffed with tickets and notes, a cassette tape and loads more.

"This T-shirt looks a right mess," says Simran, wrinkling up her nose at an enormous T-shirt with a wobbly upside-down pink triangle in the centre. "But look at these boots! Proper vintage! I bet they're your size, Jesse, go on, try them on."

The boots *are* awesome. They are dark blue, creased and well-worn with doodles in biro on the soles, and they are beautiful. Lisa must have worn these all the time.

I loosen the frayed laces and slide my feet in. It feels a bit wrong – I mean, they're not mine – but it feels right too. Just like the waistcoat, these boots feel like they were made for me. Maybe one day my waistcoat from Simran will be as well-worn and well-loved as Lisa's Docs. I snap a picture to send to Tom.

"What's this?" asks Simran, opening the cassette case. A list of songs falls out. It's not in Lisa's spiky writing, but in curlier writing with hearts instead of dots on the "i"s. I wonder if the writing belongs to Nicky, the girl in the photo, Lisa's maybe-girlfriend. I'd love to listen to it, but I've no idea how.

"I *think* it's a mixtape. A real one, I mean, not a playlist. I bet the last time someone listened to this was before we were even *born*. Anyway, there's something I want to show you in Lisa's diary…"

I've been desperate to show Simran the diary ever since I found it, but it took ages to get away from all those people at the funeral. I wanted to show her first, even before Mum.

"Wait!" exclaims Simran. "There's a diary in there? You didn't say. I hope it's worth having risked your life with all the creepy-crawlies up in that attic!"

"Kind of. I wanted to rescue it. Well, the whole box really. This stuff must be special for Lisa to keep it for over thirty years. It would be awful if it got binned now."

"Go on then." Simran puts the tape down and leans over to look. I show her the diary and the photo too. After a second, she says, "So who is this Nicky? We didn't meet her today, did we?"

I shake my head. "Dunno, but...do you think she was, well, you know, Lisa's girlfriend?" I ask. "Way back when they were in school together?"

"Well, obviously," says Simran. "Just look at them in this photo. All loved up."

"But..." I say. "I mean, you can be really good friends without going out together – look at us. Maybe Lisa and Nicky were just best friends."

"Yeah, sure," says Simran. "But I'm not drawing hearts round your name in the back of my diary, am I? Clearly, they were a couple." She looks thoughtful. "Your mum didn't say anything about her being gay."

"I've been thinking, maybe Mum wouldn't have known. The last time she saw Lisa, Mum was just a little kid."

It's a lot to take in. Even if it's no big deal to Simran that Lisa might have been gay, it is to me. Someone else LGBTQ in my family, someone who might understand

61

what it's like to be me, someone I could ask stuff or talk to about what I'm feeling. And they go and die before I even get to meet them.

"Well, let's have a look then," says Simran.

"I suppose… But do you think it's wrong to read a dead person's diary?"

"Lisa's not going to mind, is she?" says Simran. "And snooping about's okay if you're historians like us."

I reach to open the exercise book, when we're interrupted by a knock.

Mum sticks her head round the door. "Are you two ready to go?" she asks.

Simran bounces off the bed. "Come on, Jesse, read that later. We're in London, there's loads of stuff to explore, let's get out there. Anyway, I'm starving."

I reluctantly close the diary and put it back on top of the box. Simran's right. It can wait till later. It's waited over thirty years already. But, even so, I want to start reading it right now.

In the end, we don't go exploring, just grab some food and plan what we'll do tomorrow. We don't even talk much – Mum's still tired and my head's full of questions about Lisa's diary, wondering what her story is.

Back in our room, Simran and I go straight to bed. We don't bother putting away our clothes, it's too much effort, so we just dump them on the floor. My back aches from scrambling around in Lisa's attic. Even though Simran goes to sleep after about ten seconds – I can hear her slow breathing – I can't. I lie in my bed feeling hot and itchy, twisting and turning for ages.

I try to think peaceful thoughts, and to imagine that I am sailing away on a white, fluffy cloud, like in the relaxation exercises that Mum used to get me to do, but it's not working.

If I'm not going to go to sleep, I might as well start reading Lisa's diary. I move slowly and quietly across the dark room, so as not to wake Simran, and feel my way to the box. I know the diary's on top. I grab it. I don't turn on my phone torch until I'm under the covers clutching the book in my hand.

The biro scrawl is hard to read at first, especially without much light, but it becomes easier as I get used to it. There are cheery cartoons on some pages, and on others, there are angry, black scribbles and holes in the paper where she's dug her pen in too hard.

I skim through, looking for mentions of Nicky. September 1987 looks like the first one. I'll start here.

I decide to just read a little bit, but it's hard to stop turning over the next page and the next. So, in the end, I read until I can't keep my eyes open any more.

06 RESPECTABLE

Wednesday 30 September 1987

Walked home with Nicky B again after school yesterday. Last year we weren't friends at all. Back then, she was always with Claire and those other girls on the netball team. I thought they were all really up themselves, but actually Nicky's really nice. Claire still winds me up though.

Nicky made me laugh soooo much, doing impressions of Mr Payne. She can do that thing with her glasses like he does, like he's looking down his nose at everyone. We've both got RE with him on Friday, I bet I won't be able to stop laughing. And it will all be Nicky Burridge's fault.

Tuesday 13 October 1987

Dad had a real go at me tonight for spending too long on the phone. What if someone was trying to get through? What about my homework? Didn't I see my friends all day anyway – what more was there to talk about? It'd be different if I was the one paying the bill. Blah blah.

I stretched out the cord as far as I could so that it reached my bedroom. If I sit scrunched up in the corner right behind my door, it's just long enough. I wouldn't be surprised if Matthew was listening outside. He's such a creep. I wasn't on that long, at least I didn't think I was, but by the time we stopped talking, Mum was on her way to bed. It just never seems that long when I'm talking to Nicky. I know we've just got off the phone, but there's still loads more I want to say to her.

Thursday 5 November 1987

I hate today. Hate it, hate it, hate it. Everything was rubbish. Mum knew I was in a bad mood when I got home from school, but she still kept nagging me, on and on, about homework, about the length of my skirt, about my clothes on the floor, anything she could think of. I stopped listening after a while. That wasn't the worst thing though. It was

Nicky. Her and Jason. I thought we were walking home together. But I waited and waited and then I saw her and Jason coming through the gates together. She's all flicking her hair and leaning in like she doesn't want to miss a word he's saying and I don't know why but it makes me feel so rubbish. She was supposed to be with me. Should I phone her? But what if she doesn't want to talk to me?

Mum was okay in the end. She came and sat next to me on the sofa, neither of us really watching EastEnders but pretending we were. She passed me a cup of tea and a KitKat (she must have a secret stash somewhere) without saying anything, no questions, no interrogation. It was nice just to be with her, not having to talk. It's hardly ever like that. Still can't stop thinking about Nicky and Jason though.

Friday 6 November 1987

It's all okay now, at least I think so. This morning was awkward. This whole Nicky thing had got so big in my head that when she sat next to me in RE, I didn't know what to say. Normally we never stop talking.

She asked me if I was all right, but I just shrugged. She said that she got stuck with Jason after science cos they're supposed to be doing this project together. She said she tried to find me to walk home together but she couldn't see me.

I told her it was no big deal, but it was obvious I was upset. I couldn't even look at her. I couldn't stop myself saying what I was thinking – that she seemed really into him.

Nicky looked totally shocked. Then she said something like, "God, no, never. I'd much rather be spending my time with you, Lisa Scott." That made me feel, I don't know, weird somehow.

Then her voice got quieter, like she wasn't sure whether to go on or not. It was hard to hear over the noise in the classroom, so I leaned in closer, close enough to smell the strawberry shampoo on her hair, and she started saying how she thought boys were a waste of space and she'd never seen what all the fuss was about anyway. She looked right at me, her brown eyes questioning.

Then Mr Payne swept through the door and started shouting about the racket we were making.

He told us how Ms Ferraro had been talking to him about a way of making the ethics part of our RE lessons more fun.

Whenever he says "Ms", it looks like it's hurting his mouth. Nicky had noticed too and pursed her lips together just like Mr Payne does to make me laugh. It's the same when he says "fun" – I'm not sure he knows what it is.

Ms Ferraro's plan doesn't sound fun to me. At least, not how Mr Payne explained it. We're going to do debates, speaking for or against the issues in the RE textbooks. Most people got really excited, just because it's going to be a competition between the two classes. Like, who cares? I reckon the only reason Mr Payne agreed to do it was so that his class can win.

You have to research your issue, stand up and talk about it and then everyone else votes on who they agree with. Extra homework and extra embarrassment. You don't even get to choose which issue you speak on, who you work with or whether you argue for or against the statement. Could it *be* any worse? Well, later it turned out that, yes, it could.

Ms Ferraro's new this year. She's easy to spot in the corridors. She wears floaty, colourful skirts and has wild curly hair. She's not that much older than us. Whenever I've seen her, she's always talking earnestly to one of those teachers who've been around for ever while they look like they're desperate to escape to the staffroom for a smoke. This is just like the sort of idea she'd have.

Mr Payne wrote the topics on the board:

Abortion can never be morally justified.

Children should be protected from learning about homosexuality in school.

There is no such a thing as a "just war".

Animals have the same rights as human beings.

Marriage is the best place to bring up children.

Blah blah blah. And then reeled off the names of people in each group in a bored voice.

At first, the only thing I noticed was my name read out after Nicky's. We're in the same group – brilliant! Then I heard Jason and Craig were in our group too – rubbish! Then I took it in, the topic we'd been assigned – the one about protecting children from homosexuality. Mr Payne told us we were speaking against.

Even if we're the best, no one's going to vote for us. It's an unwritten school rule: if you let anyone think you're okay about gay people, that's almost as bad as admitting *you're* gay yourself. No one would be stupid enough to do that.

Then, of course, Jason starts mouthing off about how disgusting it was, and how he wasn't going to do the debate if he had to talk about queers.

Everyone looked to see what Mr Payne would say. Nicky seemed like she was going to spring out of her seat and have a go at Jason.

Mr Payne told Jason he had to do it. But you could tell by his pursed lips that he agreed with him – Mr Payne thought the whole topic was disgusting too.

The rest of the lesson was about research methods and the structure of the debates. I wasn't listening. Instead, I was thinking about what Nicky said about boys being a waste of space and how she'd rather spend her time with me.

Then Nicky leaned over and asked if I wanted to come over to her house at the weekend so we can work on the debate together!!!

I've never been to her house before, so she grabbed my hand, bit the cap off her biro and wrote her address across the back. It tickled, but her hands were cool and soft, and I didn't want her to let go.

Saturday 7 November 1987

Back from Nicky's. Not sure what's going on in my head right now. I'll just tell you all about it, right from the beginning.

I wasn't sure what to wear. I changed in and out of about five different outfits, before putting on the same jeans and baggy T-shirt that I started with. I worried about getting there too early, but in the end I was so late that I had to run for the bus.

I knocked and waited, tracing my finger over Nicky's address, faded now but still visible, remembering how it felt when she wrote it on my hand.

The woman who answered the door looked nothing like Nicky. She had cropped, dyed blonde hair, ripped jeans and a big grin. She looked far too young to be Nicky's mum, but I didn't think Nicky had a big sister. I worried I'd read the address wrong and that I'd knocked on a random stranger's door. But before I could say anything, the woman turned and called up the stairs: "Nicky, shift your lazy arse downstairs, your friend's here."

Then she grinned at me and told me to come in. She said her name was Kayleigh.

Nicky thundered down the stairs, wearing jeans and a T-shirt like me, her curls flying around her shoulders, not tied back in a ponytail like they normally are at school.

She told Kayleigh to leave it out. Then she grabbed me by the hand and pulled me upstairs. The second time she's held my hand now.

All the way up the stairs were paintings. I wanted to stop and look at them, but Nicky was going too fast.

"Kayleigh's so rude!" she exclaimed, dropping my hand to slam the door of her bedroom behind us. But she was

71

laughing like she didn't really mind. Then she explained, Kayleigh was her dad's girlfriend!

I tried not to look shocked when she told me. I didn't know if that meant Nicky's mum was dead, or her parents were divorced or what. I wasn't sure if it was okay to ask, but she told me anyway.

Her parents have been divorced for ages. Her mum married again and went to live in Holland with her new husband, so Nicky doesn't see her much. They thought it was best for her to grow up in the UK, so that's why Nicky lives with her dad. It blew my mind a bit. I've never met a family like Nicky's.

Whenever Mum sees something about divorce on the news, she mutters words like "broken homes" and "abandoned children". I tried hard not to hear her voice in my head or imagine her disapproving look. I bet she'd say that Kayleigh was a homewrecker.

I must have looked a *bit* surprised though, as Nicky got edgy, saying how cool Kayleigh was, not like an evil stepmum or anything.

I changed the subject by asking what her dad taught at the college.

It's art. How cool is that? Apparently, the paintings on the stairs are all his and Nicky even said he could give me advice about applying to art college. She kept going on about how my drawings were so good. I couldn't stop smiling. If only Mum and Dad felt the same way, instead of making out that studying art is a total waste of time.

Eventually we got round to planning the debate. We both agreed that Jason and Craig probably won't do *any* work and that even though we don't care about winning Mr Payne's competition, we don't want to look stupid in front of everyone.

Then we spent ages flicking through the RE textbook. We couldn't stop laughing at the 70s fashions in the photos.

Then Nicky started reading out bits from the book. She put on a posh voice whenever she said "homosexuality", which made me laugh, but nervously this time. When she said, "Why don't they just say 'gay' or 'lesbian'?", I stopped laughing and stared at her. Her face was flushed, and she ran a hand through her messy hair.

I didn't say anything, but what I was thinking was, *no one* just says "gay" or "lesbian" casually like that. Except as an insult. Although I guess the headlines in Dad's paper use words that are even worse.

"There's nothing wrong with the words, you know," she said quietly.

Then she reached under her bed and pulled out a magazine. It was called *Spare Rib*. Nicky said Kayleigh read it and loads of her dad's students did too. She said it was about politics and women's rights. This was a special edition about how women could do whatever they wanted, without needing men, not even for relationships or to have kids.

Nicky watched me flick through the magazine. I was more interested in looking at the cartoons than reading the articles. But she said there'd be stuff in there that we could use for the debate.

So we looked through it and I made notes. There was a whole article about this new law called Clause 28 that could make it illegal to talk about homosexuality in schools. The writer had loads of arguments about why it shouldn't happen, so making notes was easy – I just wrote down what it said.

Nicky seemed really excited we'd been given this side of the argument, saying it was okay to teach about homosexuality in school. She said it was a chance to open people's minds. But I couldn't help thinking how Jason and Craig will probably make throwing up noises when we tell them next lesson about the work we've done so far.

Later, her dad stuck his head in to say hello. I couldn't believe it when Nicky called him "Michael" instead of "Dad". She said she's always done that, that's what his students do too. Can you imagine if I started calling Dad "Norman"?! He'd have a fit.

I wished the morning could have gone on for ever. I never thought I'd say that about doing homework, especially boring RE. But it was different doing it with Nicky. She's so full of ideas about everything. I wish I could put my thoughts into words the way she can.

Nicky said how at the college, it was no big deal to be gay. There was even a Gay Soc that people could join. She said one of her dad's friends, another lecturer, was a lesbian. She kept it quiet, but everyone knew.

I hadn't really thought about it before. I don't know anyone who's gay. But the more I think about it, the more it seems stupid that you can't just love who you want to love. I mean, what's so wrong about that?

07 OUT WITH HER

"Wake up, Jesse!" calls Simran, pulling back the curtains. "It says here they do croissants *and* a cooked breakfast."

I must have fallen asleep while reading Lisa's diary. For a moment I wonder if I've dreamt it all – my imagination getting carried away about Lisa's life while I slept.

But then again, I don't think I would have made up that awful stuff about kids needing to be protected from homosexuality. I want to tell Simran about it – I bet she'll be outraged – but she won't stop chattering on about hash browns and fried eggs.

We need to get moving because today we've got to find the perfect idea for our history project, something that will really impress Ms Grant. Even if we have to search every museum in London for inspiration.

I need to focus, to stop thinking about Lisa for now. But I shove the diary into my bag anyway, just in case I get a moment to read it later.

We end up at an exhibition full of the sort of clothes that would make everyone stare at you if you wore them in the street. It's hard to pull Simran away, but eventually she comes to look at some old World War Two letters in another part of the museum.

I love how, in between the faded spidery writing, people had drawn little doodles about what life was like during the war. Even when things were so awful, people could still make fun of what was going on.

Then Mum leads us past all the shiny restaurants and fancy coffee shops, down a maze of poky little streets to a tiny basement cafe, where the three of us squash around a chipped wooden table in the corner.

People buzz in and out, talking loudly. The pictures on the wall are old and lopsided. When the food comes, there's huge, steaming platefuls of it. And it's delicious.

"Isn't this place wonderful?" says Mum. "There used to be cafes like this all round here. Cheap and cheerful. They've probably all vanished now, except this one."

I can see why Mum likes it here so much. It looks nothing like Over the Rainbow. No books for a start, or rainbow bunting. But something about it feels the same;

special. Like it's a place where anyone could come in and feel at home. I'd be happy sitting here all day and watching people come and go.

"How do you know this place?" I ask with my mouth full of chips.

"Oh, from when I was a student," says Mum. "I used to come here all the time. You could get a roast dinner and a pudding for a fiver. And eavesdrop on some amazing conversations while you ate. It's nice to find it again." She sighs. "Oh, listen to me going on, I sound so old..."

"It's all right," says Simran. "You know how Jesse loves ancient history... Maybe she could write down your memories in our project." Only Simran could get away with saying something so cheeky.

"So, yes," says Mum. "What about this project? Has inspiration struck either of you yet? Or do we need to carry on searching this afternoon?"

"And do a tiny bit of shopping as well?" says Simran. "Maybe? Please? I mean, we are in London. It would help, I reckon. Shopping's always very inspiring."

I laugh. "I don't know. Maybe we'll never think of anything."

"Of course, you will. I find food always helps," says Mum, tucking enthusiastically into her plate of lasagne. "Anyway, I was wracking my brains last night," she continues. "Trying to remember anything about when Lisa stayed with us, but not much came back. Except that when she first arrived, she was so quiet. She stayed in her room all the time, listening to music. I was shy of her at first, she was so grown-up and she looked so serious whenever she did appear. I remember that she used to draw me these cartoons – she was really good. I loved it when she did that."

"I found her diary in the box and it's *full* of drawings," I say. "She's really talented. I mean, she *was* really talented."

We all go quiet for a moment, thinking about Lisa. How everything about her is now in the past tense. History.

"Here, let me show you." I pull the diary out of my bag and move the greasy plates to make a space for it on the table.

"Oh yes," says Mum, turning the book around so she can see it better. "I mean, I don't recognize the people she's drawn, but that's definitely her style. Oh, look!" She points at one of the pages and laughs.

"That's her RE teacher," I say. "Mr Payne."

"She didn't like him very much, did she?"

"He deserved it!" I exclaim. My cheeks feel hot. Mum and Simran look at me in surprise. Am I talking too loudly? "I mean, he was awful," I add more quietly, trying to find the right words to explain. "Mum, when you were at school, did teachers let people say, like, really homophobic things?"

Mum looks thoughtful and sips her drink. "Well," she says. "It wasn't like now. People didn't really talk about things like that in school. There was no LGBT History Month or PSHE or anything. I suppose some teachers might have allowed things which aren't acceptable today. It's all so long ago. Why?" She looks concerned. "Is that what Lisa's diary says this teacher does?"

I explain about Jason in Lisa's class saying gay people were disgusting and Mr Payne basically agreeing with him, and Lisa writing about it like that was perfectly normal.

"What?" exclaims Simran, her fork crashing down onto her plate. "That's so out of order!"

Mum sighs. "That's probably how it was then. I'm glad you two are so shocked by it. It shows that things are getting better. No one would get away with that kind of prejudice today. Not without being challenged anyway."

I want to believe she's right, but I worry she's not. Maybe no teacher would say something like that in front of the whole class, but I've heard comments in the corridors from people like Jasmine and I've seen stuff online.

Mum's still looking at the cartoons in Lisa's diary.

"I hope he never saw any of her drawings!" she says.

I shake my head. "It would serve him right if he did!"

80

"Maybe *nobody's* ever seen these before," says Simran. "Until us, I mean. They're a bit like the drawings in those war diaries we saw in the exhibition this morning, aren't they?"

"What's this?" asks Mum, as a photo slips out from between the pages. She holds it up to the light and peers at it. It's the one of Lisa and Nicky, arms round each other, big grins on their faces. She turns it over. There's nothing written on the back, just a faded date-stamp: 30/04/88.

"I don't know," I say. "I'm still reading about 1987. But that's Lisa, obviously, and that's her friend Nicky."

"*Girl*friend," corrects Simran.

Mum raises an eyebrow. "Really?"

I shrug. "Dunno, maybe."

"Not maybe," says Simran, flicking through the diary. "For sure. Look, she's doodled Nicky's name all over the place! You should fast forward, Jesse, skip the boring stuff and find out when they're going to get together."

"It's not a film," I tell Simran. "It's someone's real life."

Despite this photo of Lisa and Nicky together looking loved up, I'm worried for Lisa. What if it *was* just a crush? What if they *didn't* get together and Lisa's heart got broken? I'm starting to really care about what happened to her. Even if it was years ago and there's nothing I, or anyone, can do to change it now.

I know how Lisa's story ends – it's awful that she died so young – but I hardly know anything about the life she lived first. I hope she was happy.

"I wonder what's going on here," says Mum, putting on her glasses to examine the photo. "Looks like some kind of big event, doesn't it? All those people in the background. Perhaps Lisa writes about it in her diary. It's obvious *where* they are, even if we don't know much else."

"Is it?" I ask. It's not obvious to me. "Where are they?"

"I'm not leaving here till I've had a huge slice of treacle tart drenched in custard," says Mum firmly. "But after that we can go and retrace their steps if you like. There's plenty to see on the way."

When we leave the cafe, all three of us full of treacle tart, Mum leads us through tiny streets, a crowded Leicester Square and more back alleys, until we pop out at Piccadilly Circus. There are impressive buildings on every side and tons of tourists, just like us, snapping photos of each other on their phones.

"Here we are," says Mum, holding up the photo, like a magician who's pulled off a successful trick. "I think, yes, this is where we're looking for. They were on these steps right here."

Mum passes the photo to me. I examine it closely, and then look all around. In front of us is a small statue on top

82

of a huge fancy-looking carved base, with shallow stone steps leading up to it. I recognize it from films about London. It's Eros, the god of love. An almost naked guy with big wings, holding a bow and arrow. Kind of weird when you think about it. Yes, this is the right place.

Simran grabs my hand and pulls me up the steps.

"Careful!" I squeal, holding on tight to the photo with my other hand.

She throws her arm round me and holds out her phone for a selfie. "Smile!"

And we both do.

"Go on, send it to me," I urge her.

I'm so glad I'm here with Simran. Other people might think it's weird, or boring, traipsing round London in the footsteps of a dead person you've never met. Not Simran, she never makes me feel like I'm boring or weird.

My phone buzzes. I normally hate photos of myself, but this one's perfect. I forward it to Tom to show him what we're up to in London and save it to my lock screen, so that I'll see Simran and me every time I unlock my phone.

I think about all the people who've stood in this place, posing for photos, not just Lisa and Nicky. Everyone thinking that what's happening to them at that moment is the most important thing in the world. And it is, to them.

But then another moment comes and another. And each moment disappears into history. And maybe even the people who were there at the time don't remember it. It makes me feel weightless, that I'm not really here and nothing that's happening to me is real.

I'm sure, just from looking at the photo, that something important was happening for Lisa and Nicky right then – they look so happy with each other and comfortable in who they are. But I don't know what *was* going on that day and *why* it mattered. It would be easy to skip six months ahead in the diary to April 1988 and find out, like Simran wants me to, but that feels like cheating. My fingers creep towards my bag. I want to start reading again.

"You know," I say to Simran, "if you go shopping, I could wait for you in a cafe. You know I hate it and you'd get loads more done without me moaning about being bored."

"Aw, Jesse, come on…don't abandon me," pleads Simran, but she knows I'm right about me slowing her down.

Mum looks from me to Simran. "You two are very grown-up, but I'm not letting someone else's child, or mine for that matter, wander off on their own in the middle of a huge city they don't know. We're staying together."

"You could go with her, Mum, you'd enjoy it. I'll be fine. I won't move till you come back. I'll just sit and read somewhere."

I can tell Mum's torn. She knows after years of dragging me around that I'm never going to enjoy clothes shopping like she does. I'm not the daughter she always imagined, sharing tips on hair and make-up and clothes. Ha. On so many levels, that's never going to happen.

"I've got my phone," I add. "I just need a bit of time out, that's all."

Mum nods. "Okay then, there's an art gallery down the road, you can stay in the cafe there. Just don't go anywhere or talk to anyone and call me if anything happens. Got it?"

"Yeah, all right, Mum. Got it."

"It's good to see you so interested in something," says Mum softly, once we've reached the gallery. She hugs me, then she and Simran head off together to hit the shops.

As soon as they leave, I settle in the cafe with a large hot chocolate. I pull the diary out of my bag and start reading. I want to find out if Lisa and Nicky manage to win the debate despite everything that's stacked against them. I really hope they do.

08 CAUSING A COMMOTION

Friday 13 November 1987

It's Friday the thirteenth! No wonder today was such a disaster!

RE was wild. Mr Payne came striding into the classroom like he was leading an army into battle. He gave us this talk about how we had to win the debates and Ms Ferraro's class wouldn't stand a chance against us. It was fierce. There was nothing about "taking part is what counts" or any of that stuff. He kept pulling at his tie whenever he got worked up till I thought he was going to throttle himself. My fingers itched to draw him, but there was no chance because then we had to get up and go into the hall.

Nicky thinks he's so obsessed with beating Ms Ferraro because she's a powerful woman. He feels threatened by her because she's got new ideas. Nicky says that's scary for someone old and dried up like him.

But I wasn't interested in how Mr Payne was feeling. I was more worried about how I was feeling – so anxious that my hands were shaking. And for a good reason.

I didn't want to get up and speak in front of everyone. What if I couldn't get the words out, even with everything written down in front of me? I knew I'd go bright red as soon as we started. Not just because of speaking in public, but because of what we were speaking about.

I told myself it didn't matter, it was just a stupid school debate. It would be just about okay if people laughed at me, but I didn't want them to laugh at Nicky. She was taking this all so seriously, like it actually mattered. She must've known we couldn't win, but she was acting like she thought we could.

Just as a joke, I whispered to Nicky that we should run away.

"Come on then," she smiled, giving me this look, like she honestly would, like we actually could. "Mr Payne will never catch us. Can you imagine him running down the corridors after us? Let's leg it for the doors at the back!"

We all filed into rows in the hall. There were two tables and two groups of chairs set up at the front for each side when they came up to debate.

We sat through the other debates first. I kept hoping a

miracle would happen which would stop it ever being our turn, like the fire alarm going off or someone fainting. We were supposed to have researched the topic with Craig and Jason, but really, Nicky and I had done it all – they'd just messed around in the lessons when we were meant to prepare. Each group had to decide on two speakers – for ours, that was Nicky and me. I felt sick. Maybe I would be the one to faint.

We stood up and did our bit. Nicky talked about how important it was to learn and talk about all kinds of relationships in school. Homosexuality wasn't something to protect children from, she said, it was part of life. And anyway, you couldn't make someone gay, just by talking about it. There have always been gay people, even thousands of years ago, even in the Bible, and historians had found evidence of marriage ceremonies between two men or two women. So it must be natural. I tried to be as confident as her, but I swear my voice was shaking as I talked about how all religions said love was the most important thing.

Whenever I looked up from my notes, I could see Ms Ferraro smiling at me encouragingly and Mr Payne standing with his arms folded and a smirk on his face.

Craig and Jason slowly edged their chairs away from ours, like we were nothing to do with them, like we had something they could catch.

When we sat down, after what felt like hours, Ms Ferraro started clapping. But only a couple of people joined in. Everyone just looked at their shoes, including me. At least it was over now.

Except it wasn't. It got worse. It sounds stupid now, but I hadn't even thought about what the other group might say, and how awful it would be to listen to it. Nicky and I been too busy thinking about our own arguments. How we were going to open people's minds, or whatever it was she said.

First, they quoted Bible verses. That was okay, I mean it *was* RE. I don't believe in the Bible anyway, so who cares? Then Tara, who always pushes in front of you in the dinner queue like you're too insignificant for her to even notice, said how all gay people got AIDS and that was a punishment from God, a sign that they were wrong...

Before I could stop her, Nicky leaped up and started shouting at Tara, saying she was stupid and talking rubbish. Just because I've got red hair, everyone thinks I must be hot-headed, but I'm not. Not like Nicky anyway! I wanted to crawl away and hide.

Mr Payne told her to sit down because she'd already had a chance to make her argument. He was really snooty about it. He even said something like "this is a debate, not a pub brawl". But not one word from him about what Tara had said. I thought Nicky would stop then, but she kept repeating how it was just prejudice and it wasn't true.

That's when even the people mucking about or watching the minutes crawl by on the wall clock began to pay attention. Was Nicky calling Tara a liar? Was she going to carry on talking back to Mr Payne? What would he do? Nicky didn't normally get into trouble. But today wasn't normal.

Mr Payne gave her his coldest look, said nothing, then turned to Tara and waved his hand at her to continue.

Nicky sat down, arms folded, the colour of her face matching my hair. I wanted to squeeze her hand and say it was okay, but I stopped myself. I didn't want anyone to think anything, did I?

Then Tara started again, saying how five-year-olds were being forced by teachers to read books about being gay! That's why this new law, Clause 28, was so important. It would stop teachers, or anyone, promoting homosexuality like that...

Then Jason shouted out, "It's disgusting. They shouldn't allow that in schools, it's obvious."

I hissed at him to shut up. He was supposed to be on *our* team!

"I'm not on any team with *you*," he spat back under

his breath. "Or that lez, Nicky Burridge, everyone knows she is. You should watch out, Lisa."

I thought that Mr Payne would tell Jason off, like he did with Nicky, but he just ignored him and let Tara carry on with her speech. Ms Ferraro leaned forward. I thought she was going to say something. But she didn't.

I hoped that Nicky would let it lie. Then we could finish and get out of there as soon as possible. But, guess what, she didn't.

She jumped to her feet again, complaining about Jason shouting out. Wasn't Mr Payne going to tell him off like he did her earlier?

Then Mr Payne lost it. Whenever he asks, "Who is the teacher here, you or me?" you know that someone's going to get in serious trouble.

"Like I care what he thinks, bigoted old fool," Nicky muttered quietly to me. I swear Mr Payne has supersonic hearing though. Like an evil super-villain.

He sent Nicky to stand outside the hall. She picked up her notebook and bag, and marched to the doors, looking stunned. A couple of people whistled, then everyone went quiet, watching her go. There was this hum of excitement in the air. I wondered if I should follow her, but my feet wouldn't move. I stayed in my seat.

Then Mr Payne started having a go at Ms Ferraro!

In front of everyone, telling her how he'd warned her about rejecting traditional, tried-and-tested teaching methods, it encouraged children to think they knew all the answers. Ms Ferraro just opened and shut her mouth. Like she couldn't get the words out.

Everyone was properly talking now, until Mr Payne shouted at them all to shut up because it was time to vote.

He read out the motion again, the one we'd been arguing against: Children should be protected from learning about homosexuality in school.

No one voted for our side. Except me. Not even Craig and Jason and they were on our team. It was even worse than I'd thought it would be. Not one single person. That's probably the first time I've seen Mr Payne smile; it was horrible. It seemed that he didn't mind about us beating Ms Ferraro's class after all.

I sat through the other debates, not listening, Nicky's empty chair next to mine. What would happen to her now? I wanted to make a quick escape when it was over, but instead I got stuck stacking the chairs at the back.

Andy from the other class staggered over with a pile of chairs and dumped them next to mine.

"I thought your speech was really good." He said it so quietly that it took a while to work out what he said.

I snapped back at him that if he thought we were so

good, why didn't he vote for us? It was mean, seeing as he was actually being nice, but I didn't care, I was still so angry.

I didn't expect him to sound so miserable. He muttered something about life being rubbish enough already and not needing an extra reason for Jason and Craig to pick on him. My stomach sank into my shoes. I knew Craig and Jason sometimes made monkey noises at Black kids in the corridors. Maybe that had happened to Andy. I felt even worse now about being annoyed with him.

He said, "I thought you and Nicky were really brave up there. You're really good together."

There was something about the way he said "good together" that made me feel proud and happy and anxious and confused all at once.

It suddenly seemed really important to tell him that Nicky and I weren't a couple. I mean, of course we're not.

Is that what everyone's thinking? I wanted to ask him – but I was too scared of what the answer might be.

I still felt bad about having snapped at Andy, so I asked if he wanted to hang out with me and Nicky sometime after school. He seemed really pleased. I'd rather it was just her and me, but I know she won't mind, and Andy's okay.

I rushed out of the hall as soon as the chairs were done,

but Nicky had gone. Probably getting a telling-off from Mr Payne. I wanted to call her when I got home, but Dad said I couldn't until after we'd eaten, and now Matthew's on the phone talking to one of his stupid mates. Oh wait, I think he's finished. At last.

Just off the phone. Wish I hadn't called Nicky now. Feel even worse. She said how Mr Payne laid right into her, but she didn't seem to mind about that, she sounded proud about getting her first detention. Apparently, her dad told her she did the right thing, standing up for what she believed in. She was much more upset when I told her about the vote.

I kept apologizing about not storming out behind her or even saying anything to stick up for her. But she wasn't mad at me, she said there was no point in me getting in trouble with my parents. She's right – they'd definitely be on Mr Payne's side. They think teachers are always right, whatever.

I told her about Andy being nice because I thought that might make her feel better, but she wasn't really listening.

"Right," she interrupted. "This means we've got to do more, to shout louder, to fight. How can people believe that stupid stuff about AIDS being a punishment from God, or teachers trying to turn students gay? We have to tell people the truth. If the law changes to prevent schools even talking about gay people, it's going to get even worse."

What? Today was bad enough. I never want to go through anything like that EVER again. NO ONE supported what we said in the debate. How can any new law make things any WORSE!?!

When I said that, Nicky got really worked up, just like in the debate. Matthew was lurking around. I worried that he could hear what Nicky was saying, so I clamped the receiver closer to my ear and shooed him away. He made a face but went into his room.

"We've got to fight back," she said. "It's the principle. Don't you think gay people deserve the same respect as everyone else, Lisa?"

Of course I do, and Nicky knows that. But she's wrong about us changing things. There's nothing *we* can do about it. No one's going to listen to us.

The whole phone call, the talk about fighting, it all just made me feel rubbish. Now that the RE debate is over, why can't we just get back to normal? Hanging out. Being friends. Not joining a fight that's got nothing to do with us.

I asked her why she even cared so much about it. She gave this huge sigh, like I *had* let her down after all.

Then she hung up.

I sat there listening to the dial tone, until Matthew stuck his head around the door and asked if I was talking to my imaginary friend. He thought he was so funny. I hate him. I hate everyone.

I feel so trapped in here with Mum and Dad and Matthew, doing and saying the same things that we always do and say, the TV droning on in the background. It makes me want to scream. I know I won't sleep – I'll just keep going over and over everything in my mind.

I've decided, I'll go to Nicky's house tomorrow. I'll just turn up. Even if she won't answer the door or tells me to go away, it's better than waiting and wondering if, after that phone call, we're still friends any more.

09 TOO GOOD TO BE FORGOTTEN

"Got you!"

Even though I know it's only Simran, I can't help screaming. The woman at the next table looks up from her laptop. Simran's hands grip my shoulders. I can't see her face, but I know she's grinning.

"Oh my god, Sim, you made me jump out of my skin. I nearly had a heart attack!"

"Sorry," she says. But she's so not. She loves making me jump.

She sits down opposite me and pushes a bag across the table. "Do you want to see what I got?"

I look around. "What did you do with my mum? You didn't lose her, did you?"

"Don't be daft, she's just getting a coffee. Anyway, look…"

She shows me a couple of tops and some neon nail varnish, and I try to sound like I'm interested, but my mind keeps drifting back to Nicky and Lisa.

I feel sick just thinking about that RE debate. Imagine having to listen to people coming out with all those lies and knowing that no one was going to stop them.

At least none of our teachers are anything like Mr Payne – even the worst ones, the ones who forget my pronouns and then make a big deal of it, or the ones who give tons of homework. Ms Ferraro sounds a bit like Ms Grant, full of new ideas, except Ms Grant would never let anyone walk over her like that. She'd say something. For sure.

Simran can tell I'm not giving her my full attention. She taps the diary. "So, what's going on? Did they kiss yet?"

"Simran!"

"What? I just want to know."

"No, in fact they've just had a huge row."

Simran's eyes widen. "No way. Spill. What about?"

"It's complicated," I sigh. "I don't really get it."

Mum joins us with her coffee, a slice of carrot cake and three spoons. I take a large spoonful of the icing – that's my favourite part.

I explain to them both about the debate and the argument and everything else I've read about in Lisa's diary.

"Wow," says Simran, drawing in breath and shaking her head so hard that her earrings jangle. "That's so messed up. I mean, being gay isn't something you need to *protect* people from, like a disease or something. People are what they are."

I think about the tatty "Some People Are Gay… Get Over It" posters in the corridors at school. I'm so glad not to have been a student in Lisa and Nicky's school all those years ago.

"It's like no one even imagined that anyone LGBTQ+ could be in the room!" I add. "And no one voted for Nicky and Lisa, Sim, no one. Imagine how lonely she must have felt, the only person in that whole hall with her hand up." I feel a bit choked up.

"No wonder Nicky started kicking off," says Simran. "I would have done the same as her, wouldn't you?" I don't say anything. "Jesse?" she prompts after a moment.

"Um, yeah, of course." I hope I would have been brave enough. But maybe I would have been more like Lisa, silent and glued to my seat. Especially if I knew the sort of things people might say or think or whisper about me. I honestly don't know what I would have done.

"There's more than one way to be brave," says Mum, like she's reading my mind. "I think Lisa was brave too. It's brave to stand out like that, to be the only one to vote, even when she was scared of the consequences. Especially if she didn't have support at home. Didn't you say Nicky's dad encouraged her to speak out? I'm sure that made it easier for her."

"But how could it have been okay to say such awful things? Didn't people know any better? Why didn't Ms Ferraro stop them?" The questions spill out, one after another.

Mum takes a breath. I think she's going to answer me, but instead she says, "You're the historians. Research. Find out more about it."

"Yeah," says Simran, reaching for her phone. "There's that thing that Nicky and Lisa were arguing about, 28 something."

"'28 something'?" I laugh. "That's not it, it's…"

"Section 28?" says Mum.

"It says *Clause* 28 here," I tell her, flicking through the diary. "Are they the same thing?"

Simran taps it into her phone, then reads out loud. "Section 28. UK law in place from 1988 to – what? – 2003 – that's ages! – prohibiting the promotion by local authorities of homosexuality as a pretended family relationship." She pauses and looks up. "What does that even mean?"

"1988," I murmur, leaning over to look at the screen.

"That's the year after Lisa started writing her diary."

"Local authorities run schools and youth groups and libraries," explains Mum. "So I guess it means that under this law, this Section 28, none of those places could... what did it say?"

"Promote homosexuality," repeats Simran.

"But what does promotion mean?" I ask.

"I'm not sure in this context," says Mum. She sounds like she's choosing each word carefully, as if she's trying to break bad news without upsetting us. "It could mean anything really. A ban on any books or lessons or groups for or about LGBTQ+ people."

Simran and I both stare at her.

"No way," says Simran fiercely. "Isn't that against freedom of speech or something?"

"I bet Mr Payne would have loved that," I say. My voice sounds hard and bitter. "Jason too."

"And Nicky would have hated it!" adds Simran. "She'd have tried to stop it happening."

"But how?" I ask.

"If you want to understand what happened, then you know where to start, don't you?" Mum picks the diary off the table and hands it to me. "You've got something amazing here. The thoughts of someone who was actually there. Right here in your hands."

"Ms Grant says that's called a primary source. Isn't that right, Jesse? Hey, Jesse!" Simran waves her hand in front of my face when I don't answer straight away. "Are you all right?"

I don't feel all right. I feel… I don't know what I feel. Angry, anxious, and something else… I think it's excitement. Because I've had an idea.

"Right here in our hands," I say softly, echoing Mum. "Do you think *this* could be our history project, researching into Lisa and Nicky's lives?" I ask.

Simran nods thoughtfully. "Yeah, why not? It's proper history, isn't it? I mean, it all happened ages ago."

"Excuse me," says Mum. "Not *that* long ago, I was a kid then, you know, and I'm not *that* old."

"Yeah, but still, the 1980s, that's ancient."

"But doesn't something have to *happen* to make it history?" I wonder, partly to Simran, partly to myself. "I mean, it's just their lives, school and home, it's ordinary."

"So far. You don't know what's going to happen next. And anyway, what about those diaries from World War Two we saw in the museum this morning?" says Simran, leaning forward. "They were about people's ordinary lives, weren't they? And they were interesting because they were living through something important. It's the same here. Obviously." She sits back in her chair, point made, and then darts forward again to snatch the last spoonful of cake. "Jesse, this is it! Now you can stop going on and on about what we're going to do for our project and we can finally talk about something else." She grins. I stick my tongue out at her.

"I suppose…" I say. Maybe I sound like I'm still not sure, but I'm already starting to imagine what our project could look like, on display in the school hall. I *know* we're going to do this.

"And…" continues Simran, quieter now. "It's *our* history, you know. It matters. Lisa and Nicky, it was different for them, everything they knew about being LGBTQ+ they had to work out themselves. Schools and libraries and youth groups couldn't help them, that's what your mum just said."

"They didn't even have the internet," adds Mum.

"And yet," continues Simran. "They still found each other. I think they should be remembered."

"What about all the other stuff in that box with the diary?" I say, my mind racing on. "That could all be part of our display too."

"And you can do additional research," chips in Mum. "I'm sure you could find a book or two in Over the Rainbow about Section 28."

"But what about Lisa?" I ask. "Do you think she'd mind?

If she was still alive, I mean. It's her things, her story, her private diary."

Mum sighs. "I don't know what Lisa would have thought. I wish I did, I wish I'd known her as an adult..." She sighs again. "But there we are. If it was me, I reckon I'd be flattered if someone was interested in my life. It's a kind of a tribute, a way of remembering her. I rather like that. Apart from the diary and whatever else is in that box, it's going to be tricky to find out much about Lisa's life. I was too little to remember anything. Gran and Grandpa aren't around to ask, nor are Lisa's parents."

"What about Matthew, her brother?" I wonder.

"He didn't come to her funeral," says Simran. "Maybe they weren't even speaking before she died."

"Or maybe he wanted to come, but he couldn't because he lives on the other side of the world," I reply.

"He's my cousin, but honestly I don't remember him at all," says Mum. "It does seem ridiculous to have family and hardly know anything about them. We could have got to know Lisa, but now it's too late. Matthew's my flesh and blood. I want to get in contact with him, it might even help with your history project too. I'll have a look in Gran's old address book when we get back home. Maybe there's an email address for him. If not, I'll email Lisa's friend Ali and ask her."

A waiter swoops past our table and collects the dirty plates. "You've got five minutes. Cafe's closing at six," he tells us.

"What?" exclaims Mum. "We've got to get moving! We need to pick up our bags from the B&B and catch our train home. There's a lot more to carry now than on the way here, what with Simran's new clothes and all these historical artefacts of yours."

"I can't believe it's already been two days," says Simran, as we dodge the rush hour crowds on our way back to the tube. "I wish we could stay for longer. There's loads more to see."

I know what she means, but I'm looking forward to getting home. Now that we've decided what our project's going to be about, we need to start work. But we don't have to wait till we get back – I can read some more of the diary on the train.

"First thing tomorrow," I say, putting my hand on Simran's arm, "let's go to Over the Rainbow and show the diary to Maz. Maybe she can help us find out more about Section 28." We stand in the middle of the pavement as people flow past us.

"I see," Simran replies. "You're going to go on about this project more than ever now, aren't you?"

"Yes, I am," I tell her. "Anyway, it's *our* project! Don't pretend you're not interested too!"

She grins. "Of course I am. Your idea's brilliant, Jesse. Our project is definitely going to be the best!"

"Come on, let's catch up with Mum, we don't want to get left behind in London."

"Don't we?" she says. I grab her by the arm and drag her along. The breath from our laughter makes clouds in the cold evening air.

Luckily Mum booked us seats on the train back to Hurston. There are so many people squashed in the carriage that there's barely space to move. I ease the diary out of my bag. I want to know what happens when Lisa turns up outside Nicky's house on the day after the debate.

10 WALKING DOWN YOUR STREET

Saturday 14 November 1987

Oh my god, oh my god, oh my god. I feel like, oh, I don't know what I feel like. I'm going to remember today for ever – Saturday 24 October 1987. When I got in, I ran straight upstairs. Mum was trying to tell me something, but I don't want to talk to her. I can't. If she says or does anything, this feeling I've got will shatter into a million pieces.

I was so nervous on the bus to Nicky's. I couldn't bear the thought that I might have messed everything up. Not just because, after yesterday's debate disaster, no one else would want to be my friend, but because I've never had a friend like her before. What if she hated me now? What if she thought I was as bad as everyone else? I needed to say something to make it right, but I didn't know what.

I walked up and down the road four times, promising myself that once I'd seen three blue cars, I'd ring on the doorbell. Then four, then five.

When I finally did, I felt sick. No one answered. I was just about to walk away when I saw the wobbly outline of Nicky's dad through the coloured glass in the front door.

He invited me in, even though Nicky was out doing the weekly shop with Kayleigh, and made me a coffee. It was bitter and horrible, but it felt like a grown-up kind of thing to drink. There were paintings all over the walls. Huge ones. Swirling shapes and colours and patterns.

I could imagine Mum tutting at the piles of books and dirty cups on all the surfaces – Nicky's dad must drink a *lot* of coffee – and complaining that a five-year-old child could do better than these so-called modern artists. But I loved the pictures.

Suddenly something moved. I swear I jumped about two feet in the air. A sleek black cat shot out from under the table and out of the door.

"That's Frida, she's very temperamental. A true artist's cat. She'll get used to you after a while," said Nicky's dad. I hoped he was right and Frida would have a chance to get used to me. But maybe Nicky wouldn't want to speak to me. Maybe I'd never be able to come here again.

He talked to me about the art on the walls, asking my

opinion and listening to what I said. He made being an artist feel like a real thing you could do, instead of something to mess around with before getting what Dad calls "a proper job".

All the time we were talking, I was listening out for Nicky.

Suddenly, the front door banged open. Kayleigh shouted out to Nicky's dad to give her a hand.

I saw Nicky before she noticed me. One hand holding a bulging carrier bag, the other scooping her hair out of her eyes, the sun through the window lighting up her face. And everything about her was...perfect. She looked like an old-fashioned painting. If people in old-fashioned paintings carried Sainsbury's bags. Then she saw me, and smiled, in this unsure, questioning kind of way. In that instant, she transformed from a painting back into a person.

We all flapped around, unpacking the bags, with Nicky showing me where everything went in their kitchen. Then her dad made more coffee, Kayleigh wandered off into the garden, and Nicky and I went upstairs.

She didn't ask what I was doing there or seem surprised that I'd come. We stood on each side of her room for a bit, not saying anything. And then a whole load of words came out of my mouth without me knowing what I was going to say next.

"Last night on the phone, I asked why the debate mattered so much to you. Stupid question. I think I know why. I just couldn't quite get my head round it. I didn't want to. It's cos *you're* gay, isn't it? I've never met anyone gay before, and you're not what I thought it would be like. God, that sounds stupid. I'm always saying stupid things. I'm sorry. It's just, I really like you. I really like being friends with you, I mean. I don't want to say anything to make you feel bad, not ever..."

I stopped. Something so obvious struck me. I like being friends with Nicky, of course, but actually, truly, that's not enough. I wanted to be more than friends. Could Nicky feel the same way? About me? Was that possible?

The silence grew. I stared down at my boots.

"You're right, Lisa. I'm gay."

She said that she hadn't told anyone, except her dad and Kayleigh, but that probably all of Fifth Year had guessed after the way she behaved yesterday.

I couldn't believe her parents knew.

"Michael worked it out. He kept talking about gay stuff going on at the college, and leaving newspaper articles lying around, you know, so that I would know it was okay. A few weeks ago, the news was on, and Mrs Thatcher – who Michael hates anyway – was speaking."

Mum and Dad don't talk about politics much, but they

had one of her posters up in the window at the last election.

"She was talking about how terrible it was that kids were learning about being gay at school. Just like Tara was saying in the debate yesterday, remember? Guess where Tara heard it from! Anyway, Thatcher said this one really bizarre thing about how children were being taught that they had 'an inalienable right to be gay'.

"At first, it was kind of funny. I mean, it's not like we're taught anything about being gay at school, are we? Specially not about a right to be gay! What planet is she living on? And then it felt horrible, listening to her, and knowing this was the person in charge of the whole country. I mean, how sick is that? But I didn't say anything. And Michael didn't either. Not even his usual shouting at the telly when he thinks they're talking rubbish.

"When the news was over, we sat, still not talking, all through the sport and the weather. Until finally, he said, 'I believe in rights, you know. I believe that every child has the inalienable right to be whoever they want to be, whatever that might be.' He looked right at me when he said that. And I...I started crying."

I wanted to reach over and hold Nicky's hand. But I didn't. I couldn't. I stayed still. I thought I might start crying too.

"It was the perfect thing for him to say, and he really

meant it, you know, he wasn't just saying it. I could be anything, anyone, and he'd still love me. I could be gay and that would be okay. I didn't *have* to tell him. He just knew."

She reached out and took my hand. That's the third time she's done that now. But this time felt different.

I stared at our hands, fingers laced together, then I looked up at her. She was smiling, but she looked pale. God knows what I looked like.

I didn't understand what any of this meant and what was going to happen now. I just knew I wanted to be with her.

Nicky said that all that mattered was how we felt about each other. No one at school had to know if we didn't want them to.

It was a shock, remembering about school, but right then, in Nicky's bedroom, it felt like another world, another planet, a million miles away. I wanted to say that I didn't care, that we could tell everyone. But it wouldn't have been true.

It was getting dark by the time I left. Nicky's dad asked if I wanted to stay for tea, but I couldn't. At the door, Nicky pressed something into my hand.

She said she'd made it for me but wasn't sure whether to give it to me or not.

I started listening to Nicky's mixtape on my Walkman

on the bus home. I've got it on now. They're just ordinary songs, ones that are on the radio all the time, but now it's like they're meant specially for me. No one has ever made me a mixtape before. She must have spent ages recording this. For me.

I just looked up "inalienable" in my dictionary, the one we have to have for school. It means something that's unchallengeable, something that's yours for ever and no one can take it away. An inalienable right to be whoever you want to be. How amazing is that?

11 TURN BACK THE CLOCK

I put down the diary. Could Lisa's mixtape be the one we found in the box? I want to check right now, but it's on the luggage rack above my head. I'd disturb too many people if I tried to get it down.

I don't want to keep reading now. I need time to take it all in. So many feelings. It's brilliant that Lisa and Nicky have got together, and that Nicky's family are so cool about everything. But I'm worried that things will be so tough for them, that they'll be forced to hide how they feel about each other, even from Lisa's family. My family.

I can't talk to Simran about it now because she's asleep. Or at least she's quiet and her eyes are shut. That's how she is. Either on or off, and not a lot in between.

So, instead, I stare at my reflection in the window,

trying to see a family resemblance that ties me and Lisa and Mum and Gran and Tom together. I search for the clip of Margaret Thatcher's speech that Nicky watched with her dad and watch it on my phone. It makes me want to cry.

I glance down to admire Lisa's dark blue Docs on my feet. Across from me, Simran's wearing the denim jacket that we found in the box. There are some of Lisa's badges on it, faded now. Simran's added some of her own, which stand out brightly. She's rolled up the sleeves and it looks great on her. Of course it does.

Dad picks us up at the station, drops a sleepy Simran home, and then wants to hear all about everything.

"We were only gone two days!" I exclaim, when he squeezes me into a huge hug as soon as we're through the front door.

"Two days is long enough," Dad says. "I'm glad you're back. I missed you both."

"Rubbish," says Mum, switching on the kettle. "I bet you had a great time without us, probably eating takeaway and watching TV till all hours."

It's funny to think of Dad behaving like a teenager who's been left at home alone. But he probably just worked late while we were gone.

"Who, me?" says Dad, trying to look innocent. "I went

for a run with James from work and then I just sat and pined for you, maybe nibbling on a lettuce leaf or two."

But, in the sink, I can see some plastic boxes, the kind you get from the Chinese takeaway, that have recently been washed out to reuse. Dad spots that I've noticed them and winks at me.

"So, tell me all about it," he says when the tea is made. "How was the funeral? Were you both okay?" His forehead creases with concern.

"It was strange," says Mum, still stirring her tea, even though the sugar must have dissolved ages ago. "I'm glad we went. It was the right thing to do. But I barely remember Lisa." She sighs. "The whole thing was organized by her friends. They were the ones who looked after her when she got ill. I just feel, I don't know, like her family let her down. Like *I* let her down."

Dad reaches out and takes her hand. "Don't be so hard on yourself, Jen. Your mum had been in touch with Lisa over the years, hadn't she, so she wasn't totally cut off from the family? Remember, you've had a lot on your plate. And it sounds like Lisa had people around her who cared about her. That's what matters."

A lot on your plate. I guess Dad means Gran getting ill. And Tom leaving home; I know she really misses him. But maybe he means me too, that me coming out has given

Mum something else to worry about.

"Mum," I say, reaching for her other hand. "It's not your fault. You haven't let anyone down."

Mum shakes her head. "I'm just tired. It's been a big couple of days, it's late and I've got work tomorrow. Anyway…" She turns to me. "Jesse's the one with exciting news. Show Dad what you found in Lisa's attic."

I start unpacking the box on the kitchen table. I only found it yesterday, but already the objects inside are becoming familiar. The diary, a copy of *Spare Rib*, the magazine that Lisa and Nicky used to research for their debate and, yes, the mixtape. It must be the one Nicky made, why else would Lisa have kept it for all this time?

But that's not all. There are leaflets, tube tickets, the photo I found of Lisa and Nicky, and more. Laid out on the table, they already look like they could be part of an exhibition. These are no longer disconnected, mysterious objects. They each have their place in the story. They are all filled with meaning, even if I haven't fully uncovered it yet.

Dad is most excited by the mixtape. He picks it up, opens the case, and unfolds the piece of paper with the list of songs inside.

"Would you look at that? This takes me back. I made one of these for my girlfriend in secondary school. I spent hours over it, waiting for the right songs to come on the radio so I could record them, listening to all the lyrics, imagining they were about the two of us."

"Did she like it?" I ask. I'm intrigued by this picture of my sensible dad as a lovestruck teenager, even though it's weird thinking about him having girlfriends before Mum.

"She never even heard it. She dumped me before I'd finished making it. I was distraught. All those hours wasted. What's worse, I was so upset that I pulled out all the ribbon in the tape, so I couldn't even listen to it myself. There were some classic songs on there."

"Could we listen to this one?" I ask.

"Hmm, I'm not sure what we could play it on. If Lisa didn't keep her old Walkman in the box, we could have a look in the morning to see if I kept mine."

"What about looking now?" I ask. The tiredness I felt on the train has disappeared.

"It's too late," says Mum. "We all need to get to bed. I'm not having you two turning the house upside down now. It can wait till the morning." Dad nods reluctantly, still holding the tape in his hands.

"Oh, I said I'd meet Simran in Over the Rainbow tomorrow morning. Could you give me a lift in? Please."

"What? You only just said goodbye to her. What could you possibly still have to talk about?" says Dad. "No luck,

I'm afraid. I'm working at home tomorrow, but I've got meetings, so you'll have to take the bus. It's better for the planet anyway." Dad works for the council's environmental management team, so he's a bit obsessed with stuff like that.

I carefully place Lisa's things back in the box. All except the diary. That's coming upstairs with me.

When Dad gets a new book out of the library, he always reads the last page first. He says he likes to know where things are going, so that he can be prepared for any surprises. It makes sense – his job involves preventing and preparing for floods. He *has* to be ready for whatever's coming next.

But for me, flicking to the end feels like cheating. Although Lisa's entries in November are so few and so short that I feel okay about skimming through these. Then it's December, the holidays start, and everything changes.

12 CRUSH ON YOU

Saturday 19 December 1987

Last day of term yesterday – thank God. It's so hard at school. All the pretending. When you see couples like Clare and Dan all over each other, and Nicky and I can't even hold hands. They're always getting told off by the teachers when they get caught snogging in the corridors. But it's not serious. Can you even imagine if we did that? It would be a whole different league.

Even with us keeping our distance, I worry that someone might guess. Especially Jason. I always feel like he's watching us, laughing at us. Nicky says just to ignore him, but he makes my skin crawl.

Nicky and I went ice skating to celebrate the end of term. My idea. It felt like a real Christmassy thing to do. And the first thing we've done that's like a proper date, not hanging out at Nicky's house. No one else would have known we were on a date just by looking at us. Our secret.

I used to go skating all the time when I was little. Mum would take me on Sundays and we'd have hot chocolate afterwards. I don't know why we stopped. Maybe Matthew started football and there was no time for both.

But I remembered how much I loved the feeling you get on the ice, like flying. I wanted Nicky to feel that too. Can you believe she's never been skating before? She was so nervous at first.

"I'm going to fall over in about two seconds. I know it," she said. "I saw this TV programme about someone getting their finger sliced off when they fell and someone skated over their hand. Can't we just go back to mine and watch a video?"

I promised her she'd love it and that no one would skate over her fingers. If she just held onto me, she'd be okay.

She gave me this smile, like she still wasn't sure, but she grabbed my hand anyway. Everyone was holding onto their friends as they wobbled on the ice, so we could hold hands and not worry what anyone might think.

We started really slow. Little kids zoomed past us. Even when Nicky got the hang of how to move her feet, she still refused to let go.

I told her to trust me, but she begged to go round, just

one more time, holding onto the side.

"Come on," I told her, laughing. "You'll never be ready. You've just got to do it. Don't think about it."

She let go, wobbled, and gripped more tightly to me. I thought I was going to fall with her.

But neither of us fell. We were skating. When I looked over at her face, her eyes were shining. She looked beautiful. I wanted to kiss her, but I knew I couldn't. Not there.

"We're doing it! How am I still upright? How come I've still got all my fingers?"

"*You're* doing it," I said. "Are you ready to let go of me yet?"

"No way. Don't you dare let go of me, Lisa, not ever. Okay?" I didn't argue, I didn't want to stop holding her hand.

Then I heard a voice calling my name from the side of the rink.

There was Andy, leaning by the barrier. He sounded really pleased to see me. I felt bad. When we talked after the debate, I'd said we'd hang out, but never done anything about it. I said hi sometimes in the corridors, but that was it.

I pulled Nicky with me, and we both came to a stop next to him, our skates thudding against the barrier.

I asked him why he wasn't skating. He said he was too clumsy to be out on the ice, but he was looking after his sister and her friends because his mum had to work. He pointed towards some of the giggling girls who'd swooped past us earlier on.

"Lisa's just taught me," gushed Nicky. "She's a brilliant teacher. Soon we'll be like Torvill and Dean!"

Then she suggested that I did some proper skating without her clinging onto me, while she and Andy went to get some chocolate out of the machine.

At first, I looked for her every time I went round. But the rink was starting to empty out, and soon I was just enjoying being on the ice, going faster and faster, not minding about the cold or my achy legs.

By the time I skated back over to Nicky and Andy, tired and out of breath, they were laughing together over something. I felt jealous for a moment, but only until she smiled at me. Sometimes I just don't get why someone like Nicky, who could be with anyone, wants to be with me.

When Andy's sister and her friends came over, he said he had to go.

Nicky nudged me and whispered, "You know what, I think Andy's one of us."

I wasn't sure what she meant at first, until she squeezed my hand.

I looked towards the exit, where Andy was helping his sister get her skates off. I asked if he'd said anything, or if she'd said anything about the two of us.

But she said she just "had a feeling" that he was gay. Like how she'd known about me.

"But *I* didn't know about me," I protested. "How could *you* have known? It just happened, didn't it? I *still* don't know. I just know I want to be with you."

Whenever I start to think about anything bigger than that, any words or labels, I panic. I can't think about the future for me and Nicky or what any of this really means. I can only think about now.

Nicky said that we should hang out with Andy over the holidays at her house, even revise for mocks together.

I hate thinking about exams. They are so soon. The only one I'm feeling halfway good about is Art, and Mum and Dad don't even think it's a proper subject. They want me to stay on at school and do A levels, instead of doing art at college.

"You could still do A levels," Nicky told me, like she always does. We've talked about this a thousand times. "You're clever enough, you could do them at college like me. It's your life, not your parents'. It should be up to you, your inalienable rights and everything."

"Tell that to my mum."

"Maybe I will," said Nicky, teasing me.

She told me how much she'd loved skating – she kept expecting to fall, but didn't, because I made sure she was okay. That made me feel good. It's usually Nicky showing me new things or looking after me, instead of the other way round. She said it was like I had no fear out there on the ice.

But I'm afraid of so many things. Not like Nicky. I'm afraid that Mum and Dad might stop me doing Art, or that people will find out that Nicky and I are girlfriends.

She tucked her arm into mine and snuggled in. I froze. Then checked to see if anyone was looking, but there was no one around.

It was cold and I asked her if Michael could give us a lift back to hers, but she said he was at a meeting at the college. We'd have to get the bus.

Then she started telling me all about his meeting. How there was going to be a protest march about Clause 28, right through London, and Michael was at this meeting to try and organize a group from the college to go. Thousands of people would be there. It would be in all the papers, maybe on telly. She looked at me expectantly, eyes shining.

I tried to shush her, even though there was no one around to hear us. Why was she telling me this? Then I realized. She seriously thought that *we* should go on this march! Her and me, on a gay rights march, when we can't even hold hands in the corridors at school! It was ridiculous!

When I was little, I remember Mum and Dad taking me and Matthew to the British Museum. Matthew wanted to see the mummies, even though I found them creepy. It was cute how excited he was – he wasn't so annoying back then. Mum let us both choose something from the gift shop afterwards. It felt like such a treat.

On the way back to the tube, we turned onto this side road near the station. Suddenly there were police everywhere. Behind them, you could see brightly coloured banners and hear people shouting, although I was too short to see much.

I remember Mum grabbing hold of my and Matthew's hands and marching us back the way we'd come. Matthew kept asking if he could see the police cars up close, but Mum didn't answer, she just kept walking.

I heard her mutter to Dad, "They call it Pride – *that's* nothing to be proud about." I thought it was such an odd thing to say, but I knew if I asked her what she meant, she wouldn't tell me.

Nicky woke me out of my daydream by squeezing my hand. "So, what do you think? We should be there, right?"

I sighed. "If thousands of people will be there, we don't have to be. Anyway, what if it's not safe?"

She glared at me. "God, Lisa, you sound just like your mum. I thought..."

Then she stopped. I asked her what exactly she thought. She wouldn't say at first, then finally, just as we reached the bus stop, she said, "I thought you could be fearless. That's all. But I was wrong."

Nothing was the same after that. The date didn't feel like a date any more. I'd disappointed Nicky again.

But me on a protest march? Mum and Dad would explode if they knew I was even thinking about anything like that. It's different for Nicky, with Michael and Kayleigh as parents. They don't stop her from doing anything.

But it's not just about what Mum and Dad would think. It's me. I don't want to go, not even with Nicky.

She gets so excited, talking about fighting and struggle and changing the world. But I don't feel like that. Talking about stuff like Clause 28 makes me feel small and scared and hopeless. I don't want to think about how much people hate us, just for being who we are and loving who we do. And, most of all, I don't want to think about how Mum and Dad would probably agree with them, or about what would happen if we did anything that meant they found out about Nicky and me.

13 SING OUR OWN SONG

"Morning, Jesse! Rise and shine!"

"Wha—?" I mumble into my pillow. How can Dad sound so cheerful when it's still so early? I'm half asleep. I was reading the diary till late last night. I didn't want to stop. It seems like Nicky and Lisa were always falling out over something. Over the *same* thing, I guess – how to be open in a world that wanted them to hide.

"Sorry, I know it's early, but I wanted to catch you before my first meeting. I found my old Walkman. I knew I wouldn't have thrown it away. You never know when something's going to come in handy. I've put in new batteries for you."

I sit up in bed. Dad is wearing his classic working from home outfit: a smart shirt, running shorts and socks. I've made him promise never, ever to leave the house looking like that. He is waving a small grey box in his hand and looking very pleased with himself. This time Dad's commitment to zero waste is actually coming in useful.

"Wow, thanks, Dad." He perches on the end of my bed as I fumble on my bedside table for the mixtape. He shows me the right way to put the tape into the Walkman and hands me a pair of ancient-looking headphones.

"These used to be the height of fashion," he says. I snort but give him a big hug to say thank you.

I listen to the tape when I'm on the bus into Hurston. It makes a satisfying click when I press the "play" button. The music is faint and there's a strange whirring sound in the background, but that doesn't matter. It gives me the shivers that I'm the first person to listen to this tape since Lisa. She sat on a different bus in a different town over a quarter of a century ago, listening to exactly the same songs as I am now. The diary in my bag is the invisible thread that connects us.

I don't know what happens after you die, but I don't think there's an afterlife. I don't think you go to heaven or become a star in the sky or anything like that. I thought about it a lot after Gran died.

I used to like to imagine she was somewhere looking down on us, able to see what I was doing and cheer me on, but I don't think she is, not really. It's a story to make us feel better.

But then, it doesn't make sense that she's gone either, not when she used to be so alive. So, I don't know. But when I remember one of her daft jokes or see a tree covered in pink blossom like the one she loved in her garden or smell the same spices that she had in her kitchen cupboard, I feel so close to her that I can't believe she's dead. I just can't.

So now I think, every time we remember her, she still makes a mark on the world. The same must be true with Lisa. If we remember her – what and who she loved, what mattered to her – then she won't be totally gone.

I get to Over the Rainbow before Simran. Our favourite table by the window is empty, so I bags it straight away. In fact, most of the tables are empty. When Simran arrives, her eyes dart all around the shop. She's looking for Leo, I can tell, but there's only Maz behind the counter. Simran looks disappointed. I pretend I haven't noticed.

"Listen to this," I say, passing her the headphones as she sits down. She puts them on and frowns, confused. I slide the tape box across the table to her, and she nods.

"This one's rubbish," she says after a moment. "How do you skip to the next track on this thing?" She prods at the Walkman.

I flip the cassette over to the other side and press play again.

"Oh yeah, that's better," says Simran. "My mum likes this one."

"There are a couple I know, and some of the others are all right," I say. "A bit cheesy, but super romantic. I mean, Nicky chose every song just for Lisa, it's like they tell a story."

"Ready to order?" says Leo, swooping up behind Simran. She squeals and whips the headphones off. She's usually the one to make me jump, so it's extra satisfying to see her get sneaked up on instead of me.

"I didn't think you were in today," she says. "I didn't see you when I got here."

"I was in the kitchen. I've been working all week. I picked up extra hours over half-term. Maz's got her eye on me today, so we need to pretend we're talking about the menu and you're about to order something lavish, while really you fill me in on what's new."

"It's not busy," I say. "You wouldn't be ignoring other customers if you talk to us."

"Tell that to the boss," Leo replies. He lowers his voice. "I think that's the problem actually. It's been a bit quiet lately, which gives her too much time to worry about things. Oh, Simran," he exclaims, interrupting himself.

"Is that new? It's vintage, right? I love it!" Simran beams as she adjusts the collar of Lisa's denim jacket.

"I haven't seen either of you this week," continues Leo. "Don't tell me you've found somewhere else to go. Who would eat my spiced carrot cake then?" he adds mournfully.

"We went up to London for a couple of days," says Simran. "For Jesse's mum's cousin's funeral…" Leo looks like he's trying to work out the relationship, before giving up. "We went to some museums too and we went shopping, of course."

"Was that where you got the jacket?"

"Well, kind of." Simran glances at me.

"Actually, it's why we're here. I mean, apart from the carrot cake, of course."

Leo jots down "carrot cake x 2" on his notepad. "You won't regret it, it's delicious," he says. "But what do you mean, you're here because of Simran's jacket? I'm lost."

"It's a long story," I say.

Leo looks over his shoulder at the counter where Maz is talking to a couple of customers.

"Ah, who cares?" he says, pulling over a chair from the next table and sitting down. "She's not even looking. Tell me everything."

So, we tell him. Simran and I take turns to pick up the story while Leo listens attentively.

"Here's the diary if you want a look," I say, pulling it out of my bag and putting it down on the table. "We googled Clause 28 already, but we need info from different sources for our project. We thought Over the Rainbow might have a book about it or something."

"Leo!" shouts Maz. This time, we all jump. She's moved surprisingly fast and is now standing right behind Leo's chair. "Tell me, do I pay you to serve customers or to sit and chat with your friends?"

"They *are* customers," says Leo, standing up. "I'm just finishing up their order. It's all here." He taps his notepad with his pen. "Anyway, they're looking for a book."

"What kind of book?"

"I...er..." Even though I know Maz is a real softie, talking to her still makes me feel a bit nervous. "I'm looking for a book about, um, Clause 28. Have you heard of it? It's for school."

"They're teaching you about Section 28 at school?" Maz replies, eyebrows raised. She even smiles. "Well, well, how times change."

"Not exactly teaching," I explain. "It's for a history project. We can choose what to study ourselves."

"Is it Section 28 or Clause 28?" asks Simran. "I don't get it."

"It's both," explains Maz. "Clause 28 before it became

law, and Section 28 after. But it's the same thing. Give me a minute, I'll see what I can find to help you out." Her eyes move to the bookshelves, and then back to Leo.

"Leo, you appear to be still here. Hurry along, there's a customer over there ready to pay. And these two don't want to wait all day for their carrot cake, do they?" She shakes her head wearily and turns to us. "I'm sorry about him," she says.

Leo jumps to his feet, gives us a thumbs up behind Maz's back and scampers over to help the couple at the counter.

Before our cake arrives, Maz returns with an armful of books. Some of them are huge. Simran shoots me a worried look. We won't have time to read all of these before school starts again.

"Thank you, but do you have anything shorter?" Simran asks.

"For beginners?" I add.

Maz puts her pile down on the table and pulls a thinner book out from the bottom. It looks like a graphic novel, with artwork on the front that reminds me a little bit of Lisa's drawings.

I turn it over. On the back are the words of the Section 28 law. The same words that I haven't been able to get of my head since I first read them on Simran's phone in that cafe in London: "the prohibition of the promotion by local authorities of homosexuality as a pretended family relationship".

"This should start you off," says Maz. "I just got a bit carried away. Anyway, you must know a bit about Section 28 already – you're wearing the campaign badge."

"What?" asks Simran.

"On your jacket." Maz points to one of Lisa's old badges on Simran's lapel. It has an upside-down pink triangle on it, the same design as on the T-shirt we found in the box. "Before everything was rainbows, this was our symbol. I haven't seen one of these for ages, maybe not since the march."

"The march?" I ask. I open the diary and flick back to the last bit I read. Could this be the same march that Nicky wanted to take Lisa on? "1988? In London?"

"It would have been about then," says Maz thoughtfully. "But it was up in Manchester. Maybe there was one in London too. These books will tell you. It was a long time ago. I was in my twenties back then. We wanted to change the world, rip up everything and start again. How old are you both?" she asks. "Thirteen?"

"Twelve," I say. "Nearly thirteen though."

"The eighties must seem like ancient history to you!" she says, shaking her head.

"Well…" I say and then stop. I don't want to be rude by making out like she's really old. And anyway, it's not exactly ancient history, not like the war or the Tudors.

"So much has changed since then," continues Maz. "Especially for us. Not enough though. Good luck with your research. It's important to remember – what we did, what we went through, especially now, when things are getting worse for some parts of our community, especially trans folk."

"Maz!" calls Leo. "There's something up with the card machine."

"Excuse me, let me know if you need anything else," says Maz, moving away. She mutters to herself, "That boy!"

"She'll be devastated if he ever leaves," I say once Maz has gone.

"Yeah," agrees Simran. "What was that march she was talking about?"

"Well, I know there were protests against Section 28, Clause 28, whatever. Lisa writes about how Nicky wants her to go on a march, but she's too scared. I only read that bit last night, so I don't know whether Lisa went or not. I looked online about the march, but there's hardly anything about it."

"Jesse, you've got to read more diary, see what

happened," urges Simran. "Will you have time before school starts?"

"Yeah, sure," I say. There's other homework still to do, but that can wait. "I'll read some more on the bus, unless you want it next."

Simran shakes her head. "You have it. I'll check out this book from Maz."

We eat our cake and chat. I find an old book token in my bag with just enough money on it to buy the comic book. I hug Simran goodbye and catch the bus home. But, through all of it, my mind is somewhere else.

I still can't get that word "pretended" out of my head.

It feels so familiar. I've heard some people say it about me, and I know even more people think it. That I'm just pretending to be non-binary, that I'm doing it to get attention, that it's just a phase, that the whole idea of being non-binary is a made-up thing, that the thing that feels most true, most real, most obviously right about me, is just pretend. I hate it.

14 NEVER CAN SAY GOODBYE

Friday 1 January 1988

Happy new year! Mum and Dad got all dressed up to go round to Marie and Derek's over the road. They dragged Matthew with them but let me stay over at Nicky's.

It was the best New Year's Eve ever. We didn't go to bed until after 2am. The house was full of Michael and Kayleigh's friends, the garden too, and the music was so loud, and at midnight everyone sang Auld Lang Syne and drank toasts and kissed each other. Nicky and I did too. I was a bit shy at first, but no one seemed bothered. Michael gave me a hug and said how much he liked having me in the family. He'd had quite a lot to drink, but I know he meant it too.

Just as I was drifting off to sleep, with Frida's soft warmth curled up on my feet, Nicky reached for my hand,

and asked if I was still awake.

Then, ever so softly, she said, "We're going to have such a year, you and me. It's going to be so good. Being with you makes me so happy, like I can be totally me, you know? It's the best."

I'd had this anxious feeling sitting in my stomach since we had fought about going on the march, not quite sure what Nicky really thought of me. Was I exciting enough? Brave enough? Did I understand things the way she did?

But when she said that, those feelings melted away. We were okay. We are okay, way better than okay. I could tell she was smiling, even in the dark.

I told her that's how I felt too. It's less embarrassing to say that sort of thing when you know no one can see you. Although, right then, I could have told Nicky anything.

She started saying how people were stupid if they thought that we shouldn't be together just cos we were both girls.

I don't know if she's right. Well, she is right, but maybe it's only because people have never thought about it, or they're scared of something different. Maybe that's how Mum and Dad feel.

Nicky snuggled against me when I said that and told me I was too nice.

We talked about what 1988 was going to be like. She

said maybe it would be the year that Matthew grew up and stopped being a pain. Ha ha. If only.

But who cares about Matthew? Or exams? Or deciding about college? Or any of the other things that are going to happen this year? 1988 is going to be brilliant because of Nicky, I just know it.

Friday 12 February 1988

Another late night at Nicky's. We hung out with Andy earlier, but he had to go back to his house for tea, so mostly it was just me and her. It's cool, now that there's someone else who knows about us, who we can be ourselves with. He won't give away our secrets, just like we won't reveal any of his.

I hate that bit when I know I have to go. I always try to find a way to stay one more minute and then another and then it's a real rush and I'm grabbing my coat and running before it's really, truly too late. Michael gave me a lift home tonight. I don't think Michael and Kayleigh would mind if I stayed there all night, but Mum and Dad would.

When I got in, they were sitting in front of the telly. The first thing Mum said, before I'd even taken off my coat, was, "I hope you're not wearing out your welcome at Nicky's."

Then she went on about how I was practically living over there, how I just came home to eat and sleep, they hardly ever saw me, blah blah. "You can always bring your friends over here," she said, "your father and I don't bite."

I tried to explain how it was just easier at Nicky's house, because there was more space. But I realized straight away that I'd said the wrong thing.

"Well, we can't all afford a big house on the common, can we?" she said.

That wasn't what I'd meant. I don't care how big Nicky's house is. But try telling Mum that when she's already in a mood.

Then Dad took over, complaining that they hardly know Nicky, or her family. They even think she might be distracting me from my exams.

They'd obviously planned this. They were totally ganging up on me.

I had to take a really, really deep breath right then. I slowly unlaced my Doc Martens, staring at the laces instead of looking at either of them. If I did, I just knew I'd end up shouting.

I mean, it's so ridiculous. I can't stay at home studying for my GCSEs all the time, nobody does that. But I didn't want them to get mad and say that I couldn't see Nicky or spend so much time over at hers. I had to play it right.

If all they care about is exams, well, fine. Nicky's really good at maths, I can say she's been helping me out. It's sort of true. We start doing homework together, but usually end up talking or laughing or playing with Frida. Her dad's really helped with my art too. Although probably talking about art right then wouldn't be a good idea.

Then the real bombshell! Mum suggested that Nicky and her parents could come round here one evening! For a meal! For Mum and Dad to get to know them! They hardly ever invite anyone round, except occasionally Marie and Derek from over the road. How can Mum and Dad think this is a good idea?

It's not a good idea. It's a bad idea. A very bad idea. It just doesn't fit – the idea of Michael and Kayleigh here with Mum and Dad, it would be like a meeting between creatures from two different planets. Oh god, and Matthew too. He's definitely a creature from another planet. Ha ha.

I don't think Mum and Dad would suspect about me and Nicky, but what if Michael and Kayleigh gave something away by mistake?

I haven't even told Mum and Dad that Michael and Kayleigh aren't married. They assume Nicky's mum and dad are still together. I haven't said anything different.

I said, "Yeah, maybe." But what I meant was, "No, never."

Mum kissed me on the cheek, then turned back to the TV.

"Oh," she called, just as I turned to go. "Make sure you don't leave those great ugly boots of yours at the bottom of the stairs where anyone could trip over them. I don't see why you want to wear men's boots anyway when you'd look so pretty in some nice sandals."

There was no point telling her for the millionth time that they're not men's boots, so I just kicked my Docs out of the way and stomped upstairs in my socks.

15 IT DOESN'T HAVE TO BE

"Name three different types of plate boundary," demands Simran. She's sitting cross-legged on my bed, her geography book open in front of her. She turns the pages in between scrubbing at her nails. My bedroom reeks of nail varnish remover.

"I don't even know what a plate boundary is," I say, yawning. "Are you sure we've learned this?"

"Totally sure, it's for tomorrow's test. It's not my fault if history is the only subject where you pay any attention."

"That's not true!"

"Prove it then. Three types of plate boundary. Tell me." She taps the book and glares at me. Simran can be quite fierce sometimes.

"Um...large, medium and small?" I guess.

"Ha ha. Okay, I'll start you off... The first is constructive..."

"Oh god, Sim, don't pretend you're interested in this."

"I'm interested in not failing tomorrow. My mum wouldn't be happy about that." Simran holds up her hands for me to inspect. "Does this look okay for school?" I nod. There's no trace of the neon nail polish that Simran's been wearing since we got back from London.

"I can't believe it's school again already." I've enjoyed being away from the bells and the noise and the rushing around. But I also can't wait to show Ms Grant what we've already done for our history project.

"Don't change the subject," says Simran. "It's constructive, destructive and conservative. Ready for the next question? You can have a sweet if you get it right." She holds the bag of Maltesers in the air above my head.

I sigh. "Perhaps you should give up on the idea of being a fashion designer and be a teacher like your mum used to be. You'd be so good at it!"

Simran makes a face. "You *should* be good at this. Isn't this what your dad does at work?"

"He doesn't do anything to do with earthquakes, Sim! Not in Sussex!" I laugh. "But, yeah, I guess geography's his thing. Doesn't mean it has to be mine though. I wonder what we both *will* end up doing?"

"I'll be a famous designer, like Alexander McQueen, and you can do an exhibition about me in your museum. A retrospective, featuring all the stars who've worn my outfits."

"What museum?" I ask, sneaking a Malteser out of the bag while Simran's distracted.

"You'll be this expert historian by then, so obviously you'll run your own museum, maybe have a show on TV, or you could write a book – you'll have your own YouTube channel at least."

It sounds ridiculous, just the sort of future that Simran would dream up for us, but kind of fun too.

"I hope we'll still be friends then," I say, suddenly serious. "You and me. I hope we're always friends."

"Of course we will be," she says, nudging me with her foot. "Who else would put up with you?"

I know she means it as a joke, but what if that is what she really thinks deep down? What if she thinks I'm boring or annoying?

"What is it, Jesse?" she says, noticing that I've gone quiet. "Are you okay?"

I shake my head. "Nothing. I'm fine."

She waits.

"It's just, do you really mean that?"

"That we'll always be friends?"

"Yeah. I mean, I'd understand if not." I carry on in a rush, "I know can get kind of obsessed about things, that must be annoying, and—"

"Shut up!" she says, reaching into the bag to grab a handful of Maltesers. "You. Are. Not. Boring." With each word, she throws a sweet at me. A couple bounce off the side of my face.

"Ouch!" I exclaim, seizing the bag and taking aim at her. Before long we are pelting each other with Maltesers, and we can't talk for laughing.

"See," she says finally when the bag's empty. "Not boring. But, yes, maybe a bit obsessed. Sometimes. Hey, you're not going to eat that, are you? That's disgusting."

"Three second rule, that's what Gran used to say," I tell her, popping the chocolate into my mouth. It only tastes a little bit dusty. "I know I've been going on too much about our history project," I add.

"Maybe…" She shrugs. "But I'm getting really into it too. I started a Pinterest board the other night, and printed out some bits to put in a folder…"

"What?" I interrupt. "Why have you been going on about plate boundaries for hours, when you could have been showing me this?"

"And last night, I searched for videos about Clause 28 and found this amazing stuff. I wondered whether we could even have a laptop playing them, you know, as part of the exhibition," continues Simran. "Did you know there were these lesbians that abseiled into the House of Lords to protest? They smuggled in the ropes and got arrested. I'll show you the video. One of them looks just like Maz, well, how she might have looked way back then. And some of them broke into the TV studios too. They wanted to hold up this banner on the news, but the newsreader sat on them so they couldn't, you can hear them fighting in the background. It's wild."

"Seriously?" I say. "Lisa's just worried about going on a march."

"I bet that could have been dangerous too. She was only, what, three years older than us? Would your parents let you go to something like that by yourself?"

Simran's probably right. I've never been on a proper march, only on our local climate strike one. It was fun, with our home-made banners and loads of people from school there, even teachers. We walked really slowly down the high street, then huddled in the cold outside Hurston town hall to listen to speeches. Simran and I tried to get some chanting going, but mostly we just chatted and looked in the shop windows as we went past.

The most dangerous thing that happened that day was nearly burning my mouth on some hot chocolate. But what Lisa's writing about is different.

Imagine being out on the streets, standing up against people who think you should be ashamed of who you are, knowing that everyone wants you to shut up and go away. Hoping it's going to make a difference, but knowing people probably won't listen. I mean, Clause 28 still passed, didn't it? Despite the marches, the protests, the abseiling lesbians.

I'm glad Pride marches don't have to be like that now, that it's more like a party. I know there are still protestors against Pride marches, I've seen them on TV, but there are thousands more of us than there are of them.

"Mum says that she'll take us to Brighton Pride one day to watch the parade," I say.

"Wow," says Simran. "Really? Me too? Do you think we could go this summer? Did you see Leo's videos from when he went? Did you see what people were wearing? And the music! It looked so awesome."

My mind's drifting back to 1988. "Look what I found." I pass her a crumpled scrap of paper. "It was right at the bottom of Lisa's box of stuff."

Simran smooths the flyer out on the bed. "Stop the Clause. March on London. 30th April 1988," she reads out, then turns it over a couple of times. "Where's the rest of it and why's it ripped up?"

I shrug. "I don't know, I only found this bit."

"Weird," says Simran. "Maybe it means that she decided to go on the march after all?"

"Or that Nicky gave it to her afterwards. Anyway, I'll bring it into school tomorrow so we can show Ms Grant, and the diary too. Or do you want to take it now so you can read some tonight?" I pick up the exercise book from my bedside table and hold it out to Simran. I'm gripping it tightly. I don't really want to let it go.

"Nah, you're all right," she says. "You'll be faster than me anyway. Her handwriting is impossible to read, just like yours. You can tell me what happens. I'll bring my folder tomorrow too."

"So, it's okay that this is going to be our project?" I ask, as she stretches and hops off the bed. I'm not looking at her. What if she says that she's changed her mind? "I mean, it's my family, so of course I'm going to be interested, but I don't want you to feel like you've been pushed into it."

"Jesse," says Simran firmly. She's using her teacher voice. I hope she's not going to start testing me on tectonic plates again. "If I had discovered a long-lost queer cousin—"

"First cousin once removed."

"First cousin once removed, whatever. If I had discovered them, I would one hundred per cent be making us do a project based on their diaries. But since I haven't,

150

we'll have to make do with yours! Okay? And it's true what I said before, this is *our* story, all of us. And no one talks about it. Not enough anyway. It's always Oscar Wilde and Alan Turing and people dying tragically because they're queer. It's no fun."

"Lisa died," I say flatly.

"She did and it's sad cos she was so young and you didn't even get to meet her and obviously some kind of bad stuff happened to her way back then. But she didn't die *because* she was gay. She sounds like she was cool and happy and she got to do art and be in love and, most importantly, she had great taste in jackets. Okay?"

"Okay," I agree. I feel more hopeful, but something's still bugging me. "Our project is going to be great, but is it *enough*? I mean *everyone* should know about what happened back then. Not just the people in our class or a few parents who come to the exhibition. Everyone."

"Yeah, sure." Simran looks taken aback by my sudden fierceness. "But how? Do you mean like a website, so other people can find out about it more easily?"

"I don't *know*! But there should be *something*."

"Simran!" calls Mum up the stairs. "Your dad's here."

We hug goodbye. "Constructive, destructive, conservative," she whispers in my ear.

"What?"

"I bet you won't do any more revision tonight. So, remember that and maybe at least you'll get one mark tomorrow!"

Constructive, destructive, conservative, I think to myself, as I open Lisa's diary.

I *am* going to skip ahead this time. I want to find out what Lisa's written about the march. The ripped flyer I found in the box must be important, if she kept it all these years. Maybe the diary will explain how. I flick through the pages until I get to 30th April, but she's written loads the day before, so I guess I should start there, in case I miss something important.

16 WHAT HAVE I DONE TO DESERVE THIS?

Friday 29 April 1988

Awful, awful, awful. Stayed at school late, I lost track of time in the art room, finishing off my portrait. It looks really good now, even Miss O'Keeffe says so. She thinks I'll get an A for it.

Hardly anyone was still around when I went back to my locker in the basement to get my books. It was all echoey and shadowy, not like in the daytime when it's crammed with people all talking and shouting and pushing at once. It was so empty that when my locker door swung open, the sound made me jump.

Then I heard voices, two people arguing. I froze. I couldn't see what was happening, but as soon as I heard Jason's voice, I knew it must be bad. They were getting louder and closer. There was no way I could get out without

Jason noticing me. I stayed as quiet as I could. Maybe I could wait and slip out when they'd gone.

"Come on, got nothing to say for yourself?" That was Jason, taunting someone. Silence. Then a thud.

The other person shouted at Jason to leave them alone. I knew that voice. Andy's. Out of breath and higher pitched than usual, but definitely Andy's. I heard him say, "Get your hands off me."

Then Jason repeated back his words in a lisping voice. Saying the most horrible things, shouting about how he wouldn't want to touch Andy anyway because he might catch AIDS, that Andy shouldn't even be allowed in the same school as the rest of us. I don't want to write it down. Listening to it made me feel angry and sad and messed up inside.

I had to make it stop somehow. I banged my bag against the metal lockers to try and startle Jason.

It worked. But only for a moment. Then he saw it was me and turned back to Andy, pressed against the wall next to the water fountain.

Andy looked up at me and his eyes widened. Not with relief, with something else – embarrassment, I think. Although Jason should have been embarrassed, not him. But I guess if Jason had any shame, he wouldn't have been trying to beat up someone in the basement at all.

Then Jason turned to me. "Oh, look who it is – lesbo Lisa."

My whole body tensed up when he said that. Was it just a random insult, or did Jason know about Nicky and me?

"You must be really pathetic if you need a *girl* to stick up for you," he continued. "Although she's not *much* of a girl, is she?" Jason laughed like he'd said something really funny. It echoed around the empty lockers.

Andy whispered at me to go. I shook my head at him. No way. Out of the corner of my eye, I could see Jason smirking at us. I wanted to get out, but if I stayed here, maybe he wouldn't hit Andy again.

Suddenly there was another voice. Shrill and angry. And a swish of skirts as Ms Ferraro swept round the corner, her face red, demanding to know what was going on.

Jason stepped away from Andy and stuck his hands in his pockets. Andy leant against the lockers breathing heavily, not looking at any of us.

Jason came up with some rubbish about how he was just chatting with some mates. He gave Andy a small shove, which could have been friendly but so obviously wasn't, and picked up his bag as if to go.

Ms Ferraro barked at Jason to stay still. He must be at least a head taller than her. She looked so tiny standing next to him.

She asked Andy if that was right, whether it was really just a chat, because it didn't sound like a chat to her. Her voice was soft but steely.

Andy just nodded. He didn't say anything. What could he say? Jason would only get him worse later if he did.

Ms Ferraro waited for what felt like ages in the silence. It was so quiet I swear that everyone heard my heart beating fast and loud.

Finally, she waved her hand at Jason. "Go on, Jason, go. But I'm watching you, remember. One false move."

Then, under his breath, just as he was leaving, Jason muttered something like, "It's poofs like him you ought to be watching, not me." I couldn't believe he'd said that, yet I could too, if you know what I mean. It was just like Jason.

Ms Ferraro asked him to repeat it, but he just looked all innocent and said, "Nothing, Miss."

Then he swung his bag on his shoulder and sauntered down the corridor. I could hear him whistling.

Ms Ferraro turned to me and Andy. She asked if we were okay and whether anything like that had happened before. She told us she was here to listen, that she understood, that she would do everything she could to stop it.

"Did you *hear* what he was saying, Miss?" Andy asked, ignoring her questions and reassurances.

She was quiet for a moment, then what she said made no sense. "Not everything, no. A little. But...it might be better if you didn't tell me exactly. Easier for me to help, I mean. I'm sorry. I wish..." She stopped and spread out her hands. She looked as upset as Andy and I did.

When she told us to get our books and head home, she sounded choked up, like someone trying not to cry.

Andy and I stood there, listening to her footsteps getting fainter as she walked away.

He wouldn't look at me.

Then, suddenly, he started kicking the locker behind him, hard, again and again, swearing with every kick. It was kind of scary. I'd never seen Andy do anything out of control like that before.

I grabbed hold of his arm, but he shook me off.

So I waited until he leant back, out of breath, the hardness on his face replaced with a twisted smile.

He reached down to rub his foot. "Ow, jeez, that really hurt. Do you think I've broken a toe? Ow."

I told him what an idiot he was. Then, all the tension we'd both been holding down began to bubble out. I don't know who started laughing first, but soon we were both holding onto each other, actually weeping with it.

When we could talk again without collapsing into giggles, I asked him what on earth he'd been doing.

"I don't know, I just got so angry about how Jason can say whatever he likes and get away with it. And you know why? Because we don't matter, we don't count, we're not normal. No one's going to stand up for us or let us stand up for ourselves. I try not to think about it. But just then it really got to me."

I didn't see how breaking his toe would make things any better.

I desperately tried to dredge up some of the things Nicky had told me or that I'd read about in her magazines, to show him that wasn't true. How thousands of people *were* standing up for people like us. That guy off EastEnders, the agony aunt from *Just Seventeen*, and loads more famous people.

But we both knew that none of those people, who didn't even know we existed, could really help us. They didn't know what it was like in school every day. They didn't hear the things that people said. But Ms Ferraro did.

And she can't help us. I swear it, some of our teachers, even if they wouldn't say it out loud, would side with Jason, not with us. But Ms Ferraro doesn't think like that. It's obvious that she wants to help, but it seems like, for some reason, she's scared too.

Andy was still so upset. "You know what, honestly, Lisa, I've had enough. Keeping a low profile doesn't make things any easier. It doesn't stop people saying stuff. Threatening me, like Jason did. I can't pretend for ever."

The way he was talking, saying that he wasn't going to hide any more, made me scared. He said he was going to the Clause 28 march with Nicky tomorrow. He said I should come too.

He can't really mean this. Andy had told me how his parents were like mine. They'd go crazy if he came out to them. They might even kick him out or something.

He pushed an empty crisp packet that someone had dropped on the floor out of the way with his foot. "It's not right, hiding down here in the dark, people treating us like rubbish. You know it isn't."

Then he sat on the floor, took off his trainer and started rubbing his injured foot.

What he said next really shook me. He said he'd phoned the number on the AIDS leaflet that came through the door, the one for the lesbian and gay helpline. He'd grabbed the leaflet when it arrived and hid it before his parents saw it.

That leaflet had freaked me out when I'd seen it, with the big gravestone on the front, talking about AIDS and death. I was glad when Dad chucked it straight in the bin, muttering about how it shouldn't have been sent to every house, not when kids could pick it up and see it.

Andy carried on relacing his shoes. "I had to talk to someone, anyone, who might get it. I waited till everyone was out. I was terrified that they'd come back while I was on the phone. I had a whole story worked out to tell my mum if they did. But the man I spoke to was so kind and he made me think...there's a whole other world out there, full of people like us. Why should we wait till we're adults to be part of it?"

I didn't know what to say to that. So, I linked my arm with his and we started walking through the dark corridors, relieved that Jason had gone and that we were leaving school behind us. For today at least.

But what about tomorrow? Nicky's been on at me for weeks about coming to the march, but I've already told her – I'm not going. I told Mum that I'd go shopping with her tomorrow, after she kept going on about how we hadn't spent enough "mother–daughter time" together recently. Yuck. I'm not letting her choose me any clothes though. No way.

It's just an excuse. Really, I know I'm too scared to go. Scared of people like Jason shouting abuse. Scared of someone I know seeing me there. But also scared of this other world that Andy's so excited about. What if I don't fit in there either? What if there's nowhere that I belong?

Andy and Nicky can go together. They don't need me. I hope Nicky doesn't think I'm too much of a coward.

17 MANIC MONDAY

I grab my coat, my phone and my bag, shove my feet into my school shoes and bang the door shut behind me. It's the first day of a new half-term and I'm already late.

I'm excited to show Lisa's stuff, and all our research, to Ms Grant this morning. I imagine her telling us what a brilliant discovery we've made. But I still feel shaken up by what I read last night, like a dark cloud is floating over the day.

What happened to Andy was awful, but even worse was how Lisa saw it as normal. It *was* normal. So normal that she doesn't see the point in fighting back. Her parents won't listen. Even a teacher like Ms Ferraro can't help. Knowing that I can tell their stories now, that they don't have to remain hidden any more, makes me feel a bit better. But only a little bit.

When Simran and I get to history, I think we must have gone to the wrong classroom, because there's someone I don't know standing at Ms Grant's desk. But everyone else is here, so I slowly push open the door.

"Come on in, girls, take your seats. The holidays are over now, so no excuse for dawdling."

I flinch a little when she says "girls" – most of the teachers are pretty good about using gender neutral language – but it doesn't feel like the right time to correct her, whoever she is. First, I need to find out what she's doing in our classroom and what she's done with Ms Grant.

"I'm Mrs Knight, and I'm your history teacher for this half-term. Now, I understand you've been studying the Tudors. Can anyone tell me where you're up to in the textbook so we can make a start?"

We all sit there in silence.

No one's quite sure where we are in the textbook. It's not like Ms Grant used it very often.

"No volunteers? Do I need to choose someone?" Mrs Knight asks.

Dylan puts up his hand. Of course, he's always got something to say.

"Excuse me, Miss, but, where's real Miss? Why's she not teaching us no more?"

"What's your name?" Mrs Knight asks him sharply.

"Dylan, Miss, and I—"

"Dylan, I think you mean *any* more, not *no* more, don't you?"

Dylan opens his mouth again, but before he can say anything else, Mrs Knight carries on.

"Unfortunately, Ms Grant won't be back until after her maternity leave now. I'll be teaching you until Easter, and then her official maternity cover will start in the summer term as planned. It all happened rather quickly, so there hasn't been a full handover, but your parents will all have received a message."

She makes it sound like *our* fault that we didn't know, but I'm not the only one who looks surprised. Maybe the message didn't get sent.

There's a murmur of voices. What does she mean "it" happened quickly? *What* happened quickly? Is Ms Grant all right? Unexpected changes always make me feel anxious. I start tapping my pencil nervously on the desk. Simran puts her hand on my arm to calm me down.

"Excuse me, Year Eight, I don't remember anyone saying that you could start talking."

"But, Miss, what's happened to Ms Grant? Is she okay?" Ella bursts out.

"What's your name, young lady?" asks Mrs Knight.

"Ella. Ella Bright."

"We put our hands up when we want to speak in class, Miss Bright. I would have expected that Ms Grant would have taught you that at least." I clench my fists under the desk. I hate the way she's talking about Ms Grant, like she's not a good teacher, when she's the best teacher I've ever had.

"Ms Grant is perfectly fine, just a few complications that mean she's on bed rest until her baby's due. Probably a blessed relief for her, away from all the hubbub in this classroom."

It seems like that's all she's going to say about it. I have a million questions but asking them now wouldn't be a good idea. From the amount of shuffling going on, I think everyone feels the same, but not even Dylan puts his hand up.

"Textbooks out, please," she continues. "You should be on at least chapter twelve by this stage in the year, so we'll start there. If you're already further ahead, never mind, this will be a good recap."

Everyone gets their textbooks out of their bags super slowly. We're nowhere near chapter twelve, but no one's going to tell Mrs Knight that.

"You can take turns to read out loud section by section," she says. "That will help me learn who's who too. We'll start with one of the girls and then alternate boy, girl, boy, girl. Nice clear reading, please, no mumbling. Ella, will you begin, please?"

Ella takes a deep breath before starting to rattle through something about the dissolution of the monasteries.

Simran looks at me and raises her eyebrows. "Where did they find her? This is such a nightmare!" she whispers.

"What about our projects?" I hiss back. "And the exhibition?"

She shrugs.

"You in the fourth row." I look up when she speaks. Please, no, she can't mean me. "Yes, you, young lady with the red hair," snaps Mrs Knight. "Do you have something you want to share with the class?" I glance at Simran in horror. My face must now be as red as my hair.

"No?" she asks, peering at me over the top of her glasses.

"Jesse was just wondering about our special projects," says Simran. "The ones that Ms Grant set us before half-term. We get to choose our own bit of history and—"

"That's enough, thank you. I'm sure Jesse can speak for herself, especially as she's so desperate to say something that she doesn't even have the manners to wait until Ella has finished reading."

"Miss, Miss!" says Dylan, waving his hand in the air. "Jesse's not 'she', she's 'they'."

Simran rolls her eyes. "My god," she mutters. But it makes me feel better. Dylan's sticking up for me, even if it came out a bit wrong.

"I'm sorry?" says Mrs Knight, taking off her glasses and rubbing her eyes. She looks like a mole without them. "I have no idea what you are talking about."

My voice comes out in a whisper. "I use them/they pronouns, Miss. I'm non-binary."

"Don't be ridiculous!" says Mrs Knight, pursing her lips together. "'They' is a plural. You, as far as I can tell, are only one person." A few people snigger. "Where would we be if everyone chose whatever words they wanted and used them to mean whatever they liked? Hmm?"

But it's not *like* that, I want to say. Words don't stay the same for ever. Just like people. Changing and experimenting and having more choices are *good* things. Ms Grant would never have said anything like that. But I keep quiet, because I know that Mrs Knight would just think I was answering back.

"I see we have a few basic issues with grammar to attend to in this class over the rest of this half-term, as well as keeping up with the history curriculum," she continues, shaking her head. "It's obvious that there's no time for messing around with any special projects."

"What?" explodes Simran.

"That's not fair. I've already started mine," complains Dylan.

Ella and Jasmine start murmuring to each other.

Most people look disappointed. But nowhere near as disappointed as I feel. What about Lisa and Nicky's story now?

"That's quite enough," says Mrs Knight. "Time to get on. Dylan, you can pick up from where Ella finished, and then we'll have Jesse read after that."

I can feel tears pricking behind my eyes, but I swallow hard to try and make them disappear. I don't want to read out loud, let alone as part of Mrs Knight's stupid boy/girl/boy/girl system. But there's nothing I can do to get out of it.

I make my mind go blank and focus on one word at a time. After my turn, I stop listening and let the words flow over me. I slump lower and lower in my seat as the lesson drones on. The best part of the week has now become the worst.

When the bell finally rings, at the end of the longest lesson in the history of the universe, the classroom explodes into noise. Mrs Knight claps her hands again and shouts above the din.

"Year Eight, the bell is for me not for you – *I* will tell you when the lesson is over. I'll see you next on Thursday.

That gives you plenty of time to prepare for a test on chapter twelve. You are now dismissed."

It's impossible to concentrate for the rest of the day. Although at least I get the question about plate boundaries right in the geography test, thanks to Simran. Even that doesn't cheer me up.

Simran is really cross about the projects being cancelled – she keeps tutting and sighing to herself. I know she'd want to talk about it all the way home, so I'm secretly glad that she's staying late for choir today. I need to be by myself right now; I feel too sad to talk to anybody. I was really looking forward to this half of term, but now everything feels grey and nothingy. The cloud I imagined hovering over me earlier has grown even bigger and darker.

I shift my bag from shoulder to shoulder as I walk home. It feels heavier than it did on the way in. I'm turning things over in my mind too. Ms Grant not coming back. History projects cancelled. A surprise test on something I know nothing about. Six more weeks of Mrs Knight. But worst of all, the feeling of being able to be who I am, that's built up so slowly this year, starting to crumble away. It's taken a long time to feel a little bit safe to be me, to actually enjoy it. Now everything feels uncertain again.

I cut through the park and stop at the bench by the war memorial. It sounds a bit morbid, but I've liked coming here ever since I was little. I've always been fascinated by the names carved in stone, wondering about the stories of the people who died long ago and of the people who still leave flowers here today.

I shrug the bag off my back and wiggle my aching shoulders. Then I get Lisa's diary out and sit on the bench to read the next entry.

18 WITH OR WITHOUT YOU

Saturday 30 April 1988

I feel sick. All I can think about is Nicky and Andy – making signs for the march, dashing for the train, joining thousands of other people on the streets, actually doing something to change the world. And what's *my* plan for today? Trailing round C&A and Laura Ashley with my mum, that's what.

I'm so stupid. How is it so obvious now what I should do, when last night I had no idea? Or maybe it always was obvious, I was just too scared to see it.

But I've decided. I *can* still go on the march. It's not too late. I'm just hoping I can catch up with Nicky and Andy somehow.

Dad's already taken Matthew to football, so it was just me and Mum at breakfast. She looked so happy at the thought of us spending time together. I feel a bit bad for spoiling that. I tried to look as ill as I could, slumping at the table and holding my head and sighing.

I think my acting was a bit too good! Mum looked worried and said that she should stay at home to make sure I was okay. I reminded her of all the things she had to do today, like send Jenny's birthday present to Auntie Stella in Hurston. Mum prides herself on always sending presents on time.

Mum's always saying Auntie Stella's flighty and that they don't have anything in common, but I think she loves her really. Auntie Stella may send us late birthday presents, but they're always fun and unusual ones.

I told Mum I'd be too ill to enjoy shopping today, but we could go next week. Then I coughed some more to add to the effect and, result, she sent me back to bed.

I'm lying here now, barely able to keep still, waiting for her to go out. I've packed my camera and Walkman in my bag. I'll leave a note on the kitchen table, saying I'm feeling better and have gone to Nicky's.

I think that's the door closing now. She's gone.

19 DON'T FORGET ME WHEN I'M GONE

I turn over the page.

Hang on! What? What?

I fumble through the remaining pages in the exercise book. They are all blank or just have doodles on. Nothing about the march. Nothing at all. The diary just stops.

I shiver and pull my blazer tightly around me. While I was reading, I didn't notice the cold, but now I can feel the goosebumps on my arms.

What happened next? Why didn't Lisa write anything more?

I shut the book in frustration. There must be a way to find out. I stare at the block capitals on the back cover until they start to blur before my eyes:

LISA MARIE SCOTT

LOVES

NICOLA ANNE BURRIDGE

Nicola Burridge. Nicky. Of course. Nicky would know what happened next.

"I need to find out where Nicky is now," I mutter to myself, rummaging in my bag for my phone. It's so obvious. Why hadn't Simran or I thought of getting in touch with her already?

My fingers are so cold by now that it takes me five different attempts to spell "Burridge" right.

I find an American Nicky Burridge who runs a dog grooming parlour in Colorado, a Nicola Burridge who was a famous dancer in the 1920s and a twenty-two-year-old Nicki Burridge who starred in Woking Theatre's production of *Cinderella* in December 2019.

Obviously none of these are her. Maybe the real Nicky is one of these people who hates social media and lives off-grid, like Dad wishes we did, if only Mum would let him.

I sigh. Nothing's working out for me today. I stuff the diary back into my bag and trudge home.

"It's me!" I shout, banging the front door shut behind

me. I think I'll just grab a snack from the kitchen and then look through the box again, in case, somehow, I've managed not to notice a second diary in there before.

Mum is sitting at the table, her feet on one of the chairs. She's on the phone, but she looks up and smiles when she hears me come in.

"Jesse's home," she says to the person on the other end. "Do you want to talk to them?" I give her a questioning look. "Yes. Great... I'll pass you over. It's Tom," Mum says as she hands me her phone and wanders out of the room.

"Hi, what are you calling for? Is everything okay?"

"You're as bad as Mum," laughs Tom. "I was just walking home from lectures in the cold and dark and I thought I'd call. That's all. I thought talking to you might distract me from this freezing wind!"

"Oh, okay." I pause. There's an awkward silence. "So, how are you?" I ask eventually.

I find it weird talking to Tom on the phone. I guess because, until he went to uni, we never did. We didn't need to. He was right here. But now, the pressure of him waiting for me to say something makes my mind go blank. I know it's nothing like Lisa's brother moving to Australia, but sometimes it feels that Tom is so far away.

"I'm all right," he says. "Bit knackered from rugby training yesterday, but it was good. I reckon we'll win our match next Saturday." He chats on about rugby for a while and how he's got matches for the next few weekends.

"So, you won't be coming home to see us this term?" I ask.

There's another pause. "Ah, Jesse, no, I'm really sorry. It's not just the matches, I can't afford it either. It's such a long way. I'll be back at Easter though." He does sound sorry. Now I feel bad. I didn't mean to make him feel guilty.

"It's okay. What are you doing tonight?" I ask to change the subject.

"Oh!" His voice lightens again. "You'll be proud of me. I'm going to an LGBTQ+ society thing. It's called the Big Queer Quiz."

"What? Seriously? You're not LGBTQ+! And you hate quizzes!" Tom and I are total opposites when it comes to quizzes. I love the chance to show off my obscure trivia knowledge. He's terrible at remembering facts and figures.

"I know, but my flatmate's team is one person short. I told him I'd be rubbish, but he said that didn't matter. He promised he'd buy me chips when we got there, so I said yes. Mum said you were doing this school project on LGBTQ+ history. Have you discovered anything that might give me the edge in this quiz? Go on, help me out here."

"It's more like family history," I say. "I don't think it's going to help with the quiz."

"Tell me anyway."

So I do. Whenever I stop to check that he's not getting bored, he tells me to carry on and asks loads of questions.

"So, when are you planning on speaking to Nicky?" Tom asks.

"I tried to google her," I say. "But I couldn't find her."

"Maybe she's got married or changed her name, did you think of that? Did you include her middle name? That could help narrow your search down a bit." There's a noise of a door slamming. "Got to go, I'm home, say 'bye' to Mum and Dad for me."

"Oh, yeah, right, bye. Good luck in the quiz!" But he's already gone.

I head upstairs. I'm not sure what to do first – try again to search for Nicky online or look in the box for missing diary entries about the march.

I start with the box. I try to be methodical. I take each book out one by one and flick through the pages slowly in case there's something hidden inside. Finally, I get to Lisa's history textbook, the one with the kings and queens on the cover. I turn it upside down, shake it and several sheets of folded paper, covered in Lisa's spiky handwriting, fall into my lap.

20 KISS

This has been the longest day of my life! And it's still not over. I'm shattered, but I can't sleep. No chance. Everything's buzzing. I can hardly bear to sit down to write. I keep thinking I can hear Mum's footsteps outside my room. But I am going to write about this, even if this is all that's left of my diary now.

I'm straining to hear what's going on downstairs. There's murmuring – I can't hear the words, but I know they are talking about me. Working out what to do with me. How to solve this problem.

I should storm down there and confront them. How can they decide what happens in my life without asking me? But I know they won't listen. They didn't earlier. All we did was shout, and Mum cried. I've been crying too.

When I left the house this morning, the door slammed behind me like a full stop. I had this strange feeling that anything could happen. It was exciting and unnerving, like standing on the edge of the ice rink, getting ready to skate.

I knew it was stupid, even as I ran for the bus to the station. Nicky and Andy went ages ago. How would I ever find them in London, among thousands of marchers when they didn't even know I'd be looking for them? But I had to try.

I sat on the tube, perched on the edge of the seat, the rattle of the train making it hard to think. I clutched my ticket tightly, leaving finger marks on the paper edges. Nicky had said the march started at Embankment. So that's where I was going.

There was no one to follow. No one else in my carriage looked like they were going on the march. There were families on days out, a few couples holding hands, some teenagers messing around. But I guess they wouldn't have known where I was going either, not just by looking at me. Or could everyone tell?

At Embankment, the streets were heaving. I stood, tucked in the station entrance, trying not to stare but unable to stop. I was too shy to get my camera out, so I tried to remember everything so I could draw it later.

There were men holding hands with men, without even

caring if people saw. There were women with shaved heads and bigger boots than mine, rolling cigarettes and hugging each other hello. There was a group of people, not much older than me, with a banner that said "Young Lesbians Unite" and another group unpacking trumpets and sheet music, and yet another handing out leaflets with pink triangles on them (I recognized these from the stack Nicky's dad had at her house, Nicky had made me take one), and everywhere the same slogan: "Stop the Clause".

So *this* was what a march was like. I thought it would be angry or scary, but it wasn't. It felt full of life.

But how would I ever find Nicky?

I pushed my way through the crowds, looking round me as I went. If I kept moving, maybe I'd have more of a chance of finding her.

People kept asking if I was all right. I must have looked lost or anxious, or maybe just young. The crowd kept getting bigger. I didn't *feel* all right. I felt scared. What if I *never* found Nicky and Andy among all these people?

I was ready to give up when I heard a shout. Then two.

I couldn't work out where they were coming from.

Then I looked up.

Nicky and Andy were perched on a wall alongside the pavement, their legs dangling down. The slope of the road meant that they had a great view but that I had to squint up to see them. I swear I almost cried I was so relieved to see them.

Nicky jumped down and gave me the biggest hug, squeezing me tightly. Andy pulled Nicky back up onto the wall, and then Nicky helped me up, so that we were sat in a line.

"What the hell...?" she started saying at exactly the same time as I said, "How on earth...?" We both laughed. We were holding hands from when she'd helped me up onto the wall. Neither of us let go.

I couldn't believe they'd managed to spot me.

She reached up and gently tugged my hair. "We couldn't miss you. Your hair stands out from miles away. You're like a walking 'stop' sign. But what the hell are you doing here?"

I didn't know what to say. It was hard to explain the feeling I had, that this was where I was meant to be.

Nicky pulled something small and round out of her pocket. Then she leant over and pinned it to my jacket. It was a "Stop the Clause" badge.

"You're a proper activist now," she said approvingly.

She opened her jacket and showed me the enormous "Stop the Clause" T-shirt she was wearing. It was almost down to her knees. She'd got the T-shirt in Oxfam and decorated it herself. She'd made one for Andy too, although he rolled his eyes when Nicky asked him to show me.

Nicky had made them both put on their home-made T-shirts on the tube. If anyone tutted or raised their eyebrows, she just stared them out. I could so imagine her doing that. Andy told me later that all the time they were wearing them, he was terrified they'd bump into someone he knew who might tell his parents. He tried to sound like he was joking. Ha, if only it *was* a joke.

Nicky leaped gracefully off the wall. Andy followed more carefully.

"My toe still really hurts," he muttered, landing clumsily on the pavement.

"I think those lockers had it worse," I said.

The three of us shuffled along slowly, moving with the crowd. Michael and Kayleigh were up ahead with the group from the college. There was so much to see. I wanted to pay attention to every little thing. I felt so alive, so connected to everyone else.

The music and chanting were too loud for us to talk properly, but before long we were chanting too – "We're here, we're queer, get used to it." I started laughing, it was so much fun.

We were doing something that mattered – more than that – we were doing it together. Thousands of us, all different ages, all from different places. All marching to show the world that we exist, that we matter, that we can't be swept away or ignored.

Someone behind us said that this was the biggest gay rights march ever – people were also marching in Amsterdam and in New York to show their support for us here in the UK. A few people walking past waved or stuck their thumbs up at us, and we all cheered back. Others looked down at their feet or shook their heads; one man even spat at us. I held tight onto Nicky's hand. Now I'd found her, there was no way I was going to let her go.

At Piccadilly Circus, the march slowed down. Nicky dragged us through the crowds so we could see what was happening.

I'd been here before, that time we went to the pantomime in London with Mum and Dad and Auntie Stella and Uncle Robert, when Matthew and I were small and before Jenny was born. I recognized the big lit-up wall of ads, and the tiny statue of Eros, pointing his bow into the sky, ready to fire off arrows of love. And that was the point, wasn't it? You couldn't choose who to love or who not to, it just happened. You didn't decide where the arrow would land, and no one else should decide that for you.

It looked nothing like last time I was here. There were loads of people on the steps round the statue. And everyone was kissing. I mean it. I honestly couldn't believe it.

Someone had propped a hand-painted sign under Eros. "Kiss-In" it said in big, black letters.

I took some pictures of the sign and of all the people kissing.

As I was winding on the film, something inside me shifted. I hadn't come here to watch from the outside – I had to be part of it.

I grabbed Nicky's arm and practically pulled her up the steps towards Eros. It was too loud to explain, but she quickly worked it out.

"What, you and me? In front of everyone?" she shouted, raising an eyebrow, like she was up for it but wasn't sure that I would be.

I leaned over and kissed her. People on the steps whooped and cheered. I think someone took a photo of us. I couldn't imagine feeling any happier. Like if I did, I might float up into the sky and disappear.

Andy pretended to be upset that there was no one to kiss him. So Nicky and I surrounded him and kissed both his cheeks at once!

Andy wriggled out from between us, took my camera from my hand and stepped back.

"Smile!"

Nicky threw her arm round me. Andy hadn't needed to ask us to smile. Neither of us could have done anything else.

21 SOMEWHERE OUT THERE

She did it! They did it! Lisa and Nicky and Andy were there. Marching together. Today has been rubbish, but knowing that they made it onto the streets, despite all the things that could have stopped them, shows that love and friendship and community are worth speaking up for, whether or not people want to listen. It makes me feel a bit more hopeful.

But what did Lisa mean about crying and arguing with her mum and not having her diary any more? That must be why this entry is on a separate bit of paper. But there's so much that still doesn't make sense about what happened.

There are drawings round the edges of the pages. Sketches of the different groups at the march, and some of the banners Lisa must have seen. She's so talented. She's drawn Eros at the bottom of the page, except as well as holding a bow and arrow, he's wearing a "Stop the Clause" T-shirt like Nicky's.

I reach into the box again. Simran's got the jacket with the "Stop the Clause" badge on, but the home-made T-shirt with the pink triangle on it is still here. Now I know what it means, it doesn't matter how tatty it is. I don't know why Lisa had it, but this is Nicky's T-shirt, it must be. Now it's up to me to make sure it's not hidden away any more.

I lay it out on my bed and smooth out the creases with my hands. Then, without really thinking, I pull it over my head and stare at myself in the mirror. I look ridiculous – the T-shirt is so big that it hangs down to my knees, but instead of making me laugh, looking at my reflection makes me shiver. It feels no time at all between then and now. If I'd been alive then, what would I have done? Hidden at home or joined in the march?

Lisa was so lucky, finding Nicky and Andy among all those crowds, with no idea where they were and no phone to contact or track them. It's wild. It's hard to believe it was even possible. But it was.

So surely it can't be any harder for me to track down Nicky online now. I start searching again. More carefully this time, adding her middle name like Tom suggested, using her initials instead of her full name, and looking closely at each result.

I scroll through page after page of results. Then one entry catches my eye on a university website: Professor N.A. Zielinska-Burridge, lecturer in the politics of visual communication, special research interest in queer theory. I've seen books about that in Over the Rainbow. It sounds like the sort of thing that Nicky could be into. Maybe, like Tom said, she *has* got married, but only partially changed her name.

I click on the link. As soon as I see the photo, I know it's her. It's a middle-aged woman with cropped grey hair and glasses, nothing like the teenager in Lisa's photos, and yet her smile…that's exactly the same.

"Yes!" I shout. I send a screenshot to Simran. But she doesn't reply straight away, and I have to tell someone right now. I run down to the kitchen to find Mum.

"I've found Nicky! Well, her email address. It's right here! And, guess what, she's in Brighton, that's only half an hour away. We could meet up and talk to her and show her the diary and—"

"Steady on," says Mum. "Rewind. You mean Nicky, Lisa's friend? You've been looking for her on the internet and you think you've found her?"

"I *know* I've found her. It's definitely her. Look!" I thrust the phone at Mum so that she can see too.

She peers at the screen. "Well, maybe."

I sigh. Why is she not more excited about this?

"This all happened a long time ago," says Mum. "She might not want to hear from a total stranger about something that she thought was all in the past. It's sensitive. If they didn't keep in touch, she might not even know that Lisa's died."

"But we've got to *try* to contact her, haven't we?" I plead.

"Let's think about it. There's no rush. This is people's real lives, you know, Jesse, not just a school project."

"I do *know* that," I snap.

Great. Earlier today, Mrs Knight said that the history projects were a waste of time. And now Mum's saying that my project's not important either.

"Anyway, it's not 'just' a school project," I carry on. "It's much more than that! I'd want to get in touch with Nicky, even if there wasn't a project. I'm sending an email, not turning up on her doorstep!"

"Let's talk about this properly after tea, okay? We can decide then." She turns back to the cooking. I glare at her back but she doesn't notice.

The anger bubbling up inside me reaches my throat and it makes it hard to speak. I can feel tears in my eyes,

187

which makes me even angrier.

"Yeah, whatever, I'm not hungry." I push my chair back. The harsh scraping sound makes us both flinch.

"Where are you going?" asks Mum, turning round.

"Just to my room. Is that okay? Or are you going to stop me from doing *everything*?" I shout.

"Oh come on, Jesse, don't be ridiculous. All I'm saying is, don't rush into things." Mum sounds tired. "Why don't you come and taste this?" She holds out a spoon. "Tell me if you think it's ready."

"Weren't you listening? I told you, I'm not hungry."

Mum's face hardens. "If you're going to be like that, perhaps you'd better cool off in your room, instead of staying down here having a go at me."

"I'm not…" I start, but then I realize there's no point in arguing. Who cares what Mum says? I can email Nicky myself if I want to. I've found her email address. Tom thinks it's a good idea. I don't need Mum's permission.

Mum's voice follows me as I leave the kitchen, "And don't go emailing Nicky now, okay? Not till you've calmed down and we've talked about it."

Shut up, I think silently. *Shut up, shut up.*

Dad's coming down the stairs as I'm going up.

"How was the first day back?" he asks cheerily. As if he can't tell just by looking at me. I'm not in the mood to reply, so I carry on without saying anything. He wouldn't understand anyway.

"Are you okay, Jesse?" he asks, sounding worried.

"Fine," I mumble, without looking at him. "Just, you know, going to do some homework..."

I can feel him watching me. "Are you sure?"

I shut my bedroom door.

I throw myself onto my bed and feel something crunch beneath my arm. It's one of the Maltesers that Simran and I were throwing at each other yesterday. That one is too squashed to eat, but I find another in the folds of the duvet. As the chocolate melts in my mouth, I regret telling Mum I wasn't hungry. Actually I'm starving. Whatever she was cooking smelled really good.

I look for my phone. I'm composing the email to Nicky in my mind already. She'll want to hear from me, I know she will, whatever Mum says. It's not here, I must have left it on the kitchen table. But there's no way I'm going back downstairs now.

I sit down next to the half-emptied box on the floor. Maybe there are more things hidden inside the old textbooks, waiting for me to discover. I look through geography, then French, then science.

And out falls a slim yellow wallet of photographs. I take out the prints one by one.

The first ones are eerily familiar, even though I've never seen them before. They are of Lisa, Andy and Nicky, posing together at the Kiss-In. They are hugging each other tightly and have huge grins on their faces. I've just read all about the day those photos were taken.

The rest of the photos are from some kind of family celebration. There's a picture of Lisa and a large chocolate cake. She's blowing out the candles, but with a look on her face that says "I'm much too grown-up for this". I wonder what she's wishing for.

There's a boy next to her, sticking his tongue out at the camera. That must be Matthew. He looks young, even though he must have been about the same age then as I am now. I bet he's like Dylan and Conor in my class. Messing around all the time. Thirteen going on three.

There are a couple of shots of Lisa's parents. Her dad looks uncomfortable at being photographed, like he'd rather be somewhere else, but her Mum is facing the camera wearing what must be her best photo smile.

The last photo is of a woman with a baby in her arms. The quality's terrible and it's a bit lopsided, but the look of delight on her face as she stares at the baby shines out of the photo.

It's Gran, I realize with a jolt, Lisa's Auntie Stella. Looking more like she did in the wedding photo that she kept by her bed, than she did when I knew her. I put the photos of the two sisters next to each other and try to find the similarity.

Lisa said her mum thought that Gran was "flighty". That makes me smile. Flighty is a good word for her, someone who was always on the move, never bogged down or defeated by anything. I wish I was more like her. I miss her so much that I have to turn the photo over and bite my lip so as not to cry. The baby in her arms? That's Mum.

If Gran was here, what would she do? She'd let me be cross for a bit, then she'd tell me a funny story about something Mum did when she was a teenager. Then she'd wait and listen. Then she'd give me a hug and say something about life being too short to argue or to sulk, and definitely too short to let a bad mood get in the way of a good dinner. Then we'd go downstairs.

There are more sheets of paper covered in Lisa's spiky writing stuffed in the back of the history textbook. I'll read a little bit more. Then I'll go down and see Mum and Dad.

22 HEARTACHE

Saturday 30 April 1988

By the time we reached the rally at the end of the march, we were tired and hungry. My feet hurt and Nicky needed the loo, and the stage was too far away to hear the speeches. It was getting late. Mum would have finished shopping ages ago. I hadn't said on my note what time I'd be home, but I couldn't stay out much longer, not after having been so "ill" this morning.

It took us ages to find the tube station. It felt like we'd walked for miles. We bought chips on the way. As we got on the train, Andy and Nicky were having a loud argument about whether vinegar on chips was the best combination ever or the work of the devil.

Just as the train doors were shutting, two women, one clutching a Stop the Clause placard, threw themselves into the carriage and onto the seats facing ours. They weren't looking at us, just at each other. Their faces were glowing, and their grins were as big as mine and Nicky's had been at the Kiss-In.

Nicky and Andy were still arguing about chips. I looked up, gasped and squeezed Nicky's hand.

"What?" she said, much too loud.

Then she and I and Andy and Ms Ferraro and the woman holding Ms Ferraro's hand all looked at each other at exactly the same moment. Ms Ferraro's face went from pink to white. She dropped the other woman's hand like it was on fire.

My first thought was – what if she tells our parents? My hand reached instinctively to hide my Stop the Clause badge, like that was going to make any difference, what with Nicky sitting next to me in her enormous home-made T-shirt.

Andy recovered first, saying hello to Ms Ferraro, while Nicky and I just stared at our shoes.

It's always weird if you see a teacher out of school, but this was a whole new level of weirdness. None of us knew what to say. Ms Ferraro looked even more awkward than we did. We all knew we'd been on the march, and we all knew, without anyone saying anything, that we had to pretend that we hadn't. Everything happy and free about the day started to fade away. It had only been a brief holiday from hiding. If the protestors weren't listened to, we knew things would only get worse.

Ms Ferraro muttered something. Then both women got up and scurried to the other end of the carriage. They sat with their heads together, whispering furiously.

"So that's why she was weird, in the lockers yesterday," said Andy. "And in the RE debate, like she wanted to help, but she was scared to. That's why. It's cos she's—"

I shushed him quickly. Ms Ferraro was coming back over.

She was clearly worried we'd tell someone we saw her at the march. We all promised that we wouldn't say a word to anyone else. She explained that she could lose her job, especially if the school found out students had been at the march too. It was scary seeing a teacher, someone who should have it totally together, looking so freaked out.

Could she really get sacked, just for going on a march? It's nothing to do with school what she does on the weekend! But then she told us that Mr Ryan had called a meeting last week, for all the staff, to talk about Clause 28, like it had already been passed, telling the teachers what they'd have to do and not do, and what changes there would be to school policy. Stuff I hadn't even realized, like if a student asked her about being gay, she wasn't supposed to even talk to them about it. She was supposed to ask them to talk to their parents, or even tell their parents herself!

She said that she had thought that things were getting better, but now they seemed to be getting worse.

Then she said this really sad thing – all she'd ever wanted to do was teach, to be there for students who needed her, to open their eyes to the world around them, but now, she didn't know whether she was doing any good at all, maybe she was even making things worse.

I wanted to make her feel better. I said it was good just to know she was there, that there was someone who understood us.

I didn't say that it wasn't nearly enough.

She asked if we were okay. We all looked at each other and nodded. Then she asked about our parents.

I shook my head. No way. Mum's even stopped watching EastEnders since they had those two blokes kissing, and that was only a peck on the cheek. Andy's parents never watched it anyway. His mum said it was full of sin.

Only Nicky had something good to say. "My dad's on the march," she told Ms Ferraro. "He was the one who told us about it. It *was* amazing, wasn't it?"

At last, Ms Ferraro smiled, but only for a second. "Yes, it was. Now, I'd better go back and join my..." She paused. "My friend. See you in school on Monday."

We didn't talk any more. Nicky and Andy took off their "Stop the Clause" T-shirts. They just had their normal T-shirts on underneath – now no one looking at them would know they had been on the march. I had my Walkman, so we listened to my mixtape, passing the headphones between us, and singing along to the songs. When the train pulled into our station, Ms Ferraro and her girlfriend got off first and didn't look back. Neither of them were carrying the placard any more. They must have left it behind.

Nicky walks home from the station, and Andy gets a different bus from me, so we hugged goodbye on the station steps, ignoring the shoppers grumpily pushing past us on their way home.

Nicky pushed her "Stop the Clause" T-shirt into my hands. "Take this! A memento of the day. Don't let your mum see."

I promised I wouldn't. I shoved the T-shirt right down to the bottom of my bag. My bus was rounding the corner, so I started running. I turned back to wave and Nicky was watching me with a smile on her face. I'm trying to fix that image in my mind. After what happened next, I have no idea when I'll see her again.

I opened the door quietly, wanting to avoid an interrogation about how I was feeling and why I'd gone out when I wasn't well. Luckily, Mum had the radio on loudly in the kitchen.

I creeped upstairs. My bedroom door was slightly open. That was weird. Maybe I'd been in such a hurry earlier that I hadn't shut it properly. Or maybe—

23 STAND BY ME

The knock on my bedroom door makes me jump. I fumble and lose my place.

"Jesse, can I come in?" asks Mum softly as she opens the door. I shrug.

She doesn't speak, just sits down next to me on the bed, taking care not to mess up the photos. After a moment, I pick up the one of Gran with her as a baby and hand it to her. She looks at it for a long time.

"You really miss her, don't you," Mum says. It's not a question but I nod anyway.

"Me too," she says. We carry on looking at the photo, not speaking.

Finally, she says, "Jesse, did something bad happen at school today?"

I look up at her. How does she always know?

"I meant to ask about your day as soon as you got in, but there was the phone call from Tom, and I got distracted…"

Just for a few minutes, while I was talking to Tom and searching up Nicky online, I'd forgotten how bad school had been today. Now, it all comes flooding back.

"History projects are cancelled," I tell Mum in a flat, quiet voice.

"Cancelled? What do you mean?" she asks.

When I don't say anything more, she continues. "Start at the very beginning, it's a very good place to start." It's a quote from an old musical. She always used to say it when I was little, when I'd get home from primary school, overflowing with stories that made no sense to anyone but me.

So, I do. I explain it all from the beginning – about Ms Grant going off on maternity leave early and Mrs Knight coming in and changing everything. The only thing I don't tell her about is Mrs Knight deliberately using the wrong pronouns and laughing at me when I tried to explain. I'm not ready for Mum's hurt feelings on my behalf right now.

"She does sound like a bit of a dragon," says Mum. "I'm sure there wasn't an email from the school about any of this. But, she said herself, there hasn't been a proper handover yet. Maybe you'll go in on Thursday and find that she's got the notes from Ms Grant, and the projects and the exhibition are back on."

"Maybe," I say, without much hope. I was in that classroom, and Mum wasn't. I can't imagine someone like Mrs Knight changing her mind. And anyway, even if she did, the exhibition wouldn't be the same without Ms Grant.

"Let's wait and see," says Mum. "Gran was always on about giving people the benefit of the doubt, wasn't she? Maybe that's what you need to do." I'm about to open my mouth to protest, but Mum carries on talking.

"Anyway, I've been thinking about what you said, that this is more important than a school project, and I agree. If you want to, then you should try to get in touch with Nicky."

I stare at her. "But you said…?"

"I know, but you caught me by surprise. I've had a chat with Dad. It's up to Nicky to decide whether she wants to explore this part of her past or not. But she can't make that choice unless you tell her what you've found. I can email her if you still want us to get in touch."

"Of course I still want to! Let's do it now," I say.

"Tea's ready!" shouts Dad up the stairs.

"I know you said you weren't hungry…" says Mum.

"Maybe I am a little bit hungry," I concede. "But can't we write the email first?"

"We can do it while we're eating," says Mum.

I stare at her.

"Mum!"

"What?"

"What about the whole no-screens-at-the-table thing?" This is one of Mum's big rules. It's so we can have proper conversations at the dinner table, she says. But she finds this rule harder to keep than Tom or I do. There always seem to be exceptions, like now.

Mum and I compose an email together in between mouthfuls. Dad chips in occasionally. Mum writes the first bit, about Lisa having died, explaining about how she got ill, talking about the friends who cared for her and how beautifully the funeral celebrated her life. I'm glad she did. I wouldn't have known what to say.

The Lisa in my head is still very much alive. She's a teenager with her whole life ahead. She and Nicky are in love and they are fighting for something they believe in. Her voice springs off the pages of the diary. Every single thing that she's saved in that box says something about what mattered to her. I almost feel like I've met her.

At the end of the email, we tell Nicky about the

exhibition. I badly hope that it won't be cancelled, but even if it is, I'm not ready to give up. Nicky and Lisa wouldn't have. I'll find a way, somehow, to tell this story.

I cross my fingers as Mum clicks send.

"Don't get your hopes up, okay? It might all come to nothing," she warns.

"You will tell me when she replies, won't you?"

"*If* she replies," says Mum. "And of course I'll tell you, the very second I hear, okay?"

Simran finally messages me back, so I tell her about emailing Nicky. Then, for the rest of the evening, I watch a bit of TV, do some homework and exchange messages with Tom about the quiz.

I don't read any more of Lisa's diary. I want to know what happened to Lisa after the march, but I'm also dreading finding out. I know it's not going to be good. I want to hold onto the joy that Lisa felt on the streets, not face up to whatever was waiting for her when she got back home.

So I don't read any more tonight or for the next couple of days. It's not until Wednesday night, when I'm sick of preparing for Mrs Knight's test on the Tudors, that I pick up Lisa's story again.

24 POINT OF NO RETURN

Saturday 30 April 1988

Matthew was sitting on my bed. I shouted at him to get the hell out of my room.

"Why do you always have to be so mean?" he whined. "Can't you be nice to me, just for, like, one day of your whole life? Anyway, if Mum saw this—"

I didn't know what he was talking about at first. He just stood there, staring at me, like he didn't care what I said or did. It was creepy.

Then he waved something at me. My diary.

I snatched at it, but he was gripping the book so tight that his fingers went white.

It's ages since we've had a proper fight, an actual punching and kicking one. Mostly I just try and ignore the fact that Matthew exists on the same planet as me, but I'm still bigger than him and I still remember how to hurt him. I held his wrists as he kicked at my ankles. I told him I'd let him go, if he gave the diary back.

But he twisted free, holding my diary above his head, shouting "Finders keepers, losers weepers", like he was a little kid in the playground.

I lunged for him. He stumbled backwards. It might have been all right, I might have grabbed it, if Mum hadn't come in at just that moment. Matthew almost knocked her flying.

She couldn't work out which of us to tell off first, even though it was obviously his fault, so she started on us both. Why were we behaving like toddlers? She could hear us shouting from downstairs. What would the neighbours think? On and on.

She turned to me. "Lisa, you're the oldest, you should be setting a good example." She glanced at my feet. "And what have I told you about wearing those boots upstairs and ruining the carpet?"

Matthew smirked at me. There was no way I was going to take the blame when this was all his fault. The words came tumbling out as I explained how he had snuck into my room, gone through my private things and taken my diary. Surely she'd understand.

Mum frowned. "Matthew..." she said. It was both a

question and a warning. I wanted him to get told off, but more importantly, I wanted my diary back safe in my hands.

"If you *really* wanted to keep it secret, you should have hidden it better, or written it in code. You're so stupid," he shouted. "I've read it all. You and Nicky, it's disgusting. Mum, she's got all this gay stuff in there—" He sniggered as he said the word "gay".

Mum's face went pale. I hissed at Matthew to shut up.

"She and Nicky, they've been kissing and everything. It's in her diary. She loves her," he said, making kissing noises, stretching out the word "love" so that it sounded ridiculous.

I tried to say something. But Mum wasn't listening – Matthew had her full attention. He was saying how I'd lied about today, how I wasn't really ill, how I'd been with Nicky. He shook my diary so that the leaflet Nicky had given me about the march fell to the floor. The pink triangle on the front mirrored the pink triangle on the badge, which I suddenly remembered was still on my jacket.

Matthew and I both grabbed the leaflet at the same time. It ripped down the middle. I was left holding only scraps of paper.

Mum's voice was very calm as she told Matthew to go back to his room.

He didn't want to go, but he saw there was no point arguing. She held out her hand and he reluctantly handed my diary over.

Suddenly, I wished he would stay. If he did, maybe I wouldn't have to listen to whatever Mum had to say to me.

She sat down on my bed and patted the duvet next to her. I perched on the edge of the bed, as far away as I could. Tense, waiting.

When she spoke, her voice was soft, controlled. She said that it was wrong of Matthew to read my diary, but what he'd said made her worried. Could he have made a mistake? Was there anything I wanted to talk to her about?

I didn't dare look at her. I knew how her forehead would be wrinkled in concern, her head tipped to one side. I stared at the diary resting on her lap, like a bomb waiting to go off. When was she going to give it back?

"You know, I'm not prejudiced," she continued. "But this is different. With homosexuals, we're not talking about real relationships, just sad, lonely people. It's like an illness. They need help, not encouragement." She reached over and patted me on the knee.

I thought she'd be angry with me, but then she said she thought Nicky had been manipulating me, forcing me to do something I didn't want. She thought I must be confused, that I was too young to know my own mind. She wanted me to put all the blame on Nicky.

But I couldn't do that.

Even if I did, what would be the point? Mum and Dad would stop me seeing her, and I couldn't bear that.

I finally found my voice. I shouted at Mum not to say such horrible things. Nicky wasn't manipulating me. She wasn't forcing me to do anything. I loved her. She was my girlfriend.

I couldn't believe I'd said the words out loud. I couldn't stand Mum talking about Nicky like that, like she was poison, instead of being the best thing that's ever happened in my life.

Mum drew in a deep breath. I didn't hear everything she said. The rushing of blood in my ears and the pounding of my heart drowned out her voice. I couldn't keep my eyes off the diary. My fingers were itching to snatch it back, to hide it and keep it safe so no one could ever find it again.

I only remember one thing she said clearly – she told me being gay was a terrible lifestyle because I wouldn't be able to have children, to start a family of my own.

"I don't care about having children. You just want me to be like you," I shouted. "Well, I'm not and I never want to be. I hate you."

Mum's smile disappeared. The softness in her voice

was gone. Instead, it started shaking. She got off the bed and walked to the door, telling me to stay in my room until she'd talked to Dad. They were my parents, their job was to protect me. She was still holding my diary. "I'll look after this for now," she said.

I begged her to give it back. If it wasn't okay for Matthew to read it, how could it be okay for her to do the same thing? A cold feeling crept over me at the thought of Mum and Dad reading every word I'd written.

When she'd gone, all the tears I'd been holding back came out in big, angry sobs. How could I have let Matthew find my diary? How could he ruin my life like this? What is Mum going to do next? When will I see Nicky again? I just want to hear her voice, telling me everything will be okay. Even if I know it never will be again.

25 SHATTERED DREAMS

The alarm is going off. I should get out of bed, but I don't want to. Not just because it's cold and rainy outside. That wouldn't matter if anything good was likely to happen at school today. But it's Thursday. History.

I didn't sleep well either. The argument I'd read about between Lisa and her mum kept resurfacing in my dreams. I'm so glad Mum and Dad are nothing like that.

I repeat what Mum said over and over in my head, about giving Mrs Knight the benefit of the doubt. I think about it as I put on my uniform, eat my breakfast, get ready for the day. I will try. But I can't believe that things will be any different today than they were on Monday.

There's a tiny part of me that still hopes that Ms Grant will be there instead of Mrs Knight, that it was all a mistake, and things will go back to how they were before half-term. Even though I know that's never going to happen.

History is the last lesson of the day, right after Spanish where Simran and I are in different groups. It seems like all the popular girls, the ones with their skirts rolled up and their perfect nails, are in my group. They are always whispering to each other and collapsing into giggles about something mysterious. They usually ignore me, which is fine as I never know what to say to them anyway. I find a seat near the boys and try to disappear.

I don't know if it's because I'm already feeling anxious, but the whispering and the giggling seem louder than usual today. I feel conspicuous, like people are looking at me, but I tell myself that I must be imagining it. After all, I'm not doing or saying anything to make people look. I'm just sitting here. But the feeling only grows. Each time one of the girls answers a question from Mr Quintera, it seems like they are saying the "he" and "she" pronouns, *el* or *la*, extra loudly. Each time, they nudge each other, giggle, and turn to look at me.

Finally Jasmine puts her hand up. "Sir, I've got a question. About grammar."

Mr Quintera raises his eyebrows. "Go on."

I have a bad feeling about whatever Jasmine's going to say.

"Every word in Spanish is male or female, isn't that right, sir?" She's smiling sweetly.

"Yes, Jasmine. Well, all nouns take a masculine or feminine case, that's true, we learned that in Year Seven. I know it's not always easy to remember which is which. You just have to learn it, I'm afraid. Is that your question?"

"Even for people?" she continues. "Like, when you are talking about people, it's *always* got to be male *or* female." She turns to look at me. There's no mistaking that she's trying to have a go at me. "I mean, masculine or feminine. Someone couldn't be both, right? Or not anything? I mean, that would be stupid, wouldn't it?" My face is going red. I stare down at my book.

Jasmine thinks she's so clever. Someone else might have called me stupid to my face, but no, Jasmine dresses it up as something else. An innocent question. An easy laugh.

"Well, yes, of course, that's no different from English," Mr Quintera answers.

He looks uncomfortable, shuffles the papers on his desk. I think he knows that something's going on here, and that it's nothing to do with Spanish grammar, but decides that it's too much effort to find out what.

He clears his throat. "So, after that slight digression, let's get back to page fifty-three. Have a look at the postcard from Andrea about her town, and then write your own description of Hurston in your books. Key vocab is up here on the board."

I stare at my book, but I can't see the words in front of me. I can only see Jasmine's face, how she turned round once Mr Quintera was facing the board and smirked at me.

The worst of it is, it's just a laugh to her. If I was to say anything to anyone, they'd just say I was being oversensitive, that she hadn't said anything about me. But I know different.

It feels like when I came out last year, like everyone's looking at me, everyone's talking about me, but no one ever thinks about what it's like to *be* me. It's like I'm in the spotlight and I'm invisible, both at the same time.

As soon as the bell goes, I rush to the loos. I need a minute to myself before the next lesson. But when I get to the one gender neutral toilet in this part of the school, there's someone already in there. I wait in the corridor outside the door, willing them to hurry up.

"Aren't you in my next class?" says a brisk voice behind me.

"Er, yes," I stutter. As Mrs Knight strides towards me, the small hope I was holding onto, that Ms Grant would be back today, shrivels up and disappears.

"Well, come on then," she urges. "You can help me carry these books."

"I'm just waiting for the toilet," I whisper.

Mrs Knight looks at me, then looks at the door of the girls' toilets further down the corridor, and then looks back at me. "Go on, what are you waiting for?" she says. "I don't like lateness in my lessons, it's an insult to everyone who *can* be bothered to show up on time. Be as quick as you can."

She's watching me as I walk to the girls' toilets. I slowly push open the door. I'm praying there's no one else in there. I make a dash for the nearest cubicle, closing the door behind me just as I hear two of the other cubicle doors open.

"Oh my god, that was so funny," squeals Jasmine. There's a pause, and the sound of running water. "What? Oh come on, Ella, don't look like that, you know it was!"

"I just don't think you should have said any of that, it's not fair," says Ella's voice, but she sounds uncertain.

"I don't see why you're sticking up for the class freak, the girl who wants to be a boy." I stuff my hand into my mouth to stop myself from gasping out loud. Class freak. That's how she sees me. Who else could they be talking about? "Anyway, I didn't say anything bad."

"I don't think she, I mean they, want to be a boy," says Ella. I'm shocked that she's supporting me against Jasmine. I don't think Ella's ever said a word to me, except maybe to ask to borrow a pen. "I don't think it works like that."

"I mean, if Jesse's trans or whatever, yuck, but okay," continues Jasmine. "But she can't even do it right. You know that guy in my sister's year, Leo?"

I gasp in recognition at the name. Then hold my breath again and hope Jasmine hasn't heard me. She's talking about our Leo. From Over the Rainbow.

It seems that Jasmine hasn't heard. She keeps going. "You can't even tell he's really a girl. That makes sense, but who's Jesse trying to fool? Can't she just decide what she is? I mean, what does she think she looks like?"

I look down at myself when she says that. What *do* I think I look like? I think I look pretty ordinary. Black school shoes, school trousers – which are the wrong shape for everyone – white shirt, freckles, short red hair.

Is Jasmine saying I should try to look more like a boy? Or more like a girl? I know inside that it's not up to her, or anyone, to decide what a boy or a girl should look like. And that whatever I look like, it doesn't define my gender, any more than how she looks defines hers! And yet, listening to the disgust in her voice, makes me wonder what awful thing does Jasmine see about me that I don't? And does everyone else see it too?

"Shut up, Jasmine, you're embarrassing yourself," says Ella. Jasmine's reply is lost behind the noise of the hand dryer, but then Ella says, "Oh my god, we're going to be

214

so late. That new history teacher's such a nightmare, she's going to have a right go." The door slams behind them both.

I let out a long breath. I look down at my hands. They're shaking. Should I have confronted them? There's no way I'd be brave enough. Not without Simran by my side. But I can't think about this now. I have to get to history. I can't get into any more trouble with Mrs Knight.

I catch up with Ella and Jasmine just as they reach the classroom door. Ella looks surprised to see me there but we don't speak. I slip in behind them, trying not to draw any attention from Mrs Knight.

"Sorry, Miss," says Ella. "Mr Quintera let us out late from Spanish."

"Hmm," says Mrs Knight. "Take a seat, girls, quickly." I slide into place next to Simran. She smiles at me. I try to smile back, but I can't manage it.

"Dylan, stop fidgeting! Put that energy to good use and hand out these test papers."

Groans and whispers travel round the class. "Excuse me," snaps Mrs Knight. "Did I say that you could talk?"

This is the second lesson today that's a total write-off. All I wrote in Spanish was one line about how Hurston was *un pueblo pequeño* and history is hardly any better. I'm sure I knew more about the Tudors last night, but what

Jasmine said in the toilets just now has pushed everything I revised right out of my head.

Once the tests are handed in and piled on her desk, Mrs Knight sets us homework. "I expect your essays in next Monday," she says. Dylan puts up his hand. She nods at him.

"Miss, what about the projects, aren't they for homework?"

Mrs Knight sighs. "I thought I made it clear in the last lesson. There will be no more messing around with special projects until I'm convinced that you are on top of everything you need to know for the curriculum. As yet, I see no evidence of that." The bell goes for the end of the day. We all wait, eyes on Mrs Knight. "You are dismissed," she says after a long pause.

Simran turns round to talk to Omar in the row behind. They're comparing what answers they put for the test.

Someone stops next to my desk. I look up. It's Ella. I wonder how she does it, how she fits in without even trying. Not like me. I always feel clumsy and awkward and wrong next to someone like Ella. What's her secret?

"Jesse," she says, leaning closer. "I should have said this before, but, well, anyway, what Mrs Knight said to you on Monday was out of order. About your pronouns and stuff. There's no way that was okay."

"Er, thanks…" I say.

"And that thing about stopping the projects. Well, I know some people are saying it's good, cos who wants extra homework, right? But I thought it was kind of cool, getting to do our own investigations, not just learning dates from hundreds of years ago."

"What were you going to do your project about?" I ask her.

Her face lights up. "I was going to do it about the evacuees in Hurston. Loads of kids left London during the war and came to live here. My nan says that her mum was one of them. She was evacuated to Hurston and loved it, so came back years later to live here. I thought that—"

"Come *on*, Ella," calls Jasmine from the door. "What on earth are you talking to *her* about?"

Ella looks from Jasmine to me and back again. "Sorry," she mouths at me. "I'd better go."

With that, she flicks her hair over her shoulder and swoops off. I never expected Ella to stand up for me. Even if it was when no one else could hear her.

Dylan and Conor slouch past my desk. They are talking loudly about the homework and about the test. They are obviously outraged.

"I can't believe it," says Dylan.

"Ms Grant wouldn't have set us a boring essay to write, not in a million years," agrees Conor. "I wish she was here, not off having a stupid baby."

"And we had a really good idea for our project as well," moans Dylan. "It would have been way better than boring old Henry the eighth. But what's the point now?"

It's good that other people, not just Simran and me, feel this way about the history projects. I just didn't expect it to be Dylan or Ella.

"That sucks about the projects," Simran says, once she's finished talking to Omar. "But that shouldn't stop us carrying on finding out stuff about LGBTQ+ history, right? I mean, learning about *our* history, that's for us, not just for school. Who cares what Mrs Knight thinks?"

"Yeah, okay," I tell her. "But now, let's just get out of here."

Simran tucks her arm into mine and we leave the classroom behind.

Mum's working from home today. When I get back, she's in the kitchen, tapping on her phone as she waits for the kettle to boil.

She looks the exact opposite to how I feel – all bouncy and excited about something. I guess there can't be anyone like Mrs Knight, or Jasmine, at her work.

"Tea?" she asks. "You'll be proud of me, I've managed

to avoid eating every single biscuit in the house. There's a couple left for you."

I shake my head. I don't feel like talking right now. Or even eating biscuits.

"I'm tired," I say. "I'm just going to hang out in my room for a bit, okay?" Perhaps I'll read some more of Lisa's diary. Although I'm not sure I really want to read about what a miserable time she's having, after having had another rubbish day of my own.

I turn to go upstairs, but Mum calls me back.

"Jesse," she says, waving her phone at me. "Aren't you going to ask if I've had any interesting emails today?"

She sounds so eager that I can't say no. It's like she's the child and I'm the grown-up. "Go on then, who's emailed you?" I ask in my most bored voice.

"I thought you'd be a *little* more excited than that," says Mum, pretending to be in a huff. "Seeing as, for the last few days, you've been asking me to check my emails every few minutes!"

"I haven't. Not *that* often anyway," I say, hovering by the door. Hang on, does this mean that Nicky's replied to our email? Mum's going to make me ask her. "So, are you going to tell me or not?"

"Well," says Mum. "Now that you're asking, I got an email from Nicky this morning, or should I say from

Professor Zielinska-Burridge?"

"You did? Show me! What did she say?" I ask excitedly. Nicky wrote back! Even though I've seen her picture online, I still can't quite believe she's a real person.

"She says how surprised she was to get our email and how sad she was to hear about Lisa. I was right, she didn't know that Lisa had died. And she's invited us round on Sunday. She says she'd love to meet us and to help you and Simran with your project."

"Huh," I mutter bitterly. "What project? There is no project any more."

"So your new teacher didn't change her mind?" says Mum. "That's such a shame, Jesse. You must be really disappointed. But you still want to meet Nicky, don't you?"

"Of *course*!" I exclaim. I'm not going to let Mrs Knight spoil this. Not when there are more secrets to unlock. "We've *got* to go. Can I read what Nicky says?"

Mum passes over her phone and I skim through the email. It's short, but friendly. It sounds like she really does want to meet us.

"I'll message Simran right now and tell her. You *can* take us, can't you?" I ask.

"Absolutely. Will you be bringing the box of Lisa's stuff too? You can see what memories it jogs for Nicky."

"Do you think she'll want it back?" I say, the thought only just occurring to me. "I mean, some of the stuff is hers, isn't it? Even if she did give it to Lisa all those years ago." I feel so attached to Lisa's things, like she'd saved it all in a time capsule just for me, I can't imagine giving it away.

"Well," says Mum. "That's up to you and her. I've been meaning to ask, have you finished reading that diary yet?"

"Not quite," I say. "I haven't found out how Lisa came to live with you that summer."

Lisa had been so brave, and she and Nicky had been so happy, and now it seemed like everything was going wrong for them.

"I know it sounds weird," I say to Mum. "But it's so intense what's happening. I don't want to read it by myself."

"That's not weird at all," she replies softly. "We can finish reading it together. I mean, only if you want to."

"Yeah, I do. Thanks, Mum."

While I'm upstairs getting the diary, my phone buzzes. There's a row of excited emojis from Simran in response to my message about meeting Nicky.

"We want to see her, but do you think Nicky will still want to see *us*?" I ask Mum, before opening the diary. "I mean, now that there's no project and no exhibition. Will she think we're wasting her time?"

"I doubt that. You read her email. I'm sure she'll want to meet you, project or no project," Mum says gently. "I mean, *you* still want to meet *her*. You felt a connection to Lisa right from the start. It's obvious how much uncovering these stories means to you, and to Simran too."

"I suppose," I sigh. I feel suddenly wiped out, like I could sleep for weeks. Today feels like it's gone on for ever – Jasmine saying I'm the class freak, Ella sticking up for me when I didn't expect it and Simran talking about how important our history is for us. Lisa and Nicky faced exactly the same things as me – prejudice, support, community – it just looked different, that's all. I guess that's why finding out what happened to them matters so much, because it can help make sense of what's happening in my world too. We're part of the same story.

Mum puts her arm around me. I've never felt more glad to have her by my side. There are just a couple of sheets of paper left. This is all I have still to read. This is it. So Mum and I finish the diary. Together.

26 ALONE

I woke up this morning in a right state. Eyes swollen from crying. Throat sore from shouting. Feet aching from the march, which feels like hundreds of years ago already. And since then, things have only got worse.

I can't believe what's happened. I can't think about what might happen next.

Last night, I was desperate to talk to Nicky, but I couldn't call her from the phone in the hall. Everyone would hear, and they'd stop me talking. I couldn't sneak out to hers. Mum and Dad would know straight away if I tried.

I was drifting off to sleep, with my clothes still on, when I heard a rustling. I sat up. Slowly, the edge of an exercise book appeared under the door. I ran over and snatched it.

Matthew was whispering about how sorry he was from

the other side of the door. I told him to shut up and go away. It was too late to be sorry now. How would that help?

"I got your diary back," he said. Like that wasn't obvious. I was holding it, wasn't I? "Mum and Dad were reading it. Dad said it was filth and he didn't want it in the house. I got it out of the bin for you." I didn't say anything, hoping he'd go away.

I looked at the diary in my hands, so relieved to have it back. But knowing Mum and Dad had read it, all my secret thoughts, made me feel like I couldn't carry on writing in it. Not in that book. It feels tainted.

"Please, Lisa, I didn't mean for this to happen. It's just you never want me around any more…and Mum always thinks you're better than me whatever I do and…"

I couldn't ignore something so clearly not true. Matthew was Mum and Dad's golden boy. I pushed the door open a crack. He was sitting on the landing outside the door. I beckoned to him to come inside.

He shuffled to his feet and slipped through the door. I think he'd been crying too.

"At least you don't have to worry any more about Mum liking me best," I told him. "Did you really think so?"

He nodded. "It's obvious. She's always going on about how clever you are."

I tried to think. Was that really true? I thought that was just her way of trying to get me to study more instead of spending my time drawing. But maybe she meant it.

"She's never that interested in what I'm doing," said Matthew quietly. "Not even enough to try and stop me doing it."

Then we both kind of smiled at what an awful mess this is.

Then I had an idea. I tore a sheet out of the diary, scribbled Nicky's number on it and gave it to Matthew.

Mum and Dad won't be expecting *him* to try and call Nicky. He can tell them that he's calling one of his mates. I felt a bit bad asking him to lie for me. But not that bad. Not after what he's done to me.

He slid the scrap of paper into his pocket. "I didn't read much, honest, but you and Nicky, are you really...?" He was biting his lip like he used to do when he was little. He suddenly looked much younger than thirteen.

"Girlfriends? Yeah, we are," I said. It was the second time I'd said it now. It felt more normal this time. Matthew went red. There was something that I had to make sure he understood. Something important. He mustn't believe any of that stuff he heard about being gay being wrong.

He asked more about Nicky and about the march. At first I wasn't sure if I should tell him anything. I mean, it was his big mouth that got me into trouble in the first place. But surely things couldn't get any worse than they were already and it was such a relief to tell someone about how I felt about Nicky, even if it was just my annoying little brother.

By the time Matthew sneaked back out, I reckon we'd had the longest proper conversation in years.

Mum stuck her head round the door later, but I pretended to be asleep. The diary was safely tucked under my pillow. I could hear her and Dad talking outside my room. I couldn't hear what they said then, but now I know.

I guessed they'd probably ground me. But it's worse than that. Much worse. I can hardly bear to write about it.

They're sending me away. Not right now, but as soon as my last exam is over. Oh no, god forbid I should miss my exams. I'm allowed to go into school for those. Allowed! Great, what a treat. But Mum or Dad will drop me there and pick me up, like I'm a little kid. Or a prisoner. And because it's nearly the start of study leave, they say there's no need for me to go back into school *at all* until exams start.

When I protested, Mum said I wouldn't be learning anything new now – it would be all revision and messing around. Total opposite to what she's been saying before, about how every minute of school is important and I shouldn't slack off now! She's such a hypocrite!

Then they're sending me to stay with Auntie Stella and Uncle Rob in the middle of nowhere for the whole summer. Even for my sixteenth birthday. What I want to do doesn't matter at all.

I'll miss everything. I don't care about the end of term party, but what about the last day? Everyone signing each other's shirts and playing tricks on the teachers. I've watched every year and wondered how it would be when it was our turn. The worst thing is, what if I can't see Nicky again before they send me away?

Matthew must have managed to phone her like I asked him because, just after lunch, there was a knock on the front door.

I looked out of my bedroom window. Kayleigh was standing on the doorstep in her ripped jeans, shifting from one foot to another. I opened my bedroom door a crack and sat right behind it, so I could hear when Mum opened the front door.

I realized Mum and Kayleigh had never met. Not that long ago I was stressing about Mum inviting Michael and Kayleigh round to our house. If only that was all I had to worry about now!

Mum sounded wary as she answered the door, like when the Jehovah's Witnesses knock.

Kayleigh introduced herself as Nicky's stepmum. Just hearing her voice was brilliant, like fresh air and sunshine. It's not even a day that I've been trapped here, but the rest of the world feels so far away. I wondered if she'd come on her own, or whether Nicky and Michael were nearby. I wanted to run back to the window to see if I could spot them on the street, but then I wouldn't have been able to hear what Kayleigh and Mum were saying, so I stayed put.

Mum drew in her breath. "I'm very sorry, but we haven't got anything to say to you." She didn't sound very sorry.

Kayleigh's voice got easier to hear, like she was getting nearer the door. She asked Mum if she could come in for a minute so they could talk, or whether she could have a quick word with me.

My heart leaped.

And sank again. Mum told Kayleigh that I'd already suffered enough under the influence of her stepdaughter, and the rest of her so-called family.

What rubbish. I almost came running down the stairs right then. I expected Kayleigh to argue right back – she can be really mouthy – but she didn't.

"Lisa's a lovely girl," Kayleigh said. That stopped me in my tracks. "She's bright, she's thoughtful, she's a really talented artist. But, most importantly, she knows her own mind. She's not under the influence of Nicky or me or anyone." Her voice was steady, but quiet. I had to lean further out of my bedroom door to hear her properly.

Then Mum blew up. I don't know if I've ever heard her sound so angry. "Excuse me, I don't need you coming here and telling me about my own daughter. I'm her mother, I know what's best for her."

Kayleigh must have realized that she had one last chance to speak, before Mum shut the door in her face. "I'm not telling you what to do," she said quickly. "It's just that, well, it's hard for some people when they find out their child's gay, and if we can help—"

"I think it's time you went," interrupted Mum. "There's no one here who's..." She trailed off. "And we certainly don't need any 'help' from someone like you."

The door slammed. I dashed back to the window. Kayleigh stood on the doorstep, staring at the closed door. I watched as she walked off down the street. I could see the curtains moving at Marie and Derek's house opposite. I wonder how much they heard. I don't care. But Mum will. I think she cares about that more than she cares about me.

27 DON'T LEAVE ME THIS WAY

Sunday is one of those surprising early Spring days when it feels fresh and clear and even a little bit warm. I hope the change in weather is a good sign. After a week of feeling anxious and unsettled at school, it's time things got better. And today, we're going to meet Nicky.

Mum's driving and Dad's decided to come too. He's meeting Pete, a colleague of his who lives near the beach. They'll go for a run while Mum, Simran and I visit Nicky.

I slide along to make space for Simran in the back seat of the car. She's clutching a tin.

"Mum says you should never arrive at someone's house empty-handed," she explains. "She forced me to make flapjacks last night so I had something to bring."

"We're not empty-handed," I say. "We've got a whole

box of Lisa's old stuff." But flapjacks are still a great idea, especially as we can eat the ones that didn't fit in the tin on the way.

Simran is also holding the diary, with the extra pages stuffed into the back. I gave it to her at school on Friday so she could read it all herself. We haven't had a chance to talk since. There's still so much that I don't understand.

I wasn't ready to talk about it with Mum after we read the last bit together. I couldn't quite believe the diary had finished. I searched through the box again for any more extra pages, but there weren't any. Mum seemed pretty shaken up too. She didn't say much, just gave me a huge hug.

"Did you finish it?" I ask Simran.

"Course I did! But I want to know what happened next! Did she start another diary? Did she and Nicky ever get to see each other again?" Simran sighs in frustration. "Oh, it's like Romeo and Juliet. But real life. I don't get how her parents could treat her like that. How could they even think those things?"

I've been asking myself the same questions. It feels so personal because the people doing and saying these horrible things aren't strangers – they're my relatives. Lisa's mum was Gran's big sister, my great-aunt. Matthew, like Lisa, is my cousin. They are part of me, of my family. How could

231

they have behaved like that?

"So, get me up to speed," says Dad. "It's like we're in one of those history programmes on TV, where they trace your family tree and discover you're related to royalty. What exactly have you found out?"

"Some of it's pretty grim," I say. "Lisa's parents tried to split her and Nicky up. They sent Lisa off to go and stay at Gran's."

"Here in Hurston?" asks Dad.

"Yes," says Mum. "That must have been the summer she lived with us, when I was little."

"Imagine being kicked out like that," I sigh.

"Yeah," agrees Simran. "Banished to the middle of nowhere."

"Hurston's hardly the middle of nowhere!" Mum protests.

"But it felt like that to Lisa," says Simran. I know what she means. It didn't matter *where* Lisa's parents sent her. Even if it was the most wonderful place ever, it still wouldn't be home. "I can't believe that her parents were so homophobic. It would be like if my parents made me leave home if I got a girlfriend. It's ridiculous!"

"I suppose more people *were* homophobic back then – it was more acceptable," says Dad thoughtfully. "Not that it makes it okay."

"Not Gran and Grandad," I insist. "They *can't* have

been like Lisa's parents, even if they were in the same family." I couldn't bear it if I found out that Gran had agreed with them all along.

"No," says Mum. "I don't remember hearing anything about LGBT people when I was a kid, certainly not from my mum and dad, but I don't remember them saying anything prejudiced either. It just wasn't talked about, not like now. Gran was always quick to stand up for anyone who was in trouble, you know that, whoever they were. And when you came out…"

"Yeah, I know." Gran was always in my corner. Even when Mum and Dad were still working out what me being non-binary meant, Gran never questioned it. "I might not understand it," she'd say, "but that doesn't matter. I'm not too old to learn new things, you can teach me."

Simran's still thinking about the diary. "Another thing I don't get is, why didn't Lisa just run away? Couldn't she have moved in with Nicky's family?"

"Sounds like your Ms Grant did a great job in turning you both into proper investigative historians, full of questions," says Dad. "Hopefully you'll find some answers today."

"I wish Ms Grant would come back. I can't believe Mrs Knight's not letting us do the projects or the exhibition," says Simran, as we reach the main road and start leaving Hurston behind.

Mum and Dad have listened to me moaning about Mrs Knight all week. I haven't started my history essay yet. Thursday's test was bad enough. It'll be even worse once she marks them and sees how terribly we all do. There's no way she'll let us do anything except trudge through facts about the Tudors after that.

"I can't believe the school couldn't find anyone better to teach us," I say.

"My mum says there's a real problem getting supply teachers, so I guess they didn't have much choice. Everyone's leaving teaching. Mum says it's the same in her old school. It's too stressful. That's why she left," says Simran.

"I wish your mum could teach us instead," I sigh. Mrs Gill would be a brilliant teacher. She's always so calm, whatever's going on around her, and she's really good at listening. Quite how Simran's quiet and laid-back parents produced three chattering balls of energy like Simran and her brothers is one of the universe's biggest mysteries.

"I'm not sure she knows much history, that's more Dad's sort of thing. Anyway, she says she's never going back to the classroom, even though she cried when she left all her little Year Ones."

"I wonder if Mrs Knight will cry when she leaves us."

"We'll be the ones crying," says Simran. "Crying with joy!"

We both start laughing.

"Come on, you two," says Dad. "Be fair. I know you're not this woman's biggest fans, but give it time and I'm sure you'll get used to her."

"Hmph," I say. I don't *want* to get used to her – I want Ms Grant to come back.

"It's not for ever, just for this term. Now, come on," he continues, tapping his fingers on the dashboard. "The sun's shining. We're on a road trip. Can't we have some music?"

"Hold on," I say. "I'll do it."

I've looked up all the songs on Lisa and Nicky's mixtape and made my own playlist. This should get us in the right mood.

I connect my phone to the car speakers and the music starts. There's nothing familiar enough to properly sing along to, so Simran and I just "la" to the choruses instead.

Dad, however, knows loads of the words. I have to tell him to shut up and stop being embarrassing when he starts bellowing "I've had the time of my life and I've never felt like this before" out of the window at people as we drive past.

Once we've dropped him off at Pete's, the car seems too

quiet. I start worrying about what meeting Nicky will be like.

Simran leans over. "Are you nervous?" she asks. "Your knee's jiggling up and down."

I put my hand on my knee and press it still. "Yeah, a bit. I mean, what if she thinks we've been snooping – that we had no right to read the diaries? She might even be angry with us."

"She wouldn't have invited us over if she thought that," reassures Simran. "I want to know why she and Lisa lost touch. I don't get it. I mean, wouldn't Lisa have seen her again after the summer? Perhaps she dumped Lisa or they had a big fight or something? Or the other way round? Maybe Lisa went off with someone else?"

"Great," I say. "Here we come, random strangers, raking up all this stuff from the past that she hasn't thought about for decades. I bet she's really going to love that." I can't let myself expect too much from today in case it all ends up being a disappointment.

"Here we are," says Mum, squeezing into a tiny parking space outside a little bungalow, squashed in between two much bigger houses. Even though it's only February, I can see snowdrops and primroses poking their heads out in the front garden. "Don't forget the flapjacks, Simran."

"Are you sure we're not too early?" I ask anxiously.

"We're right on time," says Mum.

She strides down the path, Simran and I following behind, and rings the bell.

28 RESPECT YOURSELF

It's only a few seconds before the door opens. But instead of Nicky, there's a woman I don't recognize, with long blonde hair swept up into a bun. I've no idea who she is but she's smiling like she knows us.

"Er, hello," says Mum. "I'm Jesse's mum."

"Hello," says the woman. "I'm Ana, Nicky's wife."

I'm so surprised that I nearly drop Lisa's cardboard box of stuff. Which is daft – I'd guessed Nicky's new name meant that she was married. It's just the Nicky I know is sixteen years old and madly in love with Lisa, not a middle-aged, married professor.

"Come in," says Ana warmly. "She's been talking about you ever since your email arrived." She ushers us in.

Mum, Simran and I all bump into each other, trying to

take our shoes off and keep hold of the box at the same time.

"So, you two must be the historians?" she asks me and Simran.

I blush. "Historian" sounds very grand.

"Yes, that's us. This is Jesse and I'm Simran," says Simran. "We brought flapjacks. I made them." She thrusts the tin at Ana.

"Then you are even more welcome here! We can always find room for more cake in this house." Ana's so friendly that I start to relax. She has a slight accent, but I can't quite work out where it's from. "Now why don't you two go through to the study? It's the first door, see?" She turns to Mum. "Would you mind giving me a hand with the tea for a moment? You can say hi to Nicky when we take it through to the others. I can't just call you 'Jesse's mum' so…?"

"Jenny," says Mum, and smiles encouragingly at me before disappearing after Ana into the kitchen. "Although most people call me Jen."

Simran's staring at the walls by the study door. There are framed prints of old posters. Simran points at one of them – the now-familiar upside-down pink triangle with "Stop the Clause" scrawled across it – and nudges me. On the study door itself, there is a poster exploding with colours and patterns encircling the words "My Body, My Rules". I push open the door.

The walls in here are even more crowded, with slogans and images and newspaper cuttings all jostling for space. It's more like a teenager's bedroom than how I expected a professor's study to be. It's hard to take it all in. I could spend hours in here and there would still be more to see. Nicky turns round so she's facing us.

I feel like I know Nicky, even though we've never met before. But I don't really know her, just Lisa's impression of what she was like. If Simran had to describe me, would she say the same things that I'd say about myself? Whose words would be more true? I can't help remembering what Jasmine said about me being the class freak – was that true too?

Nicky's eyes and her energy are the same as in Lisa's photos, but somehow, even though I've seen a recent picture online, I was expecting her to still have dark hair instead of grey. I was expecting time to have stood still for more than three decades.

It blows my mind that I'm only here because an old photo fell out of a box and caught my imagination. If Lisa had sealed that box down properly, or if Ali hadn't asked us to go into the attic, I wouldn't be here!

"Hello, both of you, come in, come in. Sorry I didn't

come to the door. I got distracted trying to finish off writing this article." She snaps her laptop shut. "I've been so looking forward to meeting you."

"I like the posters," says Simran, gazing around her. "They're awesome."

"Thank you," says Nicky. "Ana's always telling me off for bringing my work home, but I can't resist. I find them so inspiring, don't you?"

"This is your work?" I ask, surprised.

"Studying them, not designing them! I'd be hopeless at that!" says Nicky, turning to answer me. She looks at me hard for a long moment, takes a deep breath, then smiles and carries on. "Pretty good though, isn't it? It's called something fancy, but really I'm interested in how people use art to make political change… I could go on about it all afternoon, but you didn't come here for a lecture. We haven't even said hello properly. So, you're Jesse and Simran. Come on then, sit down."

Simran and I look uncertainly at the sofa.

"Just clear the files out of the way, don't worry about mixing them up," says Nicky cheerfully. "I suppose you already know a bit about me, but I hardly know anything about you. Although it's obvious you're related to Lisa."

"Really?" I ask, intrigued about what she sees in me.

"You know, I haven't seen her in more than thirty years

– not since we were kids. But looking at you, coming through that door, with that red hair… Yours is much shorter than hers of course… I wish I'd dared to cut my hair like that when I was younger… It was like seeing her again." She shakes her head. "It was such a shock to hear she'd died. She was so funny and smart, even if she couldn't always see it herself, and so full of life. Fifty-two probably seems ancient to you, but really it's so young…and there were so many things I didn't say…"

I don't know how to respond. I look down at my feet. One of my socks has a hole in, so I scrunch up my toes to cover it up. Am I intruding on her grief, stirring up memories that should have been allowed to let lie? I mean, she seems so sorted here with her wife and her job and her house – she didn't need us disturbing her nice life.

"I'm sorry," I stutter. "I didn't even know her. It's all chance really, how we found the diary and the other stuff. Maybe I shouldn't have read—"

"Don't say that. I'm glad you found it, truly. I'm glad it wasn't lost."

"I've got it here. Do you want to see?"

I hand her the exercise book. She takes it carefully, like it might fall apart in her hands. She starts flicking through the pages.

"Oh my god," she says, with a short laugh that's almost

like a sob. "That's him, that's him perfectly." She stabs her finger at the page where Lisa has drawn Mr Payne. "She could capture anything and anyone like that. Oh, he was awful. I suppose he retired long ago, probably terrorizing the other residents in a care home somewhere right now."

She keeps flicking. "Just look at this," she breathes, pulling the photo of her and Lisa at the Kiss-In from between the pages and staring at it. I don't say anything. It's like she's talking to herself, not to us.

"Up there," she says, pointing at the pinboard above her desk. "Could one of you reach up and just, it's there at the top, on the right…"

I lean over the cluttered desk and follow Nicky's directions, feeling through the layers of paper attached to the pinboard. Finally, I find what she's looking for.

A photograph. From the same day. Taken maybe a few minutes before or after, but from further away, so you don't just see Lisa and Nicky, but also all the banners and posters and people behind them. The whole story. She's kept it all these years. Lisa must have given it to her. I want to ask when and how, but Nicky carries on talking.

"That was an amazing day!" she says, her eyes shining. "Unforgettable. Full of joy. All of us united. Have you ever been on a Pride march?"

We shake our heads.

"Well, when you do, you'll know the same feeling, I promise. That march changed me. I guess it shaped the course of my life – I wouldn't be doing the work I do now without the inspiration it gave me. And I kept marching! You won't believe this, but I met Ana at another march, years later, when we were finally celebrating the repeal of Section 28. That first march changed Lisa too, I'm sure it did. She stopped being ashamed and scared of who she was, she started to feel proud. Which is why what happened next was so awful."

Simran and I exchange looks. Would it be right to ask Nicky questions about what happened? She *had* brought it up.

"We know Lisa's parents split you two up and sent her off to live with her aunt and uncle..." says Simran cautiously.

"And with my mum," I add. "Although she was only little at the time, so she doesn't really remember."

"I still can't believe they did that!" exclaims Simran.

Nicky sighs. "It still goes on, people being kicked out of home for being gay or trans," she says. "It shouldn't, but it does."

"What happened?" says Simran. "After that, I mean? If it's okay to ask."

"It was so terrible," says Nicky. "We never wanted her

parents to find out about us, we knew they wouldn't understand. So when I got this garbled phone call from her brother about her parents reading her diary and Lisa being grounded, I was frantic, I didn't know what to do. I couldn't see or talk to her, there were no mobile phones or email or anything like that. We'd been spending almost every minute together, and then suddenly, no contact." She slices the air with her hand. "I wanted to go round, but Michael, my dad, said it would be better if my stepmum did, that perhaps they'd listen to a woman." She stares over our heads out of the window. "*That* was a disaster."

It's so strange hearing all the things I've read about echoed back like this. I mean, I knew that they had all happened. But hearing Nicky talk about it makes it so much more real.

"Kayleigh coming round – that's the last thing Lisa wrote about in her diary," I say. "But why didn't Lisa just run away and come and live with you?"

"I wanted her to. I spent ages trying to persuade my dad that we should stage a rescue attempt. We should help her to climb out of the window like Rapunzel. He was normally up for wild ideas, but not this time. She was only fifteen, that's still a child. It was up to her parents what she did. If she'd run away to us, they could have called the police."

Fifteen. Lisa was only three years older than me. I can't

imagine running away from my parents, but then again, I can't imagine them behaving like Lisa's parents did.

"She wrote to me with your gran's address, and the photo of course. I did write back, but perhaps she felt too sad or too hopeless to write again or maybe her parents found a way to stop her. I don't know."

I wonder why Lisa didn't keep the letter with the rest of the things in the box. Maybe she never received it.

"At the time, I blamed her for not writing," continues Nicky. "It's an awful thing to say but I did. I thought that her parents must have persuaded her that our relationship was wrong. I thought that she'd ended up agreeing with them."

"But she wouldn't have," I burst out. "In the diary, she's so sure she wants to be with you, she knows it's the right thing." But do I really know what kind of pressure Lisa would have been under? How hard would it have been for her to stand her ground?

Nicky doesn't argue with me, she just smiles. A small, sad smile. "Later that summer, my dad was offered a job in Holland, at one of the universities. It was too good a chance to miss. We'd be nearer my mum and her husband, so I'd get to see her more often. And I'd be living and studying in a different country. By the time term started again, we'd gone. It was such a whirlwind. I meant to get back in touch with Lisa, I always wanted to, but I thought maybe she didn't want to hear from me, and time went by…"

"So you never did," finishes Simran softly.

"1988 was the worst summer of my life. It felt like everything was going backwards, getting worse. I knew there would be a new start – I would have left school anyway to go to college, even if we hadn't gone to Holland – that's all I had to cling onto. I remember the night we heard that Section 28 had passed, because it was the night before my maths GCSE. All that marching, all that trying to prove ourselves, all that possibility, then the fear and the silencing."

"You lost," I say sadly. "You lost the campaign and you lost Lisa." I look at the photo in my hand. Two girls with huge smiles. A carnival of joy and pride and righteous anger exploding around them. They did everything they could. And still they lost. It all feels hopeless.

"You know about Section 28, don't you?" she asks.

"A bit," says Simran. "We've been researching all about it."

"Of course, it was called 'Clause 28' back then. A law that told us that our families weren't real and that tried to erase us out of history. It wasn't the first time they'd tried it and it won't be the last. And we'll always fight back.

It took fifteen years to get rid of that nasty little piece of legislation. But we did it. And the fight made us stronger, it brought us together and took our message further. So we didn't lose, not really, not at all. I thought we had then, but I know better now."

She stops. Her eyes are flicking between Simran's pan flag badge and my "they/them" one.

"This really matters to you, doesn't it?" she says. "This is your fight too."

I nod. She's right.

A smile creeps over my face. My body relaxes. I glance at Simran and I know she feels exactly the same way. Without us having to explain anything, Nicky knows us. Something unseen but powerful ties us together with this person we've only just met.

There's a soft knock. The door opens slowly.

"We brought you something to drink," says Ana, putting a tray down on top of a pile of files, and resting her hand on Nicky's shoulder. "And, good news, *kochanie,* our guests brought cake. Is it okay to come in? We are not interrupting?"

Mum slips in behind Ana. She glances at me, checking I'm okay without saying anything. I give her the tiniest nod back. It's crowded in the study now, but once Simran and I squeeze up on the sofa, Mum can fit on the end. As

Nicky takes a cup of tea, I notice her hand is shaking.

"So you're baby Jenny?" she says beaming at Mum. Mum nearly chokes on her tea and the rest of us laugh. "Lisa used to have a picture of you and her on her pinboard. She was so proud of being a big cousin!"

"I'm just sorry I never knew her as an adult," says Mum. The laughter stops.

"Me too," adds Nicky quietly.

After a moment, Ana asks about the history project. "When I read about it in your email, I thought it sounded exciting," she says. "So different from when I was at school."

No one says anything. I haven't even thought about the project since we'd started talking to Nicky. I've been too wrapped up in listening to her. But now that I know more of the history, about why it matters, it feels even more frustrating that the chance to share it has been snatched away.

"What did I say?" asks Ana, noticing our glum faces.

"It's just that there isn't a history project, not any more." I explain what happened, and how Mrs Knight dismissed the exhibition out of hand. "I thought maybe we shouldn't have come here and wasted your time…"

As I'm speaking, Ana gets more and more agitated. I'm worried she's going to drop her mug of tea.

Finally she bursts out, "So how are you fighting this?"

"I...er..." I stutter.

"If you wait for people to *give* you your rights, you'll be waiting for ever. You have to be prepared to take them. With both your hands." She gestures like she's grabbing hold of something precious. She turns to Nicky, who's watching her with pride. "Isn't that right, professor? Isn't that what you tell your students?"

Ana puts down her mug with a bang and a moment later, picks it up again, waving it around as she speaks.

"I'm sorry," she says. "I just feel very strongly. Poland, my country, was one of the first places in the world to make homosexuality legal, nearly a hundred years ago. And now, what are they doing? LGBT-free zones, banning 'promotion' in schools, making us into the enemy, like Section 28 all over again."

"That's happening now?" asks Simran, wide-eyed.

Ana nods. "It is. You see why I feel this so deeply, why I get carried away. The little things matter, they are worth fighting for, because they can become big. Without telling our history, people forget it and let bad things happen again and again. Not just in my home country, but here too."

"But we always fight back," says Nicky, reaching for Ana's hand. "And when we do, we're changing history, and ourselves. It makes us stronger and more creative – it's beautiful."

"Beautiful?" says Ana. "My wife, always the idealist!"

I've a feeling that the two of them have had this conversation many times before.

"We could go and talk to Mrs Knight…" I say to Simran, even though just thinking about it makes my mouth go dry and my stomach clench. As I say it, I realize that however scared I am of fighting, there's no way I'm ready to give up. If Mrs Knight doesn't listen to us, well, we'll just have to find some other way.

"It sounds like you need to properly explain," says Nicky. "Maybe if you tell her why you're so enthusiastic about your project, she'll realize she's been hasty. Most teachers can't resist a student who's enthusiastic about their subject, I know those are my favourite ones to teach. I love a challenge, but it's tough trying to make people interested in something when they're not."

"We'll talk to her," I say. "But I don't know if she'll listen. History seems like a different subject when our real teacher Ms Grant teaches it – not all dates and battles and kings, but real people like us. Mrs Knight doesn't seem to care about any of that."

"Give her a chance," says Mum. "Maybe you'll be surprised."

"Anyway," says Ana. "What is in this box?"

We unpack the magazines and the leaflets, the rest of the photos and all the bits and pieces that Lisa kept so carefully.

Nicky can't stop exclaiming over Lisa's drawings. "Michael always raved about how good she was, how she really had an eye. When we were kids though, I don't know if she ever really believed she was that good. I used to love watching her draw."

I rummage around for the T-shirt, to see if Nicky recognizes it, but I must have forgotten to put it back in the box after trying it on. Never mind, there's so much else to show her.

I wonder how Ana feels about all of this, the evidence of her partner's life before she was around to share it. I mean, if it *had* worked out for Lisa and Nicky, if things had been different somehow, where would Ana be now? Not here. The thought makes me shiver. But she seems super interested, asking lots of questions. It's Nicky who's become withdrawn, almost silent.

"We'd better go," says Mum, once the tea is finished and the last flapjack has been eaten. "We need to pick up my husband. You've been so generous with your time, thank you."

"Yeah, thank you," Simran and I chime in. I reach over

the desk to pin the photo back in its place on the noticeboard, as Nicky whispers something to Ana. Ana nods, then slips out of the study door.

"You said that you thought you might be wasting our time?" says Nicky. "But you haven't, not at all. It's been painful looking back, but it's been good for me too. It's helped me face up to a few things, feelings and memories that I've kept shut away for years, stuffed into a box – not in an attic, but inside me. I should be thanking you. There's something I want you both to have."

Ana comes back in, holding the framed "Stop the Clause" poster from the hallway. She hands it to me.

"Oh," I say. "Oh no, but I…"

"You'd be doing us a favour," says Ana, with a smile. "I mean, look at the state of this place, we're overdue a clear-out."

"We can't…" I protest.

"Borrow it then, for your exhibition," says Nicky. "This exhibition that I know you're going to find a way to do, somehow, whatever your teacher says about it. Okay?"

There's nothing else to be said.

Nicky grabs a walking stick that's decorated like a Pride flag and follows us to the front door.

"Cool colours," says Simran.

"Yeah, it's pretty loud and proud. Would you believe

some people still assume I'm straight even when they see this? But I always enjoy challenging assumptions!" She grins, looking for a moment as mischievous as the teenage Nicky in Lisa's photographs.

Nicky and Ana watch as we load the box and the framed print they've given us into the boot. I'm terrified I'm going to drop it and smash the glass in front of everyone, but I hold it tightly and it's all okay.

They wave us off and we wave back. I'm sad to leave, but all that emotion has left me exhausted.

"Wow," says Simran.

"Yeah," I say.

"Are we *really* going to talk to Mrs Knight tomorrow?" she asks.

"I guess so."

"Do you think she'll listen?"

I shrug. "Probably not. But we've got to try. We'll do everything we can to change her mind," I say, trying to sound more confident than I feel. "Not just for us, but for Nicky and Ana too."

"And Lisa," says Simran.

"And Lisa," I agree.

29 WISHING I WAS LUCKY

I glance up from my worksheet on farming in Tudor times to check that Mrs Knight isn't looking my way. I'm safe. She's glaring at Conor and Dylan on the other side of the classroom.

"As soon as the bell goes, we talk to her," I whisper to Simran. "Okay? No flaking out."

"Of course not!" Simran looks affronted. "I'm totally up for this. We've got to get her to change her mind."

"Shhh," I murmur under my breath. Getting told off for talking now is going to make Mrs Knight less likely to listen to us later.

I'm barely concentrating on the lesson. Instead, I'm thinking about yesterday, about everything Nicky and Ana said about making history and changing history, even in small ways.

After getting home last night, I spent ages online, looking at LGBTQ+ rights in different countries around the world, wondering if I could ever be as brave as some of the people I read about. People who are imprisoned, or who have to flee their own countries just to be safe. People who write books about queer lives which are later banned or burned. And not just people in faraway places, but LGBTQ+ people in the UK, who get abuse on social media and in real life too.

But whatever gets thrown at them, they always fight back. For themselves, and for each other. For me too. So I guess I should be able to do some fighting of my own.

It was late before I remembered that I hadn't even started my history essay. I wrote something, but it's embarrassingly scrappy, especially because I finished it off over breakfast. I wish I'd thought about it earlier. A decent essay might have helped me get into Mrs Knight's good books. Although it's probably too late for that.

Compared to some of the people I read about last night, I've got nothing to worry about, but my heart's still racing.

The bell goes. Everyone sits and waits. We've learned that if we get up before Mrs Knight tells us to, she'll keep us back even longer with a lecture. No one wants that. Once she lets us go, everyone disappears. Except for Simran and me.

Mrs Knight is at the desk at the front, our essays in a pile in front of her, ready for marking. Simran and I hover next to her. Eventually she looks up.

"Yes? Can I help you, girls?"

It makes me wince every time she says "girls", but I don't correct her, not this time.

"We wondered if we could ask you something—" I start.

"It's about history," continues Simran.

"All right," says Mrs Knight, putting down her pen. "Carry on then, we haven't got all day."

I swallow. "It's about the history projects," I say. "We wondered if you'd had a chance to think about it again, or if Ms Grant had handed over anything about them or about the exhibition, because we've already started researching and—"

"The thing is, girls, I don't understand what any of that has to do with the Tudors, with the history that you should be studying, and that you will be examined upon." Mrs Knight looks genuinely perplexed.

"But it does…well…kind of. It's about using our history skills," explains Simran. "Ms Grant said it was good to do this now, in Year Eight, to build our understanding before we get started with GCSEs."

"Hmm," says Mrs Knight, like she's actually considering it. She waves her finger at me and peers through her glasses.

"So, Jesse, explain to me, what period of history have you started researching for this project?"

I remember what Nicky said about how teachers liked it when students were enthusiastic about their subject. I'll show Mrs Knight how enthusiastic I can be!

"My project's about the history of the Section 28 campaign in the 1980s. The campaign against, I mean." Mrs Knight purses her lips. It's not a good sign, but I keep going. "I've got primary source material and these, er, artefacts, from my mum's cousin." I hope using some proper history words will convince her that I'm serious. I'm quite proud of "artefacts". "It's so fascinating. We've been looking up stuff online as well, and we found this book…"

"We've been making notes and coming up with loads of ideas about how we'll display it all for the exhibition," adds Simran. "Would you like to see?"

Simran reached into her bag for the folder with our plans so far. We've kept adding it to, even without knowing whether or not the exhibition will go ahead. But Mrs Knight picks up her pen as if she's about to go back to her marking.

"I don't think that sounds like a suitable topic for a piece of schoolwork, no, not at all." She shakes her head and purses her lips again. "I'm sorry, girls, but no. That does remind me though. I'm going to be making a few changes to the classroom environment to help us focus our learning. I'll be letting everyone know next week, but you two might find these changes especially helpful."

I look at her blankly. What does that mean? Whatever it is, it doesn't sound like it's to do with the exhibition.

"As a first step, there will be weekly tests and a new seating plan. You two will no longer be sitting together. I'm sure that will help you concentrate on the topic at hand, instead of any distractions." She smiles a thin smile.

Simran and I stare at each other, open-mouthed.

"Now, you'd better run along or you'll be late for your next lesson."

"But, Miss—" protests Simran, cheeks flaming.

"I'm so looking forward to reading your essays," Mrs Knight interrupts, patting the pile on her desk. She smiles. My heart sinks even further. I don't think there's much for her to look forward to in mine.

The bell rings, and the first students from the next class start drifting in. Mrs Knight looks pointedly towards the door. It's clear that she has nothing more to say to us.

30 NEVER GONNA GIVE YOU UP

"She's just homophobic," says Simran, as we talk it through for the thousandth time. This time it's over a strawberry milkshake at Over the Rainbow on Saturday morning.

"And some," I add gloomily, stirring my milkshake and sucking the froth off my spoon.

"That's why she didn't like our project. It's so obvious. 'Not a suitable topic'… What else is that supposed to mean? And it's so ironic. Like, the whole project's about how it was wrong to try and stop people talking about LGBTQ+ stuff in school, and then what does she do…?"

"Stops us talking about LGBTQ+ stuff at school!" I finish for her.

"Exactly," she says, sounding so much like Ms Grant that we both laugh.

"I hope Ms Grant's okay," I say, suddenly serious again. "And that her baby will be all right."

"I'm sure she will. We won't see her now till we're in Year Nine, that's wild. Unless she brings her baby in, I suppose. When I was in Year Three, our teacher brought her dog in one day. Best day of school ever."

I'm confused about how we've gone from Mrs Knight's homophobia to Simran's teacher's dog, but conversations with Simran often go in unexpected directions.

"Yeah, but babies are different from dogs," I point out.

"Duh, I know that. I have got two little brothers. Although maybe there are some similarities…"

I laugh, and Simran carries on. "I can't believe she's going to split us up as well. You could tell she was making up that stuff about distractions. She just wants us to stop asking awkward questions."

"I know," I groan. "I bet I end up next to someone awful like Jasmine."

"And…" Simran pauses, fiddling with her spoon. "You know, Jesse, you should say something about Mrs Knight misgendering you. Okay, maybe if she'd just made a mistake with your pronouns, but she didn't even listen when you corrected her – that's bad. If you don't want to, I can do it. It's just not right."

"I don't know; I don't want a fuss. What if it makes

things worse?" Even thinking about it feels too hard and too heavy right now.

But Simran won't let it lie. She keeps on at me until I promise to talk to Mum and Dad about the misgendering, so that they can talk to the school.

I love that she does this. Without her, or Leo, or Over the Rainbow, I'd feel so alone.

Mrs Knight will be gone by the end of term. It's only a few weeks. I just have to keep out of her way as much as I can till then.

But even once she leaves, I've got years and years of school to go. There are always going to be more people like her, or like Jasmine, or like the girls in Spanish who laugh along at what she says. There are always going to be people who don't understand or don't want to understand. Not just in school. It's like Ana said, there are still governments making laws against us, still newspapers writing lies about us, and still books about us being banned.

And there are always going to be other LGBTQ+ kids, who perhaps want to come out in school, but don't feel safe. This isn't just about me or about Mrs Knight. It's bigger than that.

I guess it's the same thing Lisa realized – she couldn't just leave it to other people. She had to be part of the fight.

I think there's a bit of her in me. And that bit is telling me not to give up now. Her story, our story, it's all part of the same thing. It all deserves to be told, not just told, but celebrated. We just need to work out how.

"Let's not waste any more energy on Mrs Knight," I tell Simran. "If she's not going to listen, that's her loss. We need to find someone who will."

"What do you mean?" she asks, but before I can answer, Leo comes over to clear our table.

"Has Maz seen you here?" he asks in a whisper. "If not, you've still got time to hide!"

"What?" says Simran at normal volume. "Why would we want to hide from Maz?"

"She's got more books that she wants you to read. Once she gets started, she'll talk about them for hours!"

"Oh, that's cool," I say. "She was so helpful last time."

"Were the books good then? Did Ms Grant get excited about your ideas?" he asks.

Simran and I look at each other. I take a deep breath and explain everything that's happened.

Leo is outraged. "What are you going to do?" he demands, leaning across the table. "You've rescued all this fabulous real-life LGBTQ+ history from a dusty old loft, you've saved it from being chucked away and lost for ever. What now? Are you going to let yourself be silenced? Will you give up and shove it all back in the attic to be ignored for another quarter of a century? Well?" He brings his hand down on the table so hard that the glasses rattle.

"Wow, Leo," says Simran, looking at him in awe.

"No," I say firmly. "No, we will *not* be silenced, but…" I look around the cafe. Maz is heading towards our table with an armful of books. Suddenly it hits me. There is something we can do.

"Leo, what if we did an exhibition here, in Over the Rainbow? Even if we could do it at school, here would be miles better. We'd be telling *our* stories in *our* space in *our* way."

He grins at me. "Hell, yes! Of course we could."

"Jesse, that's a brilliant idea!" says Simran.

Maz reaches our table and puts down her stack of books. "I thought you two might be interested in these," she says.

"Thanks," I say. "We definitely would." My stomach is fizzing with excitement about the idea of putting on our exhibition in Over the Rainbow. But it's not up to Leo, however keen he is. Maz has to agree.

She turns to Leo. "Aren't you *supposed* to be working?"

"I *am* working," he protests. "Jesse, Simran and I have been discussing a business proposition."

"A what?" says Maz, shaking her head.

"Take a seat," says Leo, grabbing another chair. "We'll explain everything."

"I can't just 'take a seat', I'm working," says Maz. "Like you're supposed to be."

"Ah, come on," wheedles Leo. "There's no one waiting."

Maz sits down with her arms folded and nods at Leo. "Go on then. Two minutes."

"Look around you. Imagine this very place, that you know so well, transformed –" he sweeps his arm around, taking in the slightly threadbare bunting and the overstuffed bookshelves – "into a gallery space showcasing LGBTQ+ history, with national importance but a local connection. Taking people back in time, through the decades, to when our rights were being fought for on the streets, all portrayed through the experiences of people who were there, inspiring us all to take up the fight again."

He glances at the only other occupied table where a couple are sharing a salad. "Imagine this room, packed with people of all generations…laughing, talking, sharing stories, eating, drinking, posting about it on social media, spending money, buying books."

"Leo!" snaps Maz, breaking the spell. "What on earth are you talking about?"

"They've stopped us from doing our exhibition on

Section 28 at school," I say. "So I wondered…we wondered…if we could do it here instead?"

"They've stopped you?" says Maz. "Have they now?"

Leo turns to her, still full-on pitching. "We could do a special menu. Eighties' music too. I promise you, everyone loves that retro stuff."

He looks at her, beaming. "It'll be fun. And you could showcase all those history books that you're always going on about. What do you reckon, boss?"

"I hate to say it," says Maz thoughtfully, unfolding her arms. "But it's not the worst idea I've ever heard. It would be a lot of work though."

"Not *really*." Leo stretches the word out. "I could take charge of the cafe that day—"

"Oh, could you indeed?" says Maz.

Leo ignores her sceptical look. "Leaving you free to focus on the bookshop."

"We could help do some social media posts to advertise it," adds Simran.

"It would bring in new customers, I'm sure of it," says Leo. "I'm sorry, Maz, but it could do with a bit more life in here. Please can we do it?" He's bouncing around like an excited puppy. "Oh go on, Maz, please."

"Let me think it over," she says. "Now, move it, sweetheart, there's customers waiting. Go on, scarper!"

Maz watches him go. "I swear I don't know what that boy is talking about half the time." She turns to us, looking fierce. "Someone at school's told you that you can't do your exhibition?" she asks. I nod.

"You know the first thing *I* think whenever someone tells *me* I can't do something?" She waits. Simran and I just stare at her. "Perhaps I shouldn't say the exact words, I don't want to be a bad influence, but I'm sure you can guess." For a second, a cheeky grin breaks out from behind her tough, no-messing exterior. "So, yeah, let's show them. Let's do it. I'd be proud to host your exhibition at Over the Rainbow."

"Really?" I squeal, just as Simran exclaims, "Seriously?"

"Yes. Although I might regret this if it means Leo chattering on about it all the time, instead of doing any actual work."

This is real. It's going to happen. And there's nothing Mrs Knight can do about it. I can't wait to tell Nicky and Ana.

I wonder if people from school will come. That would be weird. Over the Rainbow is my and Simran's special place. What if they laugh at it? Or, if they like it, come back and then Over the Rainbow stops being just ours?

I look over and catch Simran's eye. She grins back at me. Who cares what other people think? I can't let that stop us. It's not for them. It's for us. And for everyone who needs it.

Leo glides past us with a grin, puts down two coffees on a nearby table with a flourish, then stops to lean on the back of Simran's chair. He props his chin on her head.

"So, *are* we doing it?" he says.

"Keep calm," says Maz. "Nothing's happening overnight. There's plenty to organize. Jesse and Simran need time to get their material in order, we'll need to do publicity, call in a few favours. But, yes, you've twisted my arm."

"Yes!" says Simran, holding out her hand for me to high-five. "Thanks, Maz. It'll be amazing, we promise. Right, Jesse?"

Leo moves round the table to hug Maz, but she gives him a look that makes him quickly back away again.

"I wonder..." I start. "Do you think other customers might have things they'd want to put on display? Things they've kept from the same time or the same campaign?"

"It's worth finding out," says Maz. "I can ask around. I'll have a look at home as well."

"We need to get planning," says Leo, rubbing his hands together. "We need a date. No, first we need a title. No, a date."

"It's too late for LGBT+ History Month...that would have been perfect," Maz says.

"Pride month?" suggests Simran.

"Not for ages," says Leo. "We can't wait till June."

"What about the anniversary of Clause 28 becoming law. Isn't that in May?" suggests Simran. "Nicky told us about it."

I'm enjoying sitting back and listening to them planning. I love it that it's not just me who believes in telling this story, but a whole gang of us now. History should belong to everyone. I know Ms Grant would agree.

"What about the end of April?" I say. "Around the anniversary of the big march that Lisa and Nicky and Andy went on. I think we should celebrate the resistance, the fighting back. That's the day we should mark, not the day when the law went through."

Everyone exchanges glances, and Maz nods.

"Settled," says Leo. "What shall we call it though? What should go on the flyers?"

"This exhibition is about fighting back..." I ponder out loud. I think about what Nicky said, about how fighting for LGBTQ+ equality had changed her, how these fights brought people together and made them stronger, how she saw straight away that this was our generation's fight too. "The fights that make us?" I murmur, looking down at my hands resting on the table. It's more of a question than a suggestion.

There's silence. Why is no one saying anything? Maybe they hate it.

But when I finally look up, everyone is grinning.

"To the fights that make us!" exclaims Leo, breaking the silence. He raises my empty milkshake glass in a toast. Simran clinks her glass against his and, because Leo's taken my glass, I tap both of theirs with my spoon.

Maz just shakes her head like she despairs of us all. But she's smiling too.

31 OPEN YOUR HEART

I grab Simran's arm and we hurry out of the school gate, skirting the puddles and dodging the groups of people stopping to chat. After checking that I'd done my homework and making sure I'd be back for tea, Mum said it was okay for me to go round to Simran's so we can properly start working on the exhibition. There are a few weeks till it needs to be ready, but with school and all the work we have to do, it's really not that long.

"Do you think we should start with the timeline?" I ask her. "Or with the stuff about the march? I thought we could scan in some of Lisa's drawings of the protest and print them out much bigger, along with the photos she took. We could find some newspaper reports online and print those out too."

271

"Cool. Let's start with the march, I think."

Since Maz said she'd ask her customers if they had anything they wanted to add to the exhibition, we've been trying to come up with ways to include as many stories as we can, not just Lisa and Nicky's.

"I had another idea," I tell Simran. I hope she thinks it's a good one. "We could make something like we saw in that museum – do you remember? That comments board. Anyone who comes can add a note with their own memories or questions or what they think about the exhibition."

"You know, it would look so good if they wrote the notes on coloured Post-its. We could make a giant rainbow out of them!" Simran chips in. "Because we'll be in…"

"Over the Rainbow!" we chorus together.

"'Over the rainbow!'" says a voice behind us in a mocking sing-song tone. "What *are* you two talking about?" It's Jasmine and Ella, also arm in arm.

"None of your business," says Simran sharply. We start to walk faster. I can't be bothered with Jasmine and her nasty comments right now. I don't want any hassle. I just want to get back to Simran's and get on with our project.

"Don't be so rude," retorts Jasmine. "I know what you're talking about anyway. Over the Rainbow is that sad little bookshop in town, isn't it?"

"It's not sad!" I say, spinning round. "You don't know anything about it."

"Excuse me," she replies in this smarmy, patronizing voice. "I didn't realize that's where you two freaks hang out with your other freaky friends. Makes sense though. I can't believe you're still going on about the history projects. You do know they aren't happening? They've been, like, cancelled. Although, if you're swotty enough to want to do extra homework, that's not our problem. Right, Ella?"

"Mmm," says Ella, looking away. "Come on, Jas, the rain's getting worse, let's go."

"Oh hey," shouts Jasmine, waving to some other girls at the bus stop over the road. "It's Kiera and Niamh. They've got crisps. Come *on*, Ella." Jasmine gives Simran and me a dirty look and tugs at Ella's arm.

As they pass us, Ella looks back apologetically. "Don't listen to her," she whispers. "She just says stuff, she doesn't think. She's all right really. I think that bookshop sounds cool."

When they've gone, I breathe out slowly.

"Why do people think she's so great?" I ask Simran, as I watch Jasmine hugging her friends at the bus stop. "I don't get it. And why does she always have to stick her nose into everything? Can't she just leave the rest of us alone?"

273

"Yeah. Ella's wrong, you know. She knows exactly what she's saying," adds Simran.

"Forget them, we can't let them spoil our evening," I tell her.

By the time we're back at Simran's house, with all our bits and pieces for the exhibition spread out on her dining-room table, I feel proud of myself for standing up to Jasmine, even if it was just a little bit. I could do it because Simran was there. How dare Jasmine slag off Over the Rainbow?

Simran's mum and dad are both really interested in what we're doing. Her mum uses her ex-primary school teacher display-making skills to help us plan it all out on big pieces of coloured card. Her dad suggests some good websites for finding old newspapers and checking out historical facts. Parminder and Ranveer stop watching cartoons to come and see what we're doing.

"I know it's on display for a whole week," says Simran's mum. "But are you having a launch party?"

"And, more importantly, are we invited?" chuckles Simran's dad.

"Of course you're invited!" I say.

"Only if you promise not to embarrass me," adds Simran sternly.

"As if we would," says her dad, with a wink.

"Have you invited Nicky and Ana yet?" asks Simran.

I shake my head. "I need to do it tonight. My mum's been on at me all week to send them a thank-you message for that Clause 28 poster, and for talking to us at the weekend. I keep forgetting. I'll invite them at the same time." I've not really forgotten, it's just that I haven't thought of the right words yet. I want them to understand just how grateful I am.

When Simran's parents ask me if I want to stay for tea, I'm tempted, but I know Mum and Dad wouldn't want me to stay out too late on a school night. I leave all the stuff at her house so we can do some more at the weekend. We've got some questions for Maz anyway, about what we can display where, before we can do much more.

It's great to see the exhibition coming together, but it still bothers me that the diary stops when it does. Just at the point when things are at their very worst for Lisa, before she goes to stay with Gran and Grandad and Mum. I hope that summer in Hurston helped her recover, but I just don't know. And that not-knowing frustrates me.

It's quiet at home compared to the bustle and noise at Simran's. It still feels weird, how these days it's usually just the three of us in the house. Tom hundreds of miles away. Gran no longer popping in for a cup of tea and a chat. Last year, within just a few months, everything changed. It felt like everyone I cared about was disappearing one by one.

The kitchen is warm and Dad's whistling to himself as he finishes cooking. Mum's sitting at the table, scrolling through social media. The food smells so good that it makes my stomach rumble super loudly.

"Have I got time to email Nicky before dinner?" I ask.

"Sure," says Mum, looking up from her phone. "Do you want to use my laptop? Don't send it though, not before I've put a note on the end. I want to add my own thank you for their hospitality the other weekend. And for giving you and Simran the picture... That was so generous. I wasn't sure if you should take it."

"Nicky and Ana obviously wanted them to have it," chips in Dad. "Or they wouldn't have offered."

I stare into space, trying to find the right words for the email. I type "Hi Nicky" and then I delete it. Perhaps that's too informal? I try "Dear Professor Zielinska-Burridge" instead and delete that too. Much too formal.

"I do hope they'll come – Nicky and Ana, I mean. Do you think they will?" I ask Mum.

"Well, I hope so. When we were in the kitchen, Ana told me a little about Nicky's health problems. She gets tired very easily. It varies day to day. I don't know if it would all be too much for her, but I'm sure they'd love to come if they can."

I frown. Nicky didn't look ill to me, but I guess you can't tell everything about someone just by looking. I should know that by now – so many people make wrong assumptions about me all the time.

Mum moves round the table to stand behind me, pressing her hands down on my shoulders. "Jesse, they'll only come if you actually invite them. Tea's nearly ready and you haven't written anything!"

She gives my shoulder a squeeze, then starts laying the table around me.

"Why don't you email Lisa's friends Ali and Sam and invite them too? They were the ones who got you started. If Ali hadn't asked you to go up into that attic, you'd never have got into any of this. I reckon they'll be pleased to know that Lisa's life hasn't been forgotten. It was so important to me when people shared their memories of your gran after she died. Just for a moment, it was like having her back again."

Once I've worked out how to start my message (I guess "Dear Nicky" will be fine), it's quick to write. I explain about Over the Rainbow and the exhibition launch and how we'd love her and Ana to come. I'm about to pass the laptop back to Mum so she can add her bit, when a notification for a new email pops up.

"Matthew Scott?" I say in surprise. "You're emailing

Matthew Scott? Lisa's little brother?"

"Yes, Lisa's little brother, but my cousin too," says Mum, pulling the laptop back towards her before I can see the message. "You knew I was trying to get in touch with him. I could only find a postal address in Gran's old address book, so I asked Ali for his email address." She sounds uncomfortable, like she's hiding something.

"Yeah, but I didn't know he'd replied. Or that you were exchanging secret messages with him." My voice has got louder. Why is this making me so upset?

"Don't be ridiculous, Jesse, there are no secret messages," snaps Mum.

"I can't believe you're getting all cosy with him," I snap back. "After what he did. He read Lisa's diary and told her mum. If he hadn't done that, then she wouldn't have been sent away!"

Mum runs her hand through her hair. "People make mistakes, Jesse, we all do. He was just a kid."

"So that makes it okay? Because of how old he was?"

If she thinks that the way Matthew behaved back then was okay, then what else does she think is okay now?

Jasmine's words – about Over the Rainbow being full of freaks – are still ringing in my ears. I try to push her voice away, but it's hard to ignore. It reminds me that I still haven't said anything to Mum and Dad about

Mrs Knight, even though I promised Simran I would. I just don't know how to start.

"No, I'm not saying that." Mum sounds impatient, like she thinks I'm deliberately missing the point. "Just that it was thirty odd years ago. It wasn't Matthew who kicked Lisa out. The whole situation must have been hard on him too." She looks at me, concerned. "Jesse, if this is making you upset, maybe you need to take a step back from the exhibition. You've hardly talked about anything else these last couple of weeks. I know it's really inspired you, and that's great, but you don't want to get obsessed by it."

"That's not a bad idea," chips in Dad. "Perhaps you need a break to get things into perspective."

"I'm not obsessed. And I don't need a break," I say. I can hear the wobble in my voice, which means that Mum and Dad must be able to as well. "We've only got a few weeks to get everything ready. You don't understand."

"So, help us understand," says Mum, her voice softer now. "Are you really upset because I'm emailing Matt?"

"Yes...no...sort of," I stutter. "It's not as easy as saying, take a step back from the exhibition. Sure, I could." I pause. "But I can't take a step back from being me."

Mum and Dad are sitting at the table, listening, not saying anything. The saucepan is bubbling over, but Dad doesn't get up to turn it down. They both look confused.

It's the same look they had when I first told them about being non-binary, the look they've had so many times since then. It's like they are trying hard to understand, to not say the wrong thing, but they can't quite grasp why I feel the way I do, why it matters so much to me.

I need to try and explain, but it's hard to find a way that they will understand.

"I like being different," I say carefully. The only way I can get the words out is not to look directly at Mum and Dad, so I stare at the patterns of tiny flowers on the plate in front of me. I don't want them to think I'm ungrateful or that I'm having a go at them.

"But I kind of hate it too. When I'm at Over the Rainbow, I can relax and be me, people get it. But otherwise, I don't know, everything feels really..." I pause, searching for the right word. "Fragile, I guess. Like people are understanding and nice and everything's okay, but that it could all collapse any minute. I'm always worrying about what someone might say or do, even if most of the time, there's nothing to worry about. But, I mean, look at Nicky and Lisa and Andy, how people treated them, the awful things people said about LGBTQ+ people, how they had to hide—"

"But that was the 1980s," interrupts Mum. "It's different now. I mean, look at how the school responded when you came out, they bent over backwards to help you.

No one's saying you have to hide." She pauses, then continues, sounding more uncertain. "Not here anyway."

Does she really believe this, or is she just trying to convince herself? Or does she think she's protecting me by not admitting what's really going on?

"You don't understand. It's there, you just don't see it."

I think about the looks I sometimes get when I'm wearing my "they/them" badge, the things I hear people say about trans people before they know I'm trans, the things people say even when they *do* know. Always having to worry about which toilets to use, the people who think I say I'm non-binary because I'm trying to get attention instead of because I'm simply trying to be myself.

And any of these things can happen any time, without warning. I feel like I'm always on high alert, always tense, always waiting for something bad to happen. Mrs Knight is just the most obvious example, not the only one.

Mum's about to say something, but Dad puts his hand on top of hers before she can speak.

"What don't we see, Jesse?" he says.

"Mrs Knight—" I say, but then I stop because I don't want Mum and Dad feeling sorry for me or, worse still, getting upset too. And I stop because I'm scared I'll start crying if I continue.

"Oh, if that's all…" says Mum, sounding relieved. "But

you've sorted that out now, right? You can still do your exhibition, just out of school. I know it's not what you hoped, but it sounds like it's going to be even better this way. It's all okay." She so desperately wants that to be true.

"That's not what I'm talking about!" I shout.

Dad flinches in surprise. Shouting and kicking up a fuss isn't like me. And yet this is the second time in the last few weeks that I've exploded at Mum. This time I won't storm out, this time I'll try and make them understand. I start pacing around the kitchen. "Just *listen*!"

I miss Gran so much right now. Missing her is like a stomach ache that's always there. I usually don't notice it, but sometimes, like now, it hurts so much I can barely breathe. If she were here, I know she'd listen, *really* listen, and then she'd give me one of her big hugs and we'd come up with a plan together.

Mum and Dad are watching me cautiously, waiting for me to explain. So, I try.

"She's been misgendering me, in front of the whole class," I say.

Mum opens her mouth to speak. "And, before you say it, no, it's not by mistake, it's deliberate, I know it is. It happens every single lesson. She won't listen when I try to explain. Hardly anyone even *tries* to stand up for me either. And, now there's this girl, she's been saying horrible stuff, and I don't know what to do about it. Maybe she thinks if Mrs Knight can say what she wants, then it's okay for her to do it too."

"Oh, Jesse, I'm sorry," is all Dad says. But it's enough for me to feel like I can carry on explaining, that they are trying to understand.

"And when Sim and I went to talk to her about the projects, the moment she heard what ours was about, that was it – her face screwed up, like she'd smelled something nasty. I'm sure that's the real reason why she wouldn't change her mind about us doing them, because she thinks there's something wrong with being LGBTQ+."

I slump down in a chair. I'm shattered. Simran will be pleased that I did what I promised I would – I *did* talk to Mum and Dad about Mrs Knight – but I hadn't expected it all to come flooding out like this.

I take a deep breath to calm myself down. That's when I notice a weird smell. A high-pitched wailing starts. Dad leaps to his feet, whipping the forgotten pan off the hob. Mum grabs a magazine and starts waving it frantically under the smoke detector. I open the windows and we all wait for it to stop. The noise means that none of us can think, let alone speak.

By the time it's quiet again and Dad's scraped the rice from the bottom of the pan and put extra spices in the curry to try and distract us from the burned bits, I'm starting to feel better. Mum keeps shooting me these little anxious glances though, and then looks away when I meet her eye.

"We'll go in and talk to the school," says Dad, in between mouthfuls. He's gone from listening to trying to fix things, like he does all the time at work. But this isn't a flooded street or an overflowing river. "It sounds like Mrs Knight needs some extra training. She needs to know this isn't acceptable. Right, love?" He turns to Mum, waiting for her to agree.

"Of course we will. If Jesse wants us to," says Mum, looking at me.

"I think, maybe not go in," I say, glad that she's giving me the choice. "Maybe an email to the head of year..."

"Okay, we'll send it straight after tea," says Dad, still wolfing down his burned curry.

Mum's not eating, just pushing her food round her plate like I do when I'm anxious about something.

"Jesse," she says finally, reaching out for my hand. "Maybe I shouldn't say this, but I worry so much about you. All the time. Whenever there's something in the news about trans people or LGBTQ+ rights, it's like they're talking about my family, about you. I see it, but I can't stop it. So I thought if we just carried on loving you, *everything* about you, then that might be enough to stop anything bad reaching you. But maybe I need to be better at listening to what you need from us. I'll try, I promise."

Dad stands up and pulls us both into a big hug. It doesn't feel awkward. It feels right.

"Thank you," I whisper to them both.

When it does start to feel awkward, we break up the hug and load the dishwasher. When Mum opens her laptop to email the school, Matthew's email pops up on the screen.

"Come on then, have a read of my secret messages," Mum says, trying to make a joke of it.

"Okay, okay," I say, skim-reading over her shoulder. It's full of names I don't know.

There are two photos attached to the email. Mum clicks on the first. It's of a man and a woman. They are squinting in the bright sun and the sea is behind them. There are two teenage boys in shorts towering over them on either side. The man's got pale skin and flame-red hair, just like mine and Nicky's. I wonder how he manages to avoid getting sunburned.

"That's a recent photo of Matt and his family," says Mum. "And this... Well, have a look for yourself."

She clicks on the other image. When it opens, I can see it's an old photo that's been scanned in. It has that wonky, grainy look and none of the colours are quite right. I recognize Lisa. She's a few years younger than in the other photos, her arms are around a little boy with a cheeky grin. They are both holding huge ice creams. They look happy. Not so different from the pictures that Mum has saved on her phone of me and Tom on family holidays. It's obvious from the photo that Lisa and Matthew must have been close once.

"It's good being back in touch with Matt," says Mum. "Well, it's not like we were in touch before, but you know what I mean. He's family – even if he does live on the other side of the world. You'll think I'm daft but I'm sure the universe has taken a hand in bringing our family back together somehow."

I hope the universe knows what it's doing, I think. But I'm not sure I agree with Mum. You can't rely on the universe. Change only happens if you do something to make it happen, like Lisa and Nicky and all those other campaigners did. You can't just sit and wait for the universe to sort things out.

I open a new email for us to send to my head of year. If the universe isn't going to make things better with Mrs Knight, then I guess we've got to do something ourselves.

32 VICTORY

One of the things we've learned about Mrs Knight is that she does not tolerate lateness. She tells us this every single lesson. And yet, it's five minutes after the start of today's lesson and she's still not here. Maybe she's late because she's so busy working out how to make my life as miserable as possible. Today is the first day of her new seating plan and I bet she'll make me sit next to someone awful.

But then I stop myself. I've been trying hard not to think about Mrs Knight too much over the last few days. I'd rather spend my time and energy on planning the exhibition, than worrying about what she's going to say or do next. Telling Mum and Dad what was going on and sending that email about it made me feel less powerless, like at least I was doing something to stand up for myself.

I wonder if Mrs Knight knows about it yet, and what will happen next.

While there's no teacher to stop us, Simran hands out the flyers that she and Leo designed to promote the exhibition. We've already sneaked some onto the school noticeboards. They are hard to miss – Leo and Simran used every colour of the rainbow and a few more. I love the way they've also used a couple of Lisa's drawings next to some old newspaper pictures in the design.

She gives one to everyone in the class. Jasmine says "No, thank you," in such a disgusted voice that it sounds like Simran's offered her a handful of worms. Ella folds hers neatly and puts it in her bag. Dylan and Conor make theirs into paper aeroplanes and start throwing them across the classroom. I keep an eye on the door. I don't want Mrs Knight to catch Simran giving out the flyers and confiscate them.

When Mrs Knight appears, Simran shoves the rest of the flyers into her bag. Everyone scrambles to get back to their seats. But she doesn't launch into her usual tirade, just clears her throat a couple of times. Her face is red and she seems flustered.

"All right, Year Eight, settle down," she says. "I've got your tests and essays to give back. Your work was, shall we say, mixed. Once we've rearranged the seating, there are a few points we need to go over as a class."

There are some groans, but they stop quickly under Mrs Knight's glare.

She walks between the desks handing out papers, each with a grade in red at the top. When she stops by my desk, I don't want to look, but it's impossible to miss the red scrawl and "7/20" on my test paper. Disappointing, but hardly a surprise. I turn to the essay, bracing myself for an even worse grade.

I sit up in surprise. 36/40. Where did that come from? I wrote it in a rush late at night and finished it off over breakfast. It must be a mistake. Mrs Knight is waiting by my desk. Is this a trick? Is she going to cross it out and replace it with the real mark to teach me some kind of lesson?

Instead, she gives me a brief nod and says, like it's hurting her to get the words out: "Credit where it's due. You showed some good analysis in that essay, that's why you got the higher grade, despite the abysmal handwriting." She starts walking away, and then turns back. "And, Jesse, I've a message for you. You need to go to the Deputy Head's office straight after school. Your parents will be waiting for you there."

"Oooooh," calls Dylan from behind me.

"Jesse's in trouble," adds Conor. I turn round to glare at them.

"Shut up," Simran tells them, and gives me a questioning look. I shrug.

Am I in trouble? It must be something really bad if my parents are coming in. Maybe it's giving out the leaflets, but then, if that was it, Simran and her parents would have been summoned too. And something like that isn't serious enough for the Deputy Head to deal with, is it? I just don't know.

Mrs Knight reads out the new seating plan and we all shuffle round. I'm near the front, next to Ella. Simran's right on the other side of the classroom, next to Dylan.

After that, she goes through the test answers and then it's the usual boring lesson. It's easy to let it all drift over me and to think about something else. Especially when I have something else to think about – why does Mr Wijendra want to see me?

Everything goes quiet. Ella nudges me. I look up. Mrs Knight's staring at me over the top of her glasses.

"So, Jesse?" she says. She must have just asked me something, but I had totally zoned out. I have no idea what the question is, let alone the answer.

Ella nudges me again, more gently this time, and rests her finger on the textbook page, like she's just stretching out her hand. After a moment, I realize what she's doing – she's showing me the answer.

"Er, wattle and daub?" I say, hoping that I can trust Ella.

"Hmm," says Mrs Knight, and carries on talking. I breathe out and vow to concentrate hard for the rest of the lesson. Learning about Tudor architecture is better than worrying about what might happen in Mr Wijendra's office later on.

"Thanks," I whisper to Ella.

She shrugs and examines her perfect nails. "Whatever, no big deal."

At the end of the day, Simran insists on walking with me to Mr Wijendra's office. I've been inside a couple of times before when Mrs Bailey was Deputy Head. Mrs Bailey retired at the end of last year. She used to wear fluffy cardigans and smelled of the mints she sucked the whole time. I went to see her with Mum and Dad, back in Year Seven, once we'd decided that I was going to come out at school. She's the one who said that we should come and see her again if there were any issues. But then she left. So that was that.

I don't know much about Mr Wijendra, apart from the fact he's young and wears smart suits with shiny shoes and has this habit of pulling on his cuffs when he does assemblies.

Simran whispers, "Good luck, message me later," and

then disappears down the corridor. I knock lightly on the door.

Mr Wijendra opens the door. He's smiling. Mum and Dad are already there, sitting on the edge of their chairs. On the wall are some of the posters of "LGBTQ+ heroes" that were up around school for Pride week last summer, before disappearing the following week. I wonder if he's put them up specially because I'm here.

He offers us tea, coffee or water. I say, "no thanks" to everything, because I just want to get this over with, whatever *this* is. Mum and Dad say the same, which surprises me because Mum never normally says no to a cup of tea.

Mr Wijendra takes off his jacket and puts it carefully over the back of his chair, takes a seat behind his desk and clears his throat. I can't help admiring his waistcoat, even though it's not as nice as mine.

"So," he says. "Jesse, I'm sure you know what this is about." I try to look like I have a clue what he's talking about. "Your head of year shared your parents' email with me, the one with your concerns about Mrs Knight." He picks up a printout from his desk and waves it at us. "I've been away on a conference for a few days, which is why I didn't reply before, but as soon as I got back, I wanted to see you. Nip this in the bud, as it were."

Oh, of course, the email. So, I guess, I'm not in trouble after all, unless…

"Is there anything else you want to tell me about, in your own words?" He waits, his brown eyes fixed on me. They are sharp, like they don't miss anything.

"No, thank you," I say. "It was all in the email."

"Well then, I had a conversation with Mrs Knight, just before your history class this afternoon." He pulls at his cuffs. "I've been very clear. We are not trying to change her opinion about anything. As she rightly says, everyone is entitled to their opinion—"

Even when it's a bigoted, homophobic opinion? I wonder to myself. That doesn't seem right.

"But the need to treat every single pupil at this school with respect is not up for debate. *That's* not a matter of opinion." His voice softens. "Jesse, I'm sorry. We want to be an inclusive school. We want you to be able to learn and thrive here. Nothing should get in the way of that. You use they/them pronouns, am I right?" I nod. "Hmm, there should have been a note about that in the register for Mrs Knight when she started. Everything happened so quickly when Ms Grant had to go on leave that it looks like we missed some of the usual processes. But everything should be back on track now." He smiles and leans back in his seat. "Do any of you have any questions?"

I'm not convinced that a note in the register would have made any difference to Mrs Knight. She probably would have ignored it, or decided it was a matter of opinion, mine against hers. It's good that Mr Wijendra's taking it seriously now, but who's to say this won't happen again and again and again. Maybe not for me, but for someone else. Someone whose parents aren't on their side. Someone who can't speak out.

When we came here last year to see Mrs Bailey, Mum and Dad did most of the talking. I just sat there, red with embarrassment, as the three of them talked about language and pronouns, toilets and changing rooms. Mrs Bailey tried her best, but she kept looking to us for the answers. Mum and Dad shared everything we'd learned from YouTube and support forums and educational policy papers we'd found online. I just said "yes" and "maybe" and "thank you".

But so much has changed since last year. I've changed. I think about Ana saying, "if you wait for people to give you your rights, you'll be waiting for ever" and Nicky's dad talking about "every child's inalienable right to be whoever they wanted to be" and Lisa herself, putting up her hand to vote for equality in that RE debate when no one else did.

"Actually," I say. Mum and Dad look up. Mr Wijendra's

sharp eyes are fixed on me. "That's all very good, I mean, thank you, sir. But I don't think that's enough. It's more than just using the right pronouns because you're told to, it's about understanding *why* it matters. And it's not just about Mrs Knight, it's about all the staff and students understanding gender identities better so they can challenge stuff they hear too."

"Ah yes," says Mr Wijendra, leafing through the folder in front of him. "Very important. I understand that there was some staff training and an awareness campaign in Pride week last year. I wasn't there myself, but…" His eyes flick up to the posters on the wall. Oscar Wilde stares back at him, and he doesn't look impressed to me.

My heart's beating super fast and my mouth's gone dry. But I'm determined to try again, and to keep trying until he understands me. I open my mouth to say something about how it's not enough to remember that LGBTQ+ people exist for one week in June, and then forget about us the rest of the time. But then Dad starts speaking.

"That's good to hear, Mr Wijendra. But can I share a little something with you? Something I've learned in my career. I work in environmental management, you see."

Mr Wijendra nods at him to go on. Mum and I exchange looks. Dad's seriously going to talk about flood plains and energy efficiency now?

"In essence, my job is about preventing problems, spotting where things are likely to go wrong, months or years before they will. If I waited for an area to flood, and then tried to do something about it, I wouldn't be doing my job properly. There would be a lot of angry people with their shops and houses destroyed, when simple, precautionary action could have prevented that flood damage in the first place. It strikes me that your job is rather similar to mine, that's all. And I'm sure you know as well as I do, that one training session or one week of action is not going to be enough to make this a truly inclusive school for someone like my child."

After Dad's finished, we all sit in silence.

"Thank you," says Mr Wijendra finally. "You and Jesse, you're absolutely right. How about I talk with my team and review what else is happening now, and what we can introduce on a more regular basis? This is my responsibility, not yours. I'll set up a meeting for the four of us in another few weeks to report back. Would that be acceptable?" He's looking at Dad for a response, but Dad turns to me before saying anything.

"What do *you* think, Jesse?" he asks.

I turn to Mr Wijendra. "Yes," I say. "That will be acceptable. And…" I rummage in my bag for a moment, before finding one of the exhibition flyers to hand to him.

"If you want to know any more, you're invited to this."

He thanks us again, shakes Mum and Dad's hands, and opens the door for us. Dad looks serious. Mum grins at me. I'm not quite sure what happened there, but I can't wait to tell Simran all about it.

33 NOTHING'S GONNA STOP US NOW

"Jesse, aren't you up yet?" Mum sticks her head round my bedroom door. I snuggle deeper under my duvet. It's pretty obvious that I'm not up. "Won't Simran's dad be here to pick you up in half an hour?"

I groan. Not just because I hate getting up. Or because it's the weekend when I can usually stay in bed instead of getting ready for school. It's because today's the day the exhibition opens.

I'm excited, of course I am. I really, really want this to happen, especially when it so nearly didn't. But, now it's here, my stomach feels like I've just drunk one of Maz's kale and spinach milkshakes.

What if nobody comes? Imagine if it's just me, Sim, Maz and Leo in an empty cafe? The thought of that makes me want to hide under the duvet and never come out!

Or what if *everybody* comes? That's a terrifying thought too. There have been posters up in Over the Rainbow and in the library and loads of stuff on social media, as well as the flyers that Simran and I brought into school.

And then there's Nicky and Ana, Ali and Sam and all the people that Mum and Dad have invited. All those different worlds in one place. Dad's emailed round his team at work and Mum's posted about it in the WhatsApp group for our street.

I love that they're proud and excited, but I think they are trying so hard to make sure everything goes okay because they want to protect me. Their worries sometimes feel like an extra burden to carry.

"Here, tea and toast," says Mum, putting a plate and mug down next to my bed. "Big day. It's important to keep your energy levels up."

"Thanks," I say, sitting up and reaching for the mug. It makes me smile – it's the one which says "LGBTea" on it in rainbow writing. Simran gave it to me for my birthday.

"But you might want to eat and drink it *while* you're getting dressed," continues Mum sternly. "You're cutting it a bit fine, you know. And you are planning on having a shower, aren't you?"

"Uh huh," I say, through a mouthful of toast.

We need to start early so that we can set everything up before the cafe opens at ten. As much as it can be, it's all ready. We spent last weekend mounting photographs, badges and copies of diary entries onto big boards, alongside extra info and a timeline, as well as space for people to add their own memories, thoughts or questions on rainbow Post-its. I've been over and over everything in my mind, but I can't think of anything we've forgotten.

I'm brushing my teeth when Simran rings the doorbell. I dash down the stairs at twice my normal speed. Simran's dad's car has an enormous boot and most of the stuff is already in there. The rest will be packed around our feet or on our laps. I can see Ranveer's face pressed against one window and Parminder grinning out of the other.

"I'm sorry it's such a squash, but they insisted on coming too," says Simran. "Dad's taking them swimming and then they're coming to Over the Rainbow after. Mum too. She says a couple of the teachers from her old school might drop in later too."

"That's good," I say. "It means that at least one or two people might come."

"What? Of course people will come to our exhibition!" says Simran. "Loads of people are going to be there. Just wait and see."

It's only once I'm in the passenger seat and we're just

about to leave, that I realize what I've forgotten. There's not really time, but I have to go back.

"I'm sorry, Mr Gill, I've just remembered something…" I unclip my seat belt and leap out of the car.

I unlock the front door, shout to Mum that it's me, and sprint upstairs. I find my waistcoat and slip it on over my T-shirt. Now I feel complete. Comfortable in who I am and how I look. The day that Simran bought this for me was the day when the letter about Lisa's funeral arrived, the day when all of this really began.

Mum catches me at the bottom of the stairs and pulls me into a hug.

"I'm really proud of you, Jesse," she says.

"Mum, I'm late, I haven't got time—"

"And you should be really proud of yourself too," she continues.

"There won't be anything to *be* proud of unless I go now," I say, pulling away.

There are a series of loud beeps from the car. I'm guessing that's Simran. It's not the sort of thing Mr Gill would do.

"Dad and I will be there in a couple of hours, okay?" Mum shouts after me. "Text if you remember anything else you want us to bring."

I dive into the car and we pull away. As soon as I sit

down, Ranveer starts poking my shoulder. "Jesse, Jesse, what happened when the red sauce chased the brown sauce?"

"It couldn't ketchup!" shouts Parminder, unable to wait to deliver the punchline. Ranveer scowls at him.

"Very clever," says Mr Gill, even though I'm guessing he's heard this joke a hundred times already.

"Come on, Dad," urges Simran. "There's no need to drive this slowly. We're practically going backwards."

Mr Gill doesn't drive any faster. He just nods and says, "All in good time, don't worry."

Simran sighs and flings herself back into her seat. "At this speed, by the time we get there, I'll be old enough to drive myself," she mutters. "Only four and a bit years. I can't wait."

Mr Gill parks outside the cafe so that we can unload everything. Maz is outside on the pavement, with a bucket of soapy water and a cloth, rubbing energetically at the window. When she hears us, she turns round and stands with her back to the glass.

"Are you spring cleaning, ready for today?" asks Simran, as we get out of the car.

"Something like that," she answers. She looks grim, even for Maz, who doesn't smile much. Maybe she's stressed about today. "Why don't you two take everything in? Leo's inside. He'll make you a drink while I finish up here." She stays standing by the window, not moving, watching us as we lug everything through the cafe door.

The covers are over the counter, the sign on the door is turned to "closed" and the signboards are waiting inside the door. It feels special to be allowed in before the cafe properly opens. Like we've got private, behind-the-scenes access. For the first time today, my excitement is starting to outweigh my anxiety.

"Hey, you're here! At last!" squeals Leo, emerging from the door to the kitchen and swooping in to air-kiss us both. "Have you got everything? Are you ready?" He carries on without waiting for us to answer. "Look at what I've been making... Ta da!"

Simran and I stare at a row of foil-covered balls stuck with cocktail sticks, before Simran finally asks, "Er, what are they?"

"Cheese and pineapple hedgehogs, of course," he says. "It's all part of the 1980s theme. It's very authentic. Go on, take a stick, I've made loads. We've got tons of retro crisps as well. And everything else...well...we're sticking with our normal menu." He wrinkles up his nose. "I did google, but food in the eighties, it all looked so boring. Or just weird. Or weird and boring. If that's even possible."

Leo seems a bit too hyper, even for him. Like he's trying too hard to be cheerful. It feels fake. The opposite to Maz, who looked like Christmas had been cancelled.

"Leo," I say, giving him my best stare. "What's up?"

"What do you mean 'what's up'? Nothing's up." He giggles.

"Leo…" I repeat.

"Oh, all right, but Maz didn't want to tell you." Leo flops down onto a chair, like a balloon that's just been popped.

"So, *are* you going to tell us?" asks Simran.

"Whatever it is, it can't be that bad," I add, sitting down opposite him and staring him out.

He sighs. "When we got here this morning to open up, there were some stickers on the window."

"Stickers?" I repeat, not understanding what he's talking about.

"It's not the first time," he says.

"What are you talking about? What kind of stickers?"

"Really…" he pauses, like he really doesn't want to go on. "Really horrible ones, with nasty slogans. Stuff about trans people. It wasn't nice. Maz's scrubbing them off now. They'll be gone in a minute, it'll be like they were never there, I promise." He stares at his hands.

I shiver. Simran reaches over and puts her arm around

304

me, but I shake it off. I can't bear someone touching me now, not even my best friend.

"I'm so sorry," she says, glancing from Leo to me and back again.

"Why are *you* sorry?" I ask her. "You didn't do it." My voice sounds far away, like someone else is speaking, not me. I just want to crawl away and hide.

"It just feels horrible," she says. "Knowing that someone out there thought it was okay to do that in a place that's supposed to be safe for all of us."

"The worst thing is that it probably made them feel good, being mean to someone else," says Leo. His voice cracks. "I just don't get it."

"We shouldn't waste our time on people like that," interrupts Maz. We turn to see her standing in the doorway, filling the space. "On people who are trying to divide our community. People who have learned nothing from our history. What they don't realize is that we're always stronger together, right?"

"Yeah, I suppose," says Simran. She sounds subdued, so different from her excitement when she came to pick me up just a few minutes ago. I can't get any words out.

"Yes, but—" starts Leo.

"No buts," says Maz, cutting him off gently. "I thought you'd know better than to argue with me, Leo. I'm your boss, remember." She puts her hand on my arm. I don't move away. "I know this hurts but we can't let them win. Every time someone's tried to pull us apart, it's brought us closer together. And that's what's going to happen today. That's why this exhibition is so important. It shows that we've always been here, and that we're not going away. We're going to tell our stories. We're going to celebrate the fights we've won, and we're going to carry on fighting, until everyone's included. No one's going to stop us."

This is a side of Maz I've not seen before. That was like a political speech, like you might hear at a march or a rally, not the usual practical, no-nonsense Maz.

"Is that what you've been worrying about?" I ask. "Not just about not having enough customers, but about this place being attacked for welcoming trans people?"

"Who says I've been worrying about anything?" she asks, staring accusingly at Leo.

He holds up his hands. "I didn't mean—"

"Never mind. Look, I have been worried about both of those things, but *you're* not to worry about them. Times are tough right now, for lots of different reasons. But, well, perhaps Leo's relentless cheerfulness is finally rubbing off on me, or perhaps seeing you all so enthusiastic about our history has warmed my frozen heart, but today I don't feel worried at all."

She looks round at us. "Now come on you lot, get off your backsides, it's less than an hour till we open. And stop nibbling on that hedgehog! That's for paying customers."

The Maz we know and love is back.

34 THE FINAL COUNTDOWN

Just before Maz unlocks the door and puts the signboards out, we all step back to look at the exhibition.

There's our giant timeline of the campaign, a laptop playing video clips, copies of Lisa's drawings and diary entries and newspaper articles and pictures mounted on rainbow card, including some that Over the Rainbow customers have brought in to share. There's even a picture of a much younger Maz at the Manchester Stop the Clause march, which she says was even bigger than the one in London!

Next to the empty comments board are piles of pens and Post-its for people to share their thoughts and responses. We even found space for the Stop the Clause poster and Nicky's home-made campaign T-shirt.

Thanks to Mrs Knight, we've produced something that's far bigger, bolder and brighter than anything we would have been able to do at school!

At first, it's just what Leo calls "the regulars". The people who are always here on a Saturday, grabbing coffee or brunch to ease themselves into the weekend or recover from the night before.

He greets them all with a smile and, every time he takes an order or sells a book, he points out the exhibition. They nod politely, a few wander over and take a look, but otherwise it's quiet. Our specially chosen eighties' playlist sounds far too loud.

"Stop it," says Simran, when I sit down opposite her. I'd just gone to check if there were enough Post-its for people to leave comments on the exhibition. There were.

"Stop what?"

"Fussing. It looks great, like a proper museum. There's no need to keep jumping up and rearranging things. It's stressing me out. Here, swap seats with me, so you're looking at the door, not at the exhibition."

"It's just…" I say, glancing over, as I reluctantly do what Simran tells me and change seats. "There's this one bit where—"

"No," says Simran, putting her hand on mine to stop me getting up again. "When's Nicky and everyone arriving?"

"Not sure exactly."

"Then let's walk around town instead of sitting here. I saw this top I might get in one of the windows on the high street, it's like twenty per cent off, but I'm not sure about it. I want to know what you think."

"No, you don't," I say. "You know I'll just say 'buy it' whatever. Even if it's disgusting."

"But that's what I want – I want you to come and say 'buy it' and then I'll buy it." She grabs my hand and pulls me to my feet. "Come on."

Simran's right. I do feel better after getting out. Although I can't stop staring at everyone we pass and willing them to turn down the little side street to Over the Rainbow. But they all just walk past.

I tell Simran to buy the top, and she does, but not until she's searched through all the sale racks for something better.

We're almost back at the cafe, when we see three women huddled together on the pavement just before the turning. They are checking a map on one of their phones and arguing about which way to go. I recognize Sam's curls and Ali's short hair, but not the tall, Black woman with them. They've come all this way because of me. I suddenly feel shy. Simran runs right up to them, pulling me by the arm.

"Are you looking for Over the Rainbow?" she asks them. "You're only, like, one minute away." They look up, relieved, and Ali's face breaks into a smile when she recognizes us.

"Hello, you two. It's great to see you again. I'm so glad it's on a happier occasion this time. I can't wait to see what you've done with the contents of that dusty old box! If it wasn't for you, it probably would have ended up in the dump!"

"Well," I say, looking at my feet. "I don't know, it's nothing much really."

"Shut up," says Simran. "Let them see it and then decide." She lowers her voice to a whisper. "It's really good."

"Come on then, I'm dying for a coffee," adds Sam and Ali's friend.

"I'm so sorry," says Ali. "This is Andi, she's an old friend of Lisa's—"

"Less of the old, thank you," corrects Andi. I wonder why, if she's such an old friend, we didn't see her at the funeral.

"This is Jesse, Lisa's cousin, and their best friend Simran," continues Ali, ignoring Andi's interruption. "Andi will definitely have a story or two to add to the exhibition," she tells us.

"Too right," says Andi. "Just try and stop me. Though some of them won't be suitable to repeat in public, that's for sure." She raises her eyebrows at me and laughs this rich, knowing laugh which makes me blush.

I glance at the window as we go in. The posters advertising the exhibition look great, and so does the banner that says, "The Fights That Make Us". There's no trace of the stickers. I'm glad I didn't see them, even if I can imagine what they said.

It's now definitely busier than on a normal Saturday. Mum and Dad are sitting at a corner table, eating slices of Leo's home-made Battenberg cake. Sam and Ali join them while Andi goes to the counter to order. I hope Maz's pleased with all the extra business she's getting today.

I say hello to Mum and Dad, then I can't help going to check on our exhibition. Some people have already added Post-its to the board, although it's probably just my parents doing their best to be supportive as usual. I can't get close enough to read what they say, because a man laying out leaflets along one of the shelves is blocking my view. He steps back to check how they look – and slams right into me.

"Ow!" We both stumble backwards and, at exactly the same time, both start apologizing.

"I'm so sorry. Are you okay?" he says, looking more

shaken than I am. "I'm from the local library. I've brought some leaflets about our Read with Pride collection. Would you like one?" I take a leaflet. "I didn't mean to flatten anyone in the process," he apologizes.

"I'm fine," I say. "Really. I'm not even a little bit flat."

"Have you looked at the exhibition?" he asks eagerly. "What do you think of it? I guess you weren't born during any of this."

"Oh, I…er…yes…" I'm not sure how to answer. When I don't reply, he carries on.

"It's really well-curated, very professional. We should do more of this sort of thing in the library – local history, you know," he says. "Anyway, I'll get out of your way and leave you to have a look round in peace. I have to get back to work, although I might swipe another one of those cheesy pineapple sticks on my way out. Excuse me. And sorry again."

Professional, well-curated, I repeat silently to myself. And I feel my face breaking into a smile. Wait till I tell Simran.

I turn round and see Nicky and Ana hovering uncertainly in the doorway.

I feel a sudden stab of worry. It's Nicky's opinion about the exhibition that matters most. It's her life that's on display. Her story, and the story of the time that she lived through, up there for everyone to see. If I've been feeling anxious – how must she be feeling right now?

Mum spots them too, and is at the door before me, talking to Nicky. Nicky's smiling, but she looks nervous too. She's holding tightly onto Ana's hand.

"So, Jesse," Nicky says after we all say hello and Mum's found her a chair. "Take me back in time. I'm ready to see this exhibition of yours."

35 HOLDING BACK THE YEARS

I step back so that Nicky can take it all in.

"Oh my god," she says, pointing at one of the boards. "This T-shirt. I made that. I'd forgotten all about it. I made it and I gave it to Lisa after the march. The lettering's a mess – you can tell I didn't inherit Michael's artistic genes. Although I did nick some of his paint to create it. So, she kept it all this time…"

"I knew it. I knew it was you, Nicky Burridge," comes Andi's jubilant voice from behind Nicky, followed by a rich peal of laughter. "You made me wear one of those ugly, home-made T-shirts too! I've never forgiven you for that."

So Andi knows Nicky too, which means they must have all been at school together, which means…

I don't know how long Nicky and Andi stare at each other without saying anything, but it feels like for ever. I'm holding my breath, waiting for someone to speak.

"Andy Williams?" says Nicky. "I was expecting to see a few ghosts today, but this, but you—"

"I'm no ghost."

"You're Lisa's friend Andy from school?" I ask her. "I've read about you."

"The very same. I've always wanted to be famous!"

So, this is Andy. Wow. Not what I expected, not at all. It makes me feel good, to see how happy she looks, and to know that it's down to me that she and Nicky have found each other again.

"It's been what, thirty years?" says Nicky.

"More like thirty-six," replies Andi. "I looked you up, you know, on Friends Reunited, you and Lisa both."

"What's Friends Reunited?" I whisper to Mum.

"Like Facebook, but before Facebook," she whispers back.

"You weren't on there, but Lisa was," continues Andi. "So, we reunited! We've been friends ever since. We've had some great times, and Lisa's friends became my friends. They were there for me, right from when I first started thinking about transitioning. Along with my sister, of course. She was awesome."

316

"Your sister? That makes me feel old! Last time I saw your sister, she was in primary school," says Nicky.

"Well, she's all grown up now. Seeing how supportive she was when I first came out helped my mum and dad to get on board with it too."

"Really?" asks Nicky. "That's amazing. You always used to be so scared about them finding out you were gay."

"Yeah, I should have known better, but it made sense to worry back then. I mean, look at how Lisa's parents went off at the deep end when they found out about you two. But my mum and dad, once they got used to the idea, they became my biggest defenders. They could see I was still the same person they'd always known. I wasn't like those scary gay people on TV, you know. I was their child. When I came out as trans a few years later, well, by then they were ready for anything." She laughs, but her laughter soon turns into a sigh, long and deep. "I really miss Lisa, you know. I couldn't make it to the funeral – I wasn't well – so when Ali and Sam told me about this, I was determined not to miss it."

"I'm so sorry that I lost touch with you both," says Nicky. "I feel terrible about it. And to know that it's too late for Lisa…" She's choking up.

"Don't, honestly, no one blames you," says Andi.

"It's just, Amsterdam was so incredible, and after that, well—"

317

"Life happens, I get it."

"When you were looking for me online, that must have been about the time I got my diagnosis. MS. I was so stunned. I retreated into myself. I cut myself off from everybody, which, I know now, was a pretty stupid strategy. I certainly wasn't on social media then, whereas now, well, Ana will tell you, I spend far too much time in the virtual world! It's been an absolute lifeline."

"I'm sorry," says Andi, her face softening.

"There's no need to be. I'm fine, it's just part of life. I mean, the pain's not much fun, and I get so tired all the time. But, once I worked out that I needed other people, and they needed me – I could just get on with life. And, you know what, life's been pretty good to me." She clears her throat and tries to smile. "Getting a bit deep for a sunny Saturday morning, aren't we?" It's obvious that she wants to change the direction of the conversation. "So, what do you think about being part of history? Jesse and Simran have done a brilliant job." She waves her hand at the exhibition, and then shoots Andi a mischievous look. "Aren't you worried about what Lisa might have written about you in her diary?"

Andi shrugs. "I can't believe it all happened so long ago. I still feel like a teenager most of the time. Maybe it's because I spend all day with them! I'm a secondary school teacher, would you believe? Maths."

"But it sounded awful being queer when you were in school!" I blurt out. "Why did you go back and work there? I would never have done that, not in a million years."

"I didn't want any other kid to go through what we did, simple as that," says Andi. "Section 28 only made it worse. As a teacher, there was always the fear that if you spoke out, your job was on the line. But there were still ways to make a difference, if you were careful. I thought I could change things from the inside. And maybe I have. A little. With a bit of help." Andi turns to Nicky. "You remember Ms Ferraro?"

"Your teacher?" I ask, before Nicky can reply.

"My friend now," replies Andi. "I would never have imagined calling her 'Irena' instead of 'Ms Ferraro' when I was a teenager! We met at an LGBTQ+ teachers' conference a few years back. Kept in touch ever since. She's a bit of an inspiration, actually. She does loads of work to support LGBTQ+ students in her school. But she still regrets not being able to help us more."

"She was young, she did what she could. We *all* wished things had been different, that we could have done more," says Nicky. "But today we're celebrating what *has* been achieved."

Simran nudges me hard in the ribs. "Look!" she hisses. "Look who's just come in!"

Ella is standing in the doorway. She's clutching a flyer in her hand and looking round uncertainly, like she's not quite sure what to do next.

"What's she doing here?" I ask Simran. Seeing Ella in Over the Rainbow feels wrong, like spotting a polar bear in the middle of the jungle.

"We gave out flyers to everyone," Simran reminds me. And now I remember how Ella put hers carefully into her bag.

"I'm going over to say hi," I tell Simran.

"Do you want me to come with you? Just in case she says anything mean," Simran asks.

"It's fine," I say. "She's not like Jasmine. She's nice. And anyway, she's by herself." I'm relieved there's no sign of Jasmine or any of her other friends. I wouldn't be surprised if they decided to come along just to make fun of us.

"She's not by herself," says Simran.

Simran's right. There's someone behind Ella. I blink and look again. Seeing him here is even weirder. More like, I don't know, seeing a polar bear on Mars.

"Hey, Jesse! Simran! We're here!" shouts Dylan, grinning and waving frantically. We weave our way through the people milling around the exhibition until we reach the doorway.

"Cool title," says Dylan, waving his crumpled flyer. "Conor and I were going to do our project about fighting too."

"Oh?"

"Yeah, Conor's dad was going to take us to Brighton to see the plaque for the Brighton Boy boxer and to go to where he used to train." Dylan waits. I think we're supposed to look impressed.

"I'd never heard of him either," says Ella. "But Dylan's been telling me about him *all* the way here." She rolls her eyes. "He was a heavyweight champion, born near here, and used to be really famous, like 150 years ago."

"He was a legend," says Dylan, his voice full of respect. "Only ever defeated once."

"You do know *this* exhibition isn't really about fighting?" says Simran.

"Course I do, I'm not stupid," retorts Dylan. "Still sounds all right though."

"You two came together?" I ask. I've barely seen Ella and Dylan talk to each other at school.

"Nah," says Dylan. "We just both got off the same bus."

It's joyful, and kind of unnerving, all the unexpected

ways that this exhibition is connecting people who wouldn't otherwise have anything to do with each other.

"So, where do we start?" asks Ella.

"Come with me," I say. I leave them looking at the timeline, while I check out the final exhibition board, which is now covered in a rainbow of brightly coloured Post-its. So many people have left their comments.

I start reading them. There's "Love the abseiling lesbians!" stuck next to the article that Simran found. "Trans rights are human rights" with a hand-drawn trans flag beside it, and another which says "QUEER JOY!!!!". There are long notes with tiny writing crammed into every corner which must have people's stories and memories on.

And there are really brief ones that make me want to find who wrote them and ask more questions: "This is *my* story, please remember it"; "Why did no one tell me any of this?!!" and, shortest of all, "Thank you". I'm not sure if it's a thank you for the exhibition, or a thank you to everyone who fought for our rights. Maybe it's both.

I will read the rest later. The adrenaline is wearing off. Now I really need to sit down.

36 RUNNING IN THE FAMILY

Mum pats the chair beside her. I collapse into it gratefully and grab some of her chips.

"It's going well, isn't it?" she says. "Are you pleased?"

I nod, my mouth too full to reply.

"This arrived after you left this morning." Mum reaches into her bag and produces a parcel with brightly coloured Australian stamps and my name and address written on the front in spiky handwriting.

My first thought is, I don't know anyone in Australia. Then I realize, yes, actually, I do.

Simran's dad leans over the table. "I must say, this is an excellent exhibition. You should both be very proud of yourselves. It's good to have another amateur historian in the family. Perhaps Simran will start taking an interest in my military history books now."

"Yeah, yeah, Dad," says Simran, edging herself onto my seat, so that we're both perched half-on, half-off, and helping herself to the last of the chips. "Dream on."

"My daughter," sighs Mr Gill, shaking his head, but still smiling. "So disrespectful to her elders."

Simran leans across the table and kisses her dad on the side of his beard. "Sorry, Dad. You know I love you really."

"Simran's told me about your books, Mr Gill. They sound really interesting. I'd love to see them some time," I say. Simran makes a face. But I'm not just sucking up, I genuinely would be interested.

"Well…" says Mr Gill, beaming. "I would love that too, Jesse, but let's see what's in your parcel first."

"Oh, yes," I say, looking around for a clean knife to slit the tape open.

"You don't need a knife, just rip it," says Simran. "Here, let me!"

I let her. I can't wait to see what's inside either.

It's a plastic folder, stuffed with yellowy-brown newspaper cuttings. A letter flutters out. It's handy that I'm now an expert at deciphering Lisa's handwriting, because Matthew's is almost identical.

Dear Jesse,
I hope these arrive in time for your exhibition. Although

it's up to you whether you use them or not. I hope you will find them interesting nevertheless. Your mum told me what you were doing. It's strange to think that our lives have become history, but it makes me happy to know that campaigns for equality are not being forgotten. They are needed today more than ever.

Perhaps you'll be surprised that I say that. You probably don't think much of me. You'll know about the trouble I caused for Lisa and her girlfriend when we were kids and the consequences for them both. Lisa and I hadn't been close for a long time before that, but things were never the same for anyone in our family after that summer.

I'm in awe of how bold Lisa became. After leaving home, she carried on campaigning for LGBTQ+ rights, at a time when that wasn't an acceptable thing to do. I thought she was brave. I never had the courage to stand up to my parents like she tried to do. Because of that, and because of how I behaved that summer, we drifted apart.

When I met Katie, my now wife, she suggested we move near her family in Western Australia. There was nothing keeping me in the UK, so I went. I always thought there'd be time to make it up with Lisa but kept putting it off. Another regret.

But I always followed the campaigns she cared about. When I was in the UK and when I moved away, I got into the habit of cutting out relevant bits from the newspapers. It made me feel closer to her. I've kept them all. As you can see, she wasn't the only hoarder in the family!

I'll sign off now, but I hope we'll stay in touch.

Your cousin, Matt

I look through the folder. He must have been collecting these for years. There are articles about marriage equality and about gay vicars, about kiss-ins and parliamentary debates. There's a short, factual piece, dated November 2003, about the end of Section 28.

"Why did he post them?" asks Simran. "He could have taken photos of them and emailed them to you, then they would have arrived in time."

"It's because they're the real thing," I say. Mr Gill smiles at me. He understands. "The real paper from years ago, like the real handwriting in the diaries, not just a copy or something written in a book. Oh, but I don't know how I'd add these into the exhibition now. There are so many!"

"Save them for the next exhibition," says Mr Gill. "I am sure this one is only the beginning. Now, isn't that your brother I see coming through the door? I thought he was at university, in the north somewhere?"

"Yeah, Newcastle," I say, looking over to where Mr Gill is pointing. Tom shouldn't be here. But he is. Mum and Dad look surprised to see him too, so I guess he didn't tell them he was coming either.

"Couldn't miss this! I thought I'd come down for the weekend," Tom says, dumping his backpack on what must be the only free bit of floor space left in the cafe. "Journey took hours though. I'm starving."

He looks wistfully at the empty bowls just as Leo sweeps them off the table and disappears back to the kitchen. I've hardly seen Leo today. Even with Maz bringing in a couple of extra staff, he's been rushed off his feet.

He's grinning though, like seeing the place buzzing is well worth any amount of extra work. I wonder if Maz will give him a pay rise for coming up with the plan for today. I hope so. I'm sure he's already polishing his pitch for the next bright business idea on his list.

Mum orders food for us all and, while we're waiting, I show Tom round the exhibition. He'd been really encouraging over the Easter holidays when Simran and I were working on it, but I had no idea he would come back for the launch.

Knowing more about how Lisa and Matthew grew apart makes me determined to get better at staying in touch with Tom when he's at uni.

"It sounds like everyone's here," Tom says, after I explain about Andi and Sam and Ali and Ana and Nicky all turning up.

"I hoped our history teacher would come too, especially because she was the one who gave us the idea. But she hasn't."

"Maybe she'll come later," he says, leaning forward to read one of Lisa's diary entries.

He sighs. "I bet Lisa could never have imagined any of this. It's weird that she can't see people's reactions to her things or the memories they spark in them. But I suppose if she were still alive, all of this stuff would still be stashed in her attic and none of this would be happening."

"This sounds strange," I say. "But I feel like she *is* here in a way. That she lives on through the things she decided to keep or to write down – is that daft?"

"No, of course not," says Tom. "It's like with Gran. She's still part of our lives, even though she's no longer here. She'd have loved this. She would have been so proud of you."

We both stare at the exhibition boards, not saying anything. I blink as it all starts to swim before my eyes.

"You're just the same as her," says Tom so quietly that I have to lean in to hear him over the voices and laughter and clatter of plates around us. "She really cared about people, and so do you. And once she had an idea about something, there was no stopping her. You're like that. You wouldn't let anything stop you turning something bad into something good…"

"It wasn't just me," I interrupt. "Sim and Leo and Maz and Nicky and everyone, they all made it happen too."

"That's exactly what I mean!" exclaims Tom. "That's just the sort of thing Gran would have said, right? Totally proves my point. It's *you* who brings out all those good things in people, just like she used to do. So, no more arguing, little sibling, let's go and eat."

But before I can sit down, Maz puts her hand on my shoulder, and whispers something in my ear.

37 (I'VE HAD) THE TIME OF MY LIFE

"No," I tell her. "No, no, you should ask Simran or Leo, they'd both be really good. Much better than me."

"I asked Simran what she thought," says Maz firmly. "And she agrees. Your idea. Your cousin. Your speech. No arguments."

"That's not fair," I say. "You can't ask me to make up a speech on the spot. Not in front of everyone." I feel my hands starting to shake and my throat going dry.

"It's the best way," says Maz. "It means you'll speak from the heart. And you won't have time to get nervous. Come on, get up here so everyone can see you."

Before I've realized what's happening, I'm standing on a chair and Maz's piercing whistle has silenced everyone. Every single face is looking at me.

"Well, er, hello," I say. Maz was wrong about not having time to get nervous. I'm absolutely terrified.

"Hi, Jesse!" shouts Dylan. And then everyone else starts joining in. There are "hi"s and "hello"s, and whoops and cheers too, coming from all over the bookshop, from people I've known all my life, those I've got to know thanks to this project, and those I've never seen before today.

There's one thing that every face has in common though. None of them are laughing at me or waiting for me to mess it up – they all want to hear what I have to say. I stand up a little bit taller.

I tell the whole story. I talk about Ms Grant's history lessons and about finding Lisa's diary in the attic. Researching in Over the Rainbow and visiting Nicky in Brighton. I make Simran come and stand on the chair next to mine, so that everyone can clap for her too, and between us we thank every single person who's helped us. It's a long list.

"The fight's not over," I say. "I don't think it ever will be. But just because it can take a long time to change things, just because sometimes it even feels like progress is going backwards, it doesn't mean we should give up and go home. We can't. All these stories..." I point towards the exhibition and nearly wobble off my chair as I do.

Simran grabs my arm to steady me.

"All these stories," I say again. "They are *our* stories. And they deserve to be remembered and celebrated. So, together, we need to keep on remembering, and celebrating...and fighting. It's the fights that make us."

Everybody starts clapping and cheering. Mum and Dad are both wiping their eyes and beaming. Every bit of me is tingling with joy. I'm so glad now that Maz forced me to stand up and speak. If I can do this, I can do anything.

At the back of the cafe, a baby cries.

"Thank you," I say, as I jump off my chair and walk over to the door – where Ms Grant is standing.

"Jesse, that was impressive," she says, beaming at me. "I'm sorry I'm late, but I'm glad I arrived in time to hear every word of that magnificent speech."

She lifts the tiniest baby I've ever seen out from its sling. It has big blue eyes that stare right at me, a wrinkled red face and a tiny rainbow hat on its tiny head. As soon as Ms Grant sits down and lifts up her shirt to feed the baby, the crying is replaced by a loud sucking noise.

"Getting out of the house with a baby is like undertaking a polar expedition," she sighs. "At least it is for me. Elizabeth Fry had eleven children and still found time to reform the entire Victorian prison system, but somehow it's taken me three hours just to get across Hurston. My respect for those female pioneers gets bigger every day. Although maybe they all had nannies."

I can't think of anything to say. But that doesn't matter because there are never any awkward silences when Dylan is around.

"We miss you, Miss," he tells her earnestly, bounding up to us. "You were the best. When are you coming back? That other teacher she—"

"Well, Dylan, that's nice to hear. I miss you all too. But you can see I've got my hands full at the moment." She glances at the baby, now asleep in her arms.

Everyone is fascinated by the baby, asking questions about names and weights and sleeping patterns. Even people who I didn't imagine being particularly into babies, like Maz, or people who don't even know Ms Grant, like Simran's mum. If I were Ms Grant I'd want everyone to back off, but she doesn't seem to mind.

I'm so pleased that she's come. But she's not quite how I remember from Year Eight history lessons. She's someone with a life outside school, someone who has given birth to a whole new human being since we saw her last! And, now that she's here, what will she think of the exhibition?

Ms Grant turns to me and Simran. "I've been hearing lots about you," she says. "It sounds like the two of you have been stirring things up." She looks deadly serious for a moment, like she's about to tell us off, and then breaks out in this big grin.

"Did you hear about me too?" interrupts Dylan.

"Mmm," says Ms Grant. "Would you be pleased if I had?"

"Who did you hear about us from?" asks Simran.

"I have my sources," says Ms Grant, tapping the side of her nose. "Teachers do talk to each other, you know, even outside school. I'm on maternity leave, not on the moon. Which reminds me, Sahan – I mean, Mr Wijendra, says he's sorry he can't make it today, but wishes you luck."

She sighs. "I'm sorry about leaving so suddenly in the middle of term. I'd truly intended to see those projects through. I was really excited about what you lot were all going to uncover, but this little one was so determined to see the world, there wasn't much I could do about it. But now I'm here, I'd love to see the exhibition, if you're ready to show me."

"I'll take the baby," offers Mum, stretching out her arms eagerly. "If that would help."

"Thank you," says Ms Grant, sliding the sleeping bundle into Mum's arms.

I'm nervous at first, but once I start to relax, our words tumble over each other as Simran and I share what we've found out and what it means to us.

Ms Grant keeps nodding. "There's nothing more exciting than reading old diaries," she agrees. "It's like someone reaching out from the past with a message just for you. You've both done such a great job in researching the context. This isn't just one person's story. I mean, that would be nice, but only interesting to a handful of people. You've looked at what that story tells us about a whole period." She shakes her head. "Listen to me, I sound like I'm marking your work. That's not my job right now. I'm here to appreciate two fellow historians, not to give you a grade."

"I wish we had been able to do this for school," I say. "I wish you'd still been our teacher and not Mrs Knight."

At least Mrs Knight didn't come back after Easter. In the weeks after her meeting with Mr Wijendra and before term ended, she didn't misgender me even once. The new supply teacher who started this term seems all right. Even if he's nowhere near as good as Ms Grant.

"Let's not talk about other teachers," she says quickly. "This was my responsibility. I should have prepared a proper handover. And maybe not taken you all quite so far off-curriculum quite so fast. I got overexcited and raised expectations, but that left you, well, the whole class, and Mrs Knight, in a difficult position."

Mum comes over to give Ms Grant back her baby. She

tells me we'll be getting a takeaway and Simran can join us if she wants. It's time to go home soon, she says.

The exhibition will be on display for the whole week. Simran and I are planning to come in after school each day and see what new things people have brought to add to the story. Someone from the local paper said they'd visit in a couple of days' time and take photos for their website. So, it's not over. Nowhere near.

But I'm already starting to feel sad. It will end sometime and, after this week, everything will be normal and boring again. The feeling that's been so strong today, of togetherness, of being part of a community, of sharing our stories, will fade away again.

It could so easily never have happened. If Ms Grant hadn't been our teacher, then I wouldn't have been so interested in history or looking at Lisa's old stuff in the first place. And if I hadn't done that, we wouldn't be here today. Andi and Nicky wouldn't have found each other again. And Mum might not have contacted Matthew and discovered a new branch of our family on the other side of the world.

Everything we do has an impact, but you don't know what it's going to be till much later. Maybe never. So how do you know the right thing to do?

What if Matthew hadn't read Lisa's diary? If Gran

hadn't taken her in when she got sent away? Or if the campaign against Section 28 had been successful back then and Andi and Lisa and Nicky and so many other kids had been safe to be themselves at school? Or if my parents had acted like Lisa's parents and thrown me out when I came out to them?

Each one of those "what if"s makes ripples that spread further than I can imagine. And they're still spreading, wider and wider. I guess that's what being a historian is – trying to understand where those ripples start and the difference it makes when they melt and merge and collide with each other. Doing anything at all feels like too much responsibility, too much risk. But being a person means more than just watching from the outside. It means getting involved too.

"Jesse, Simran, oh and you too, Leo," says Ms Grant. Leo stops wiping the counter and comes over. "I want to sound you out about something. It's not something we can do right away – well, I certainly can't, I have a few other priorities at the moment."

Just as she says that, the baby lets out an enormous burp. We all laugh.

"I wondered what you think about us starting an LGBTQ+ group at school. To build on the work you've been doing about our history." I note the way she says "our", not "your". "But also, to talk about the issues that LGBTQ+ students are facing today in our school. And what we can do about them, together. And, of course, to have some fun, to celebrate what's amazing about the diversity in our school."

"That would be awesome," says Simran. "Do you really think we can? Will they let us?"

Andi breaks off her conversation with Maz to join in. "My school has one," she says. "And so does Irena's. We could give you some tips."

"You see, we wouldn't be on our own," smiles Ms Grant. "But I think if anyone could make it happen, it would be the three of you. I mean, look at what you've achieved here today. There will be support from the staff, but you'll have to be the ones to get it going."

Support from the staff? Okay, perhaps Mr Wijendra had a hand in this too. We've got our follow-up meeting with him next week. I'm guessing that an LGBTQ+ group might be one of the things on his list. If not, I decide, we're going to put it there. Right at the top.

"Er, Miss," interrupts Dylan from the table behind us. I turn round. I hadn't realized he and Ella were still here. They are sharing a slice of Leo's chocolate cake – Ella eating her half delicately with a spoon while Dylan's face is smeared with icing.

"Yes, Dylan?" says Ms Grant.

"Can me and Ella join?" he asks. "I mean, it would be for allies too, right?"

I try to hide the surprised look on my face, but Ella sees it anyway. "I'm done with listening to the stupid things that people say because they don't know what they're talking about or because they think they're better than everyone else," she says. "It's boring. And annoying. But, if you two are organizing this group, it's bound to be good. When the exhibition got cancelled, no one else was bothered, or they just moaned about it but didn't *do* anything. Me too. But you *did*. Like Ms Grant said, you make things happen." She gestures towards the exhibition boards. "I didn't know any of this stuff before, and you made it feel, like, real, not like history, like something happening now."

Does Ella really see me like that? Someone who makes stuff happen. I think of all the time I've spent worrying about whether people like Ella Bright think I'm weird or awkward or annoying. What a waste of energy.

"Of course," I say, smiling at her. "The group will be for everyone."

"So, you think it's a good idea? I mean, you're ready for your next project?" asks Ms Grant.

A few weeks ago, I wouldn't have been sure. I would

have waited for someone else to do it, someone more confident than me to take the lead. But now, it feels different. I smooth down my waistcoat, wiggle my toes in Lisa's boots and look around at my family and friends.

I don't feel like I'm struggling to keep my balance any more. I'm not worrying whether I might fall. Not because I think everything's always going to be okay, I know it won't be, but because, if I do wobble, there will be someone to steady me, or even catch me if I need it. Just as I'll be there to catch them. It all seems possible, here, with all my favourite people in my favourite place, and with my new friends too, allies that I didn't even know I had. I glance over at Simran and she gives me the smallest of nods.

"Yeah, okay," I say to Ms Grant, to everyone. "Let's get started."

AUTHOR'S NOTE

I can't remember when I first heard about Section 28.

It wasn't when I was at school, even though all of my secondary education took place under its shadow.

It might have been when I was at university. Some friends invited me to join a candlelit vigil calling for its repeal. We stood in silence, filling the square outside Sheffield City Hall.

But it took at least another four years, by which time I had come out, graduated, met and moved in with my partner, for Section 28 to finally be abolished. This was 2003. Other laws followed quickly – same-sex couples could now form legal partnerships or adopt children, trans people gained legal gender recognition and it became illegal to treat LGBTQ+ people worse than anyone else at work or school. It felt like a new beginning.

Twenty years ago. Ancient history. Why is it relevant now?

When I visit schools, sharing my LGBTQ+ centred stories and chatting with readers, I often ask what they know about Section 28. Like Jesse and Simran at the start of this book, few students have heard of it. When I explain what it was, many look like they don't believe me. They just don't get it. Which is brilliant.

Yet LGBTQ+ history in the UK is shaped by Section 28. The introduction of this law, and the way people united in opposition against it, touched so many lives.

To learn more, I visited the Bishopsgate archives in London and leafed through newspaper cuttings and campaign material that felt ancient, even though it was produced in my lifetime! I devoured books about LGBTQ+ culture in the 1980s. I listened to podcasts, while I cleaned out the rabbit hutch or did the washing up, to hear people telling the story of this time in history in their own words.

As I found out more, stories that I half knew leapt out at me – could it really be true that lesbians broke into the BBC studios or abseiled into the House of Lords to protest against Section 28? Yes, it was! Why didn't more people know about this? Hearing these voices made it all feel so real, so connected to our lives today. What could I do to help share their stories?

While researching *The Fights That Make Us*, I was also very aware of growing media and political hostility towards LGBTQ+ people, and trans people in particular, right now. It seemed like every day, another public figure would say something hateful, further abuse would be piled onto LGBTQ+ charities, more government promises to protect LGBTQ+ rights would be broken.

As I write this, rumours are circulating about worrying new government guidance for schools concerning trans pupils. Guidance which would make life much harder for someone like Jesse, especially if their parents didn't support them.

Section 28 is remembered because of the damage it did. The way it took one group of people and told them, and everybody else, that they were abnormal and their relationships weren't real. The way it shamed and threatened people into silence. The way it stoked fear and prejudice.

But Section 28 is also remembered because of the way it united people in fighting back. People were so outraged that they did everything they could to stop it, and when they succeeded, they said "never again". Even if that took 15 years.

Things are very different now – the strength and confidence of LGBTQ+ organizations today owes so much to that fightback. But things are also disturbingly similar. The rights we've won are under threat.

I believe that we need to remember our past. To draw strength and anger and hope from it so that we can carry on the fight today. *The Fights That Make Us* is a small contribution to that act of remembering.

We fight for ourselves, for each other, for people we don't know but who need someone on their side. How we fight will look different for each of us. But we'll do it together. And we'll win. And, as Jesse says, it's the fights that make us.

ACKNOWLEDGEMENTS

This book has been tugging at my heart for a long time, asking to be written. And now, after years of slowly taking shape, here it is! Getting to this point would have been impossible without the help, whether they realized it or not, of so many inspirational people. Any mistakes, misinterpretations and tweaking of the facts to fit the story are all mine.

I don't remember the 1980s very well (I was only nine in 1987 when Lisa's story is set) so I needed to do research in order to properly represent the time I was writing about. In particular, I was so grateful for:

"The Log Books" podcast, which brings voices from LGBTQ+ Switchboard alive.

The Bishopsgate LGBTQ+ History Archive, where

anyone can examine newspaper cuttings and other source material – as I did – for free.

Books, including *Gay in the 1980s* by Colin Clews; *Outrageous* by Paul Baker; *Protected* by Catherine Lee; and *Good As You* by Paul Flynn.

The people who shared their experiences of being #LGBTatSchool on Stonewall's hashtag.

Conversations with Terry Purkis, Paul Matthews and Jenn Matthews about their experiences.

I also needed to try to understand about being a non-binary young person today. As well as reading research papers, I listened to young people in the schools I visited, especially the Diversity group at Fairfield High School, who generously shared their thoughts and answered my questions. Thank you to Edel Cronin for making that conversation possible. The podcasts "NB: My Non-Binary Life" with Caitlin Benedict & Amrou Al-Kadhi, and "Pride and Progress" with Jo Brassington and Adam Brett were also invaluable.

Once Jesse's story was almost complete, Kym Deyn and Tora Brumalis provided valuable insights as sensitivity readers, pushing me to think broader and deeper. Thank you, Kym and Tora.

As well as managing archives, the Bishopsgate Institute runs courses. I attended Siobhan Forshaw's brilliant

History of Protest course while I was writing *The Fights That Make Us*. This introduced me to new histories and informed Ms Grant's approach to history teaching.

Lisa, Nicky, Jesse and Simran are campaigners, committed to changing things for the better, however dangerous, uncomfortable or difficult that is. I've worked with some amazing campaigners at CAFOD, Christian Aid and Stonewall. I've admired and learnt from many more from afar, especially Lisa Power, one of Stonewall's founders and Gay Liberation Front pioneer (it's no coincidence that one of my main characters is called Lisa!). My greatest hope for this book is that it inspires more people to speak up for what matters to them, to challenge injustice where they see it, and to imagine a better way of living – the world needs you!

The Fights That Make Us also celebrates queer and/or indie bookshops and cafes, like Over the Rainbow. Each of these spaces is a lifeline for people in finding community and finding themselves. They are run by hard-working people with a passion for what they do. Please go and show them some love!

Death hangs over this book. Two of the main characters – Lisa and Gran – have died before the story starts. You never meet them, yet their legacy shines brightly and their influence shapes Jesse's life and choices. While working at Poppy's funeral directors, I've learnt from my colleagues that death is a natural part of life, grief is normal, and the importance of honouring each unique life. I like to think that Lisa's funeral was a Poppy's funeral.

This is my fourth book with Usborne and I couldn't ask for more from the team there. Jacob and Jess on the marketing side, Will on design, and my editors, Stephanie King and Alice Moloney, who made the book so much better, gently pushing me to cut, rewrite, restructure. Even when I didn't want to do it, I knew it was the right thing! You really know your stuff. Thanks also to illustrator Caribay M. Benavides, whose gorgeous cover beautifully captures Jesse and Simran's fighting spirit.

Thanks as well to Chloe Seager and the team at Madeleine Milburn for championing this story and making it all possible.

My partner Rachel, my children Esther and Miriam, my mum Mary, are all some of my first readers, full of encouragement and with a sharp eye for a typo. More importantly than that, they are my favourite people!

And finally, *The Fights That Make Us* is dedicated to the memory of three remarkable women. Two I knew, and one I didn't.

My friend and former colleague, Mary Milne, whose pragmatic, compassionate and patient campaigning taught me so much.

The author of the first LGBTQ+ book I ever read, Nancy Garden. Without *Annie on My Mind*, I couldn't have written Nicky and Lisa's own love story.

And my very own first cousin once removed, Sally Cline, author, activist, and fierce feminist.

And really finally this time, thanks to you, and all the readers, for allowing me to share these stories with you. I hope they encourage and inspire all of us to stand up for each other and for LGBTQ+ equality whenever we see it under threat. We truly are stronger together.

DISCUSSION QUESTIONS

1. Did you know what Clause/Section 28 was before reading this book? What did you learn about it, and did it surprise you?

2. Mrs Grant tells Jesse's class that their emails and social media posts may all one day be seen as historical record: "that's all history...the details of what your lives are really like." What do you think future historians could learn from your own diary, messages and social media?

3. The box of Lisa's possessions acts as a time capsule, and the objects inside help Jesse to uncover the truth of what Lisa's life in 1987 was really like. If you were creating a time capsule for the future, to show what your life now is like, what would you put in it and why?

4. Lisa and Jesse each find it difficult to stand up for themselves at various points throughout the book. Why can it sometimes be hard for people to speak up for what they believe in?

5. Jesse comes to the conclusion that "change only happens if you do something to make it happen". Using the examples in the book to help you, brainstorm ways of fighting for change.

6. Ms Grant wants her class to do a history project on something that matters to them, especially looking at voices that are missing from lots of history books. What kinds of topics do you think you would investigate, if you were in Jesse's class?

7. Jesse and Lisa are teenagers in the same family, thirty-five years apart. What are some of the similarities and differences between their lives, and what does this tell you about how history impacts us?

8. Think about the idea of community in *The Fights That Make Us*. How can places like Over the Rainbow be important for communities, especially for LGBTQ+ people?

If you have been affected by some of the issues raised in this book, the following organizations can help or provide further info:

Stonewall is a charity which supports equality for all LGBT people and prevents discrimination – at school, at work and in communities. They produce education materials and information and have an advice line.
www.stonewall.org.uk

Gendered Intelligence is a national trans-led charity that works to improve the lives of transgender people in the UK, specialising in supporting young people up to the age of 21. GI delivers trans youth programmes, support for parents and carers, and educational workshops for schools, colleges and other educational settings.
www.genderedintelligence.co.uk

Do you have a question about sexuality or gender identity? **Switchboard**'s team of trained LGBTQ+ volunteers are here to help. Contact us 10am to 10pm, 365 days a year.
Helpline: 0800 0119 100
Instant messaging: www.switchboard.lgbt
Email: hello@switchboard.lgbt